Survival of the fittest is fin… you're the one on top…but the family that has everything is about to lose it all…

The Montagues have found themselves at the centre of the *ton*'s rumour mill, with lords and ladies alike claiming the family is not what it used to be.

The mysterious death of the heir to the Dukedom, and the arrival of an unknown woman claiming he fathered her son, is only the tip of the iceberg in a family where scandal upstairs *and* downstairs threatens the very foundations of their once powerful and revered dynasty...

August 2012
THE WICKED LORD MONTAGUE – Carole Mortimer

September 2012
THE HOUSEMAID'S SCANDALOUS SECRET – Helen Dickson

October 2012
THE LADY WHO BROKE THE RULES – Marguerite Kaye

November 2012
LADY OF SHAME – Ann Lethbridge

December 2012
THE ILLEGITIMATE MONTAGUE – Sarah Mallory

January 2013
UNBEFITTING A LADY – Bronwyn Scott

February 2013
REDEMPTION OF A FALLEN WOMAN – Joanna Fulford

March 2013
A STRANGER AT CASTONBURY – Amanda McCabe

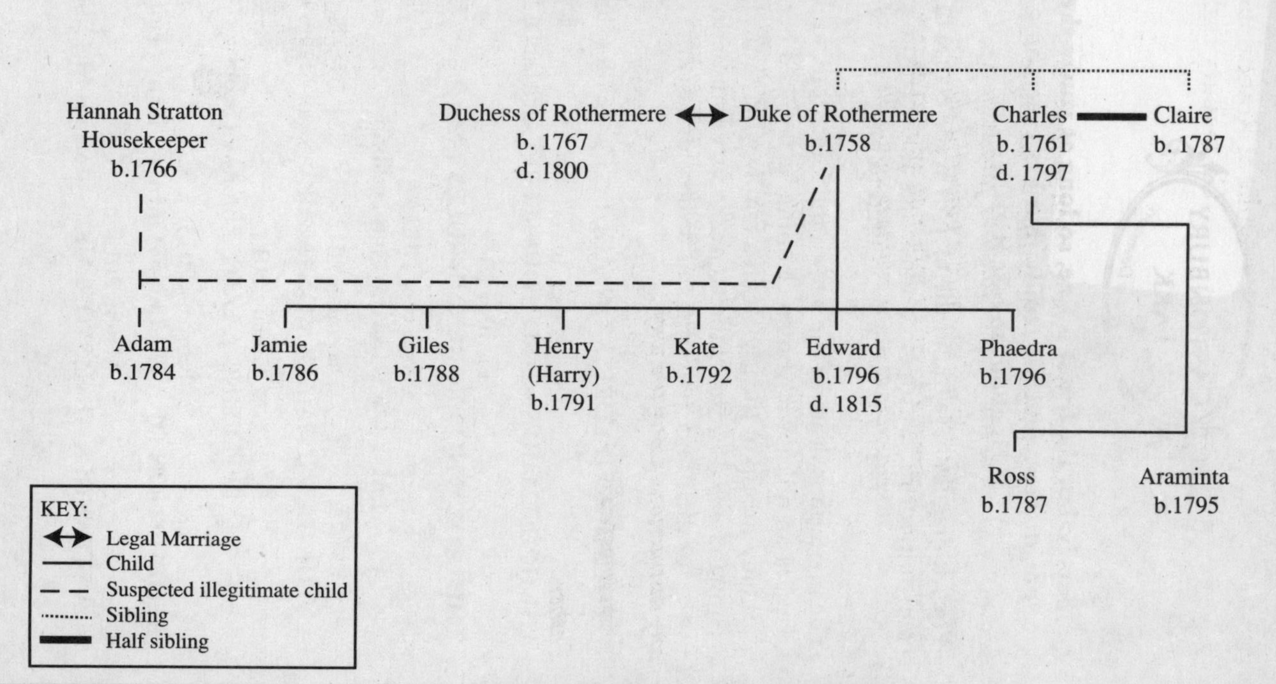
Montague Family Tree
Hannah Stratton
Housekeeper
b.1766
Duchess of Rothermere
b. 1767
d. 1800
Duke of Rothermere
b.1758
Charles
b. 1761
d. 1797
Claire
b. 1787
Adam
b.1784
Jamie
b.1786
Giles
b.1788
Henry
(Harry)
b.1791
Kate
b.1792
Edward
b.1796
d. 1815
Phaedra
b.1796
Ross
b.1787
Araminta
b.1795
KEY:
Legal Marriage
Child
Suspected illegitimate child
Sibling
Half sibling

Duke of Rothermere
Castonbury Park

Harry,

It is with much regret that I must admit we have wasted precious time in the hunt for the truth. What might have become of Jamie is still unclear and our family name remains in tatters. What was once a powerful dynasty is fast crumbling around us and I fear that we may have to give in to the demands of the woman who calls herself Jamie's wife.

Harry, I beg of you to stop the rot which is fast taking over the Montagues and discover once and for all what has happened to Jamie. Time is, as ever, of the essence, and I urge you from the bottom of my heart not to find any distractions along the way…

Yours hopefully,

Father

First published in Great Britain 2012
Mills & Boon, an imprint of Harlequin (UK) Limited,
Eton House, 18-24 Paradise Road, Richmond, Surrey TW9 1SR

ISBN: 978 0 263 90191 7

52-0213

Harlequin (UK) policy is to use papers that are natural, renewable and recyclable products and made from wood grown in sustainable forests. The logging and manufacturing processes conform to the legal environmental regulations of the country of origin.

Printed and bound
by CPI Group (UK) Ltd, Croydon, CR0 4YY

Redemption of a Fallen Woman

JOANNA FULFORD

For the Old Guard in Madrid

Chapter One

Elena Ruiz stared out of the window letting her gaze range across the rooftops of the city towards the open countryside and thence to the foothills of the Sierra de Guadarrama, shimmering in a dusty haze. Out there, beyond the jumble of pantiled slopes and chimneys, lay freedom. It was an emotive word. Her fellow countrymen and women had spent eight long years freeing themselves from the French invaders. She had played her part in that, and gladly too. When the conflict ended she desired no more than to live a quiet country life, but such freedom was not permitted women of noble birth. For them the choice was simple: marriage or the cloister.

Betrothal had taken place in a past life when she had been a different person. Young, naive and hopeful she had never questioned her pre-ordained role. The war had seemed far off then. It had caught up with her eventually, of course. As a result marriage was out of the question. No man of good family would want her now. In any case the thought of intimacy filled her with dread. Men did not touch her and the only one foolish enough to try had found himself staring down the barrel of a pistol. Even then it took a bullet crease in his arm to convince him she wasn't bluffing. The incident was sufficient to keep the rest at a respectful distance. Memories were another matter. By day, useful employment kept them at bay but at night the dreams still returned, less often now but no less violent for that. She would never be entirely free of those. Her hands clenched at her sides and she turned away from the window to resume her slow pacing of the floor.

Her companion surveyed her keenly. Although of a similar age to Elena, her dress revealed her to be of the household servant class. In spite of unfashionable olive skin, her face with its high cheekbones and pointed chin was not ill-looking, though the mouth was too large for conventional beauty. However, the dark eyes were shrewd and intelligent and, just now, expressive of concern.

'What are we going to do?'

'I don't know, Concha, but somehow we have to get out of this house.'

'Your uncle's servants are vigilant.'

'Vigilant, but not infallible. I'll think of something.'

'Better to think quickly, then. We have only a few days more.'

'I will not spend the rest of my life shut away just to suit notions of family honour.'

'If we don't find a way out of here you may have no

choice. Your uncle is powerful and, as we have already seen, he has the means to compel obedience.'

That was undeniable, Elena reflected. He had no qualms about bringing her to Madrid against her will, and he would have none about expediting the rest of his plan either. As the head of the family now it was his responsibility to guard its reputation, a duty he took most seriously, and she had become a liability.

'I'll think of something,' she replied, as though repetition might make it true.

Since their arrival two days earlier she had racked her brains trying to think of a viable plan. The only person whom she knew would help her was Dolores, but her beloved older sister was married and settled in England now. She might as well have been on the moon. As for Luisa and Estefania...they were lost to her for good. Even after four years the memory was still painful and she pushed it aside, along with all the others pertaining to that time. The past was done with, and if she didn't put her mind to the present problem the future would be irrevocably blighted too.

'At least you are not without means,' said Concha.

'Money is not the problem. There's enough and to spare, but it will be no use unless we can get out of Madrid.'

'If...when...we do leave, your uncle is certain to mount a search.'

'We'll worry about that when the time comes,' said Elena. 'In the meantime we must not give any reason for suspicion. Being under house arrest is bad enough. I don't want to be locked in my room as well.'

Concha nodded. 'You are right. Let it be thought that you are becoming resigned to your uncle's will.'

'Exactly.' Elena made a vague gesture with her hands. 'I have no wish to be at odds with him, or any other member of my family, but as it is…there's no choice now.'

The sound of iron-rimmed wheels and horses' hooves distracted her momentarily and she glanced out of the window to the street below to see a carriage approaching. Instead of driving past as she expected it stopped outside the house. To judge by the heavily sweating horses and the dust on the bodywork the vehicle had travelled some way. All the same, under the grime, it was a handsome equipage and certainly the property of a nobleman.

As she watched, a servant jumped down to open the door and let down the steps. A single passenger emerged, a gentleman, very elegantly dressed. He paused on the paved walkway and glanced up at the house. Elena caught her breath. Problems temporarily forgotten, she stared, arrested by a face in which strong lines accentuated the chiselled planes of cheek and nose and jaw. The hair visible below his hat was dark. He seemed to be tall too, certainly much taller than the servant with him, and carried himself with the air of one used to command.

Concha came to join her by the window and now stared in her turn. '*Dios mio!* Who is that?'

'I don't know. One of my uncle's acquaintances from the embassy, perhaps?'

'I imagined all his acquaintances must be old and ugly but I take it back now—unreservedly.'

They had no time for further observation because the unknown caller entered the house and was lost to view. Elena turned away from the window. She must be in more mental turmoil than she'd realised to be staring so at a complete stranger. Men were of no interest other than in a purely professional capacity. Besides, as things stood, she couldn't afford to let herself become distracted, even briefly. All her thoughts had to focus on a means of escape.

Having presented his credentials, Harry Montague waited in the marbled hallway. It was cool and quiet in here, a welcome relief from the jolting rhythm and stifling heat of the carriage. He had almost forgotten the power of the Spanish sun. Forgetting had been deliberate and, mostly, successful, though he had been aided in that by work. Spain was a land of contrasts—a beautiful and blood-soaked land that was associated with some of the best and all of the worst days of his life. When the war had concluded he hadn't expected that he would ever return, would never have chosen to—until circumstances made it imperative.

One swift glance around at the elegant furnishings was sufficient to suggest that the man he had come to see was both wealthy and possessed of impeccable taste. Whether he would be able to help as well remained to be seen. Coming here might be a fool's errand but he had to try. He had promised his cousin Ross. Besides, the revelations of their last conversation were burned into his brain. Until then he'd had no idea how seriously compromised the family's financial situation was. If he couldn't obtain the proof he needed about Jamie's death… He pulled himself up sharply. He would get the proof, one way or another.

Presently, the servant returned. 'Don Manuel will receive you now, *señor*.'

Harry was shown into a downstairs *salón*, also elegantly furnished, where his host was waiting. Don Manuel Urbieta was in his middle years, his thinning hair more grey than dark, like the neat goatee beard he wore. Though slightly above average height, he was still several inches shorter than his visitor. For all that he had the proud, upright bearing that proclaimed a grandee of the hidalgo class.

When the necessary courtesies had been observed the don invited Harry to sit and, having plied him with liquid refreshment, took the chair opposite.

'Now, my lord, won't you tell me how I can be of service?'

Harry nodded. 'I have come to Spain on urgent family business. It concerns my elder brother, James. He served with the British army during the war, but he was lost during the push into France.'

'I am sorry to hear it.'

'He was apparently swept away while crossing a flooded river.'

'Apparently?'

'My brother's body was never found. The news of his death was by report only. The only witness, a man called Xavier Sanchez, disappeared shortly afterwards.'

'I see.'

'I made enquiries at the time, but the situation was chaotic and all attention was on the push for Toulouse. No one at headquarters was able to tell me very much, giving only the briefest account of the accident. When I tried to find the witness he had vanished too. It was like being confronted by a stone wall.'

Don Manuel eyed him shrewdly. 'I think you have some doubts about this matter, no?'

Harry nodded. 'There are questions in my mind, although they may just be the result of wishful thinking.' He paused. 'In the first place, my brother was an excellent swimmer. In the second, he worked for the Intelligence Service.'

'Interesting.'

'As time went on and we had no word, the family lost hope and assumed the worst. However, not long ago we received a letter from a solicitor, acting on behalf of a lady who claims to be Jamie's wife. This lady has a young child, a son....'

Understanding dawned on Don Manuel's face. 'And this son stands to inherit the title if his claim proves to be legitimate.'

'Exactly so.'

'Have you reason to doubt this lady's story?'

'She may be what she claims.'

'But you have reservations.'

'I'm trying to keep an open mind. In view of the circumstances though, it is essential that I discover the truth.'

'That is quite understandable.' Don Manuel set down his glass. 'I have contacts in the Intelligence Service here. They may be able to help. I will see what I can find out.'

'I would be most grateful.'

'In the meantime let me offer you the hospitality of my house.'

'You are most generous, but I couldn't possibly impose on you in that way.'

'Nonsense. It will be my pleasure. *Mi casa es su casa.*'

'Then I accept.'

'Good. That's settled, then.' The don rose. 'A room will be readied on the instant. Then, after you have rested from your journey, we will dine.'

The chamber to which Harry was later conducted proved to be large and comfortable. It was a courtesy he had not expected and, he admitted, far better than anything he would have met with at an inn. After the rigours of travel it would be a luxury to sleep in a decent bed again. He shrugged off his coat and then sat down to remove his boots, glancing across the room to where his manservant was unpacking a trunk.

'I'd like to bathe if that can be arranged, Jack.'

Jack Hawkes looked up and nodded. 'I thought you

might, so I took t'liberty of bespeaking a bath for you, my lord.'

'Wonderful. I'm beginning to smell rank.'

'I reckon we've both smelt far worse.'

Harry grinned. 'True enough.' He tugged off a boot and then set to work on the other. 'All the same, we're not on campaign now and I'm not sitting down to dine in polite company until I've washed off all the dust.'

'Aye, t'roads haven't improved much since we left, have they?'

'Unfortunately not.' The other boot came off and Harry began to loosen his neck cloth. 'Still, we're here now and if there is any evidence of what happened to my brother this is where it'll be.'

'Let's hope summat comes to light soon, then, my lord.'

Relaxing in the tub soon afterwards, Harry wholeheartedly endorsed that sentiment. Coming here was a long shot but it had to be done. One way or another, the doubt must be resolved. He hadn't realised until then just how far he had been keeping hope alive. If anyone could find the information he needed it would be Don Manuel and, indeed, the man had shown himself to be a model of courtesy thus far. With his help Harry would find the answers he sought.

On the practical side there was Jack Hawkes. Ordinarily no manservant would have dreamed of or been permitted to address his master with such easy familiarity. But then, Harry reflected, there was nothing remotely ordinary about him. War formed a bond between men and, as a former member of Harry's company during the Peninsular War, Hawkes had proved his worth a hundred times over. When the war ended and the force was demobilised he'd stayed on in the capacity of personal valet. Harry was glad of it; there were few men who were as discreet and none he trusted more.

As he dried himself and dressed he wondered whether there would be other company at dinner that evening. He had assumed that Don Manuel was married but had no idea if the wife was still living, or whether there were other relatives in the household. On arrival earlier he thought he had detected someone at an upstairs window, but the angle of view and the reflection on the glass made it hard to be sure. It would be interesting to find out.

Concha finished fastening her mistress's gown and then stepped back, eyeing it critically. 'It looks well, but...is red the best choice, under the circumstances?'

'Under the circumstances it's the only choice.'

'I thought you would say that.' The maid smiled wryly. 'Your aunts won't like it.'

'They disapprove of me anyway. Besides, virginal white would be inappropriate now.' Elena glanced at the clock and sighed. 'I wish I didn't have to go down there. The thought of another meal in that company has no appeal whatever.'

'I know. All the same, it will be better if you do.'

'Lull them into a sense of false security, you mean?'

'If you appear to be following domestic protocols

they are less likely to suspect anything. Then, when you have conceived your plan, they will be taken by surprise.'

Elena thought she could probably manage the protocols part, but the plan was another matter. In spite of racking her brains for a solution she had still not come up with anything feasible.

'I'd better go. Wish me luck.'

'Always,' said Concha.

Elena squeezed her arm gently and smiled. Then, taking a deep breath, she headed for the door.

Chapter Two

When Harry arrived in the *salón* just before the appointed hour, it was to find Don Manuel already present. With him were four others. The two gentlemen, both with greying hair, appeared to be in their late forties. Both were of short stature and tending to corpulence. The two ladies looked older and both were expensively if severely gowned in black. If either ever had pretensions to beauty it was no longer evident. Nor was this deficiency ameliorated by their haughty and unsmiling demeanour. Don Manuel introduced them as his sisters, Doña Inéz and Doña Urraca. The gentlemen, Don Fernando and Don Esteban, were cousins.

As the introductions were performed Harry made a formal bow. Doña Inéz inclined her head in acknowledgement and offered a faint condescending smile that stopped well short of her dark eyes.

'You honour us with your presence, Lord Henry. I trust that your journey here was satisfactory.'

'Thank you, yes.'

'I do not care to travel myself,' she replied. 'It is too fatiguing and the state of the roads leaves much to be desired.'

He agreed that they did. Thus encouraged, Doña Inéz went on to cover the hazards of ruts, dust, brigands and heatstroke. She was just embarking on a comprehensive condemnation of all the inns she had ever stayed in, when the *salón* door opened again. Harry glanced round and then, as he set eyes on the newcomer, all other thoughts went out of his head.

Elena paused on the threshold, hoping that her composure wouldn't desert her now. Concha was right; it was important to play along for a while. Her gaze swept the room in distaste. With their dark clothing her relatives reminded her of nothing so much as a gathering of crows around their prey. They had shown about the same amount of compassion too. Then she noticed the tall figure standing beside Aunt Inéz. The man had his back to her but, as the conversation died down around him, he glanced round to find the reason.

Elena caught her breath, recognising him at once. However, that former fleeting glance through the window hadn't done him justice; to begin with he made all the other men in the room look short, even her uncle. The lean, broad-shouldered frame suggested both strength and energy and was shown off to advantage by formal evening dress. It was severe, almost austere, and a perfect complement for his dark hair. The face, which she had formerly thought arresting, was rather more than that, like the cool grey eyes that were now surveying her steadily. The effect was to create an odd fluttering sensation in the pit of her stomach.

The silence intensified. Then her uncle stepped forward. 'Lord Henry, may I present my niece Elena?'

Harry stared, taking in the slender and willowy figure in the deep red gown. Ebony hair framed a face whose sculptural beauty was accentuated by a complexion that reminded him of ivory and roses. Her brown eyes were flecked with purest amber and, just then, expressive of some strong emotion that resisted precise identification. Curiosity stirred. Then, recollecting his manners, he made his bow.

She returned a graceful curtsey. 'I'm delighted to meet you, my lord.'

'The pleasure is mine,' he replied, with perfect sincerity.

'May I ask what brings you to Madrid?'

He summarised his mission briefly. 'Your uncle has kindly offered his assistance.'

'Then I hope his enquiries will be successful.'

'Thank you, although after all this time I dare not hold out great hope.'

'Even a little hope is better than none,' she replied.

'You are right, of course.' He smiled wryly. 'But enough about business for now. Tell me something of yourself. For instance, do you reside here with your uncle or are you just visiting?'

Before she could reply, Doña Inéz interposed. 'My niece is visiting for a short while only.'

Beneath the irritation caused by that unwarranted

interruption, he was conscious of a stab of something much like disappointment. 'What a pity.'

'It is a necessary deprivation for us all,' said Doña Inéz, 'since, in a few days' time, she is to enter a convent and commence her novitiate.'

Elena made no reply, although her dark eyes revealed a brief flash of anger, then were swiftly veiled.

Harry was dumbfounded. The very idea that such a lovely young woman should become a nun seemed absurd—more than absurd, a criminal waste. Then he reflected that customs were different here, and that if she had such a vocation she should be entitled to follow it. Besides, it was none of his business.

'In that case,' he replied, 'I wish you well on your chosen path.'

Elena looked up and again he caught that flash of anger in her eyes. However, her face remained otherwise impassive.

'Thank you. That is most kind.'

The smooth tone held an inflection that was much like irony, and in spite of himself his curiosity mounted. He would have liked to pursue it, but not in Doña Inéz's company. Unfortunately she showed no sign of moving away. The woman was acting like a strict *dueña*, almost as though she were mounting guard over her niece, though goodness only knew what she thought might happen in a room full of people.

Just then dinner was announced and Don Manuel suggested he might like to take Doña Inéz in. Good manners dictated gracious acquiescence. To his chagrin he found himself seated next to the lady at table as well. Elena took her place opposite, beside Don Fernando.

The conversation at table ranged over various topics, all of them innocuous. Everyone was perfectly civil and nothing could have been more refined than their manners, but Harry became aware of something rather different underneath, an undercurrent of tension that he couldn't pin down. He reminded himself again that it was none of his business, that he had come here to obtain proof of Jamie's death. Interference in family politics was no part of his plan.

After the meal, when the ladies had withdrawn, and the gentlemen had settled down to their port and cigars, the conversation turned to other matters. Harry listened politely, though in truth his mind was preoccupied with his quest rather than the current political situation. It was only the mention of Elena's name that drew his attention squarely back to the company.

'...and so, after we have seen her safely admitted to the convent, I must return to my estates,' said Don Fernando. 'There are matters requiring my attention.'

Their host nodded. 'Of course. It was good of you to take the time to come at all.'

'I felt it to be my duty.'

'A duty we all share,' said Don Esteban. 'The restoration of our family honour is dear to us all. A life of reflection and piety will atone for sin.'

Harry's glass paused in mid-air and he shot a quizzical glance at the speaker. Don Manuel intercepted it.

'You are no doubt shocked, my lord, that sin should be mentioned in the same context as my niece.'

'I was surprised,' Harry admitted, wondering what possible sin so lovely a creature could have committed. He could think of a few that men might want to commit with her, but such a thing would be unthinkable for a highborn young woman and one so zealously guarded.

'My niece's story is not one that we would wish to be generally known.' Don Manuel eyed him keenly. 'I am sure we may rely on your discretion.'

'Of course.'

'When Elena was eighteen she was betrothed to a nobleman of high standing, indeed one of the highest in the land. Unfortunately it was during a period in the war when the action intensified. My brother-in-law, her father, was killed by enemy soldiers. His death fired a young girl's imagination with misplaced patriotic zeal and she ran off and joined a *guerrilla* band.'

Harry regarded him in genuine amazement. Whatever he might have imagined it wasn't that, but then Elena seemed to defy convention in every way.

'War affects people strangely,' he replied, mentally including himself in that category.

Don Manuel nodded. 'Many unfortunate events occur in times of conflict and, goodness knows, our country has seen enough of such things. They leave a bitter legacy.'

'Yes, they do.' Harry felt his gut tighten. The topic came too close to home, reviving memories he'd tried to bury.

'Elena's sisters were models of exemplary conduct. They were originally intended for marriage but, after their father's death, they chose to enter a convent. She did neither of those things, electing instead to live with a group of men like any common drab.'

Harry barely managed to conceal his astonishment. It seemed quite incongruous to think of Elena in such a role. He had seen quite a few common drabs in his time—the army had its camp followers—but she didn't resemble them in any way.

'In fighting for her country her role was perhaps unusual,' he replied, 'but surely not dishonourable.'

'For a woman to take up arms is unnatural. That she should live among men in that way is utterly shameless.'

Harry was tempted to probe further. Had Elena taken a lover from among the *guerrilla* band? It was entirely possible and yet it didn't seem consistent with what he had seen. She was courteous and friendly but there was not the least hint of flirtatiousness in her manner. All the same, he knew better than to ask. Instead he shifted the focus of the conversation a little.

'What of her betrothed?'

'When he learned of her shame he ended the betrothal.'

'I see.'

'Elena remained with the *guerrillas* for two years.' Don Manuel made a vague gesture with his hand. 'Of course, there is no possibility of marriage for her now, and she cannot be permitted to live as a single woman.

Such a thing is unheard of. The only honourable course is for her to enter a convent.'

'We have arranged it,' said Don Fernando.

Harry's fingers tightened on the stem of his glass. 'Am I to understand that Doña Elena is not in accord with this plan?'

'She is a wilful and stubborn young woman who has erred most grievously,' Don Fernando replied. 'It is the responsibility of her family to put a stop to such folly. The convent will do the rest. It is a closed order and a strict one. From now on she will lead a life of piety and prayer away from the eyes of the world.'

Don Esteban nodded. 'The discipline will be highly beneficial and will help her to atone for her behaviour. In time she will come to realise that our decision was made in her own best interests.'

Harry's jaw tightened. There were many things he could have said, indeed wanted to say, but he bit them back even though it went against the grain. The affair was none of his business. Things were done differently here and much stricter controls exerted on young women of good family. Nor was it uncommon for daughters to be given to God, with or without their consent. The latter proposition had always rankled with him. Entry into the religious life through choice was one thing; entry under compulsion was quite another. To use a convent as a means of incarceration was indefensible in his eyes, and he pitied any young woman caught in that situation.

'The family are gathered to witness the ceremony of

admission,' Don Esteban went on. 'When it has taken place we shall all breathe easier.'

Don Fernando nodded. 'Indeed we shall.'

The conversation remained with Harry long after he had left the company and retired to his room. More than ever their plan seemed like a criminal act even though, in the eyes of the law, it was perfectly legal. It was certainly a criminal waste. He had no illusions about why it was happening in spite of all the pious cant he had heard that evening. In the eyes of her family Elena had become a liability and they meant to put her quietly away for good. It was a harsh penalty for something that, presumably, had been a matter of conscience. However, war spawned many atrocities.

Harry shut his eyes, trying not to think about Badajoz, but the darkness was suddenly filled with flames and gunfire and the shouts of drunken soldiers—British soldiers. For three days they had run amok in an orgy of murder, arson, rapine and plunder. Filthy, blood-stained, crazy with drink and consumed with greed, they spared none. When their officers tried to intervene the mob turned on them too. He swallowed hard, feeling sweat start on the palms of his hands, once again watching helplessly as a man fell under a rain of blows from the butt ends of muskets, the scene backlit by the ruddy glow of burning buildings. And in one of those buildings was Belén....

Work held the memories at bay most of the time, along with the social round. For a while it was possible to forget. It was only when he lay in bed at night that the memories revived, often in terrifying dreams. Time had helped, of course, but had never entirely eradicated them. And then fate had taken a hand and brought him back to Spain….

He turned over and thumped the pillow hard. In spite of everything, he had promised Ross to do all in his power to find the proof they needed about Jamie's death. But what if the proof he sought couldn't be found? What if Sanchez was dead now? Harry pushed the thought away, unwilling to contemplate the thought of failure. Too much hung in the balance. He had a job to do and past demons couldn't be allowed to get in the way.

Chapter Three

It was pleasantly warm in the garden, the morning air scented by late roses in the borders adjoining the high walls. Elena scanned the latter covertly. Without a rope or a ladder there was no way to scale them; the gate that led into the lane beyond was made of iron-studded oak and kept securely locked. In spite of its shrubs and flowering beds and attractive fountain, the garden was as much a prison as the house.

She had carefully reconnoitred the property as far as she had been able, making a note of all doors and windows. Concha had filled in the gaps, assessing those areas frequented by the servants.

'All the downstairs windows are barred, Doña Elena. The only possibility is to use one of the bedrooms, preferably the one that looks out over the lane yonder.' Concha jerked her head towards the garden wall that bordered the narrow roadway in question.

'My thought exactly.'

'A pair of knotted sheets should serve. After all, it wouldn't be the first time, would it?'

'Hardly.'

'The only problem is that the Englishman is currently using that bedroom.'

The Englishman! Elena bit her lip. Heaven knew she had met enough of them, but this man was different somehow. Everything about him proclaimed noble birth and education, but it was more than that. He lingered in the mind, conjuring all manner of unexpected and disturbing thoughts. Of course, such a man would attract the attention of women. It shocked her to find that she was not immune, after all. With an effort she forced herself to concentrate on what Concha was saying.

'We'll find a way. We have to.'

Elena nodded. 'Yes, we do.'

'I made sure to pack all the necessary clothing before we came. I put it in the bottom of my own box. I thought it less likely to be searched. The weapons are concealed in thc usual place.'

'Well done. What would I do without you, Concha?'

The maid regarded her steadily. 'I think the boot is on the other foot. But for your honoured father my mother would have hanged and I would have perished. His compassion saved us both and gave us the chance of a future.'

'Some future,' said Elena. 'Look where your loyalty has brought you. Your mother is dead and you…'

'We have been through many trials together, you and I, and we will come through this. After all, we have escaped captivity before, and we have been threatened by experts, no?'

'True.'

'Remember El Lobo and his bandit thugs, to say nothing of the French?'

'How could I forget?'

'Well, then, how should your relatives intimidate you now?'

Elena grinned. 'You're right, of course. I…'

She broke off as her companion gave her arm a warning squeeze. Darting a glance along the path, she fully expected to see one of her aunts approaching. Instead it was a very different figure that hove into sight, a lean and virile figure whose presence caused her pulse to quicken. She drew a deep breath, collecting herself. Then she rose to greet him.

'Lord Henry. What a pleasant surprise.'

Surveying her now Harry thought he could say the same. The blue morning gown became her well, emphasising the curves of her figure and enhancing her warm colouring and the lustrous coils of dark hair. This close proximity did nothing to abate the admiration he had felt at their first meeting, on the contrary. London had its share of beauties, but none who held his attention and certainly none who had such a very kissable mouth. She aroused sensations he'd imagined long dead. He caught himself there. This woman had no interest in him and anyway she was destined for a convent. All thoughts about her physical charms were completely inappropriate. Feeling distinctly guilty now, he adopted an expression of polite attention.

'It seemed too fine a day to remain indoors. I hope I'm not disturbing you.'

'Oh, no, not at all.'

'This is a pleasant garden,' he went on. 'I don't wonder that you should choose to sit out here.'

'I prefer to be out of doors as a rule.'

'So do I.' He paused, unwilling to lose her company but not wishing to overstep the bounds of propriety either. He was well aware that the place was visible from the house and that if he invited Elena to sit with him it might well be misconstrued. Something more subtle was required. 'I wonder if you would care to walk a little way.'

Elena hesitated but then inclined her head in acquiescence. 'As you wish. Concha, you will accompany us.'

Harry hid a grimace. The maid was entirely *de trop* but, under the circumstances, an inescapable encumbrance.

As they set off Elena was careful to keep a foot of clear space between them. Concha fell in behind at a discreet distance. If anyone were to observe them from the house it was all above reproach. They strolled a little way in silence, though from time to time Elena shot a sideways glance at her companion. His proximity made her feel self-conscious—aware of his closeness to her fingertips, a feeling so unaccustomed that she felt unwontedly awkward.

'I regret the need for a chaperone,' she said then. 'It isn't because I don't trust you.'

He smiled. 'I'm glad to hear it.'

'It's just that I must be seen to observe the required forms of behaviour. My aunts…'

'You don't have to explain. I understand perfectly.'

She gave him another sideways look. 'Do you?'

Unwilling to reveal his knowledge about her past, he slid over it. 'Your admission to the convent is to take place very soon, I collect.'

She nodded. 'My uncle has arranged it.'

The words jarred and aroused a sense of impotent anger. Suddenly he wanted to find out more, to hear Elena's side of the matter.

'And how do you feel about the new life you are about to enter?'

'As a man might feel on learning that he is to be imprisoned for the rest of his life.'

The words confirmed what he had suspected from the conversation at table the previous evening. It made the implications all the more unpalatable.

'Then you have no vocation?'

'No vocation, or even a belief in God any more. However, that makes no difference to my family.'

He heard the suppressed anger in her tone, saw it in her eyes. He could well understand it too. More than ever the whole business seemed criminal.

'I'm truly sorry. Is there nothing that can be done to change their minds?'

'They are quite resolved and will not bend.'

'They might show some compassion.'

'They have none. I am twenty-three years old, unmarried and with no prospect of being so. I am therefore a liability they mean to be rid of, and a convent is the ideal place. The method is respectable, discreet and permanent.'

He knew she was right and, even though it was none of his affair, he could not help but feel pity for her predicament and disgust for the perpetrators.

Elena lifted her chin. 'I think that you have heard quite enough of my woes. Let us speak of something else.'

'Certainly.'

'Tell me about your brother, the one whose death has occasioned this visit. I think you must have been very fond of him to travel so great a distance.'

'Jamie was the brother I looked up to most. He was a hero to me when we were younger. I wanted to be just like him.' He smiled wryly. 'It always seemed like a big pair of shoes to fill.'

The smile, albeit transitory, suggested hidden warmth behind the cool English reserve. She sensed there was more here than met the eye and was intrigued.

'Have you other brothers and sisters?'

'Two sisters and three brothers, although Jamie is gone now and the youngest, Edward, died at Waterloo.'

'I'm sorry.'

'It was a terrible blow to all the family, but our father took it hardest. He'd already lost Jamie, you see, and when he received the news of Edward's demise… well, it affected the balance of his mind.'

'It must have been a terrible time for all concerned.'

He sighed. 'It was. Because his body had not been found there was always a little gleam of hope that, somehow, a miracle might happen and Jamie might come back but, as time went on, hope began to fade. Eventually we had to face the facts, of course.'

'But you have not given up hope of obtaining the proof you need.'

He shook his head. 'No, I have not. As for the rest, it's still hard to accept. I always thought I would know if he were really dead, that I'd feel it in my heart. I suppose that was just a form of denial. A foolish one at that.'

'Not foolish at all, only human. There is not a day goes by that I don't think about my father.'

The empathy evident in her look and tone touched something deep inside him. These were things he had never discussed with anyone, until now. Being accustomed to keeping his stronger emotions out of sight this unwonted openness made him feel exposed and yet, paradoxically, comforted too. It also felt like dangerous ground. He needed to return to a surer footing.

'I hope I haven't come on a wild-goose chase.'

'I think you will discover the truth eventually.'

'I hope so.' Harry sighed. 'Besides, it is only just that the estate should pass to the rightful heir. I need to establish who that is.'

'Of course.'

Discovering the facts relating to Jamie's death was only part of the problem, but Harry knew it would not be fitting to discuss such intimate details here. All the same, it was surprisingly easy to talk to Elena. Disarmingly easy. It behoved him to be careful. Whatever his view of the matter she was forbidden fare in every way. What might be regarded as acceptable attentions to a lady in England might well be regarded as familiarity in Spain where interpretation was much stricter. When marriages were arranged here it was not unusual if the bride and groom didn't meet until their wedding day.

That thought engendered others and he wondered what manner of man Elena's betrothed had been that he would abandon a woman in that way. Did he know what he was losing? Had they even met? He could hardly ask her, but all the same his curiosity increased.

'Tell me about your home,' she went on. 'In what part of England does it lie?'

'The family seat is at Castonbury Park in Derbyshire. That's roughly in the middle of the country.'

'The Montague name is an old and respected one, I think.'

'Our line goes back to the Norman Conquest. One of our ancestors came over with Duke William and was rewarded for his service with lands in England.'

'Do you live in a castle, then?'

'No, although there has been a house at Castonbury since the Middle Ages. The original one changed over time as bits were added to provide more living space.

Eventually it was demolished to be replaced with the present house.'

'It must be very grand.'

He smiled faintly. 'Grand enough, I suppose.'

'Do you live there all the time?'

'No, I reside in London for the most part. My work requires it. I visit Castonbury only occasionally now.'

'Your work is with the diplomatic service.'

'That's right. It's how I was able to obtain letters of introduction to your uncle and so begin my investigations about Jamie.'

'I wish you good fortune with that.'

'Thank you. I…' He broke off, seeing the familiar figure of Doña Inéz advancing down the path towards them.

Elena followed his gaze and her smile faded. Her aunt's face suggested stern disapproval, but then it was habitual for her to look that way. Composing her own expression to impassivity, Elena waited.

Doña Inéz acknowledged Lord Henry with a curt nod and then turned to her niece. 'You must come into the house directly, Elena. Sister Maria and Sister Angela are come to give you instruction. They have received special dispensation to do so and should not be kept waiting.'

Elena's jaw tightened and she fought down the urge to refuse point blank and consign both the holy sisters and her aunt to perdition. However, to do so would be a serious mistake. She must continue to play along for now.

'Very well,' she replied. 'I will come.' Turning to

her companion she added, 'I hope you will excuse me, Lord Henry.'

'Of course.' He bowed politely, then watched the two women walk away. More than ever he felt sorry for Elena's predicament, but unfortunately there was nothing he could do about it.

Elena maintained her impassive expression for the next hour as the two elderly nuns schooled her in preparation for entry into the convent. She kept her gaze lowered lest they should read the anger in her eyes. This wasn't going to happen. Concha was right. Somehow they would find a way out.

Meanwhile, the nuns would almost certainly report back to her aunt so a meek and quiet demeanour seemed the best policy for now. If everyone thought she was becoming resigned to her fate, so much the better. Thus she sat without comment through a homily about the sins of pride and disobedience and the need for repentance and reparation through a life of abstinence and prayer. When at length it ended there was a detailed explanation of what would be required on admission to the holy order. That was followed by a period of compulsory prayer in which the nuns expressed the hope that she might be guided back to the path of righteousness for the salvation of her immortal soul. Elena bit her tongue. They knew, because her aunt had evidently told them, that her niece had no vocation for the religious life, but it seemed not to trouble them a whit. So far as they were concerned Elena was a fallen woman. All that mattered now was that she should comply with the wishes of her family and quietly disappear from public view. If they ever got her within the convent gates that would most assuredly happen. She gritted her teeth. Over her dead body…

When eventually it ended and she returned to her room she sent for Concha. The maid eyed her sympathetically.

'I thought they'd never let you go. What could the old crones find to say that took so long?'

'Don't ask. I don't want to insult your intelligence by repeating it.'

'What now, Doña Elena?'

'Can you get out of the house on some pretext or other?'

'Of course.'

'We need to purchase horses and have them in readiness somewhere close at hand. When we make our escape it will have to be fast and we daren't risk taking the animals from my uncle's stable.'

Concha grinned. 'Leave it to me.'

'All that remains, then, is to choose the hour. By the time these pious hypocrites realise what has happened we will be long gone.'

When Don Manuel returned home later that afternoon he sought Harry at once and found him ensconced in the library. On seeing his host enter, Harry laid aside the book he had been reading and got to his feet. Don Manuel smiled.

'I have news which I hope will help you, Lord Henry.'

'You have word of my brother?'

'His name was indeed known to the Intelligence Service here. It seems that he was highly regarded by those with whom he had contact.'

Harry was quite able to believe it. Whatever Jamie had done, he had done well. 'Did your contact know anything about my brother's mission?'

'Only that it was highly sensitive. However, I did discover that the Spanish cell at that time was run by a man called Pablo Garrido. Among those who worked for him was Xavier Sanchez.'

'The person who was with my brother when the accident occurred. He must know exactly what happened. I should like above all things to speak with him and Garrido.'

'The whereabouts of Sanchez are not known,' replied Don Manuel. 'As for Garrido, he retired from the service after the war and returned to his home in Seville. If you seek him you will have a long and dangerous journey.'

'No matter. It's a chance and I must follow it.'

'Then I think you will wish to depart quite soon.'

'Tomorrow,' said Harry. 'The sooner I set off, the sooner I may learn what happened to my brother and obtain the proof I need.'

'I anticipated as much. For that reason I have prepared this.' His host took a small packet of documents from his coat pocket. 'It contains a map which I think you will find useful, and a list of the most reputable inns in the larger towns along your route.' He gave a deprecating smile. 'I fear I cannot vouch for any of the other establishments you may find.'

Harry accepted the packet gratefully. 'I can't thank you enough for your help in this matter.'

'It is my pleasure,' replied Don Manuel.

'I shall travel faster if I ride. My manservant will accompany me and we'll take only the essentials with us. As for the rest…'

'I shall arrange for your carriage and the rest of your luggage to be returned to Santander. From there it will be a simple matter to arrange the necessary transportation to England.'

'That would be most kind. My driver and footman are reliable fellows but they don't speak Spanish.'

'I will provide all assistance to expedite the matter,' said Don Manuel.

'One day I hope to be able to return the favour.'

His host smiled. 'If ever I need a favour I will know where to come.'

After his companion had left him, Harry paced the library floor and tried to order his thoughts. The evidence he needed was out there somewhere. Garrido would be able to shed light on Jamie's mission and might even know where Sanchez could be found. That alone would make the journey worthwhile. Before he left he must write a letter to Giles and apprise him of developments. He resisted the urge to write to their father; it would be wrong to raise hopes in that quarter until he knew more. Given their parent's fragile mental state it would be downright cruel. It might unbalance him even further, something Harry didn't want to be responsible for. He knew he could trust to Giles's discretion. He too might judge it better to keep quiet until Harry had spoken to Garrido. In spite of the obstacles still in his path, Harry experienced a sense of optimism. As Don Manuel had said, the journey to Seville would be long and arduous, but now that there was even a particle of hope, it must be undertaken.

Glancing around his attention fixed on a large desk across the room. He could already see ink and blotter so the chances were good that there would also be notepaper. A swift search revealed it to be the case. Accordingly he sat down and began to write his letter.

He was so preoccupied with his task that he failed to hear the door open. It was only when he heard a familiar voice that he realised he wasn't alone.

'I hope I'm not disturbing you, my lord. I just wanted to return this book but I can come back later if...'

He turned quickly to see Elena standing on the threshold. Her presence was so completely unexpected that it took him aback. Moreover, she had changed her gown for an elegant sprigged muslin creation which looked particularly fetching. Privately he thought she looked good enough to eat. With an effort he gathered his wits and rose quickly.

'No, you're not disturbing me.' He gestured to the shelves along the walls. 'Please, feel free.'

'Thank you.' She crossed the room and replaced the volume, then turned towards him. 'I saw my uncle return to the house earlier. Has he made any progress in his enquiries about your brother?'

'He brought good news.' He gave her the gist of the conversation.

Her heartbeat quickened and, as she listened, the germ of an idea began to grow. 'Then you will be leaving very soon, my lord.'

'Tomorrow, early.'

'I see.'

Harry regarded her steadily. 'I wish that you had news as good to tell me.'

'Alas, I do not.'

'When do you…'

'In two days' time.'

'That soon?'

'My family is eager to see the matter concluded. I will do what I must, my lord.'

'Yes.' He didn't make any attempt at consolation; nothing he could say would be of comfort to her now, given what was about to happen, and she certainly didn't need platitudes. It sickened him to think of any young woman being forced into something so contrary to her desire, and saddened him to know he was powerless to prevent it.

'I am glad that you have some news at last,' she said. 'I hope your journey will prove to be worth the effort.'

She smiled and he felt his throat tighten. In two days' time she would be lost to the world for good, her youth and beauty shut away. He could only hope that, in time, she might somehow become reconciled to her lot, but no matter how hard he tried he couldn't imagine how. His gaze followed her to the door. Then it opened and she was gone.

He sighed and returned to his letter. When it was finished he sanded and blotted the page and then sealed the document before writing the direction. His driver could take it back when he left. It would doubtless be just as fast as sending the missive any other way.

Having dealt with that, he directed his thoughts into other channels. First he needed to speak to Jack and make arrangements for the journey. They could lead a spare horse apiece to carry what they required. Saddlebags and a couple of small boxes would suffice. They'd need provisions, of course. Where possible they could make use of inns along the way; where it wasn't they would camp. After years in the army it wouldn't be any hardship. If it meant that he would finally learn the truth, Harry was prepared to take on whatever came.

Elena hurried off to her room, her mind buzzing with the details of that last conversation. As Lord Henry outlined his plans her own had finally taken shape. The result was mingled hope and excitement. If it worked she would be free. It had to work; she couldn't afford doubt or fear. If she hoped to have a future, then this opportunity must be seized. On reaching the safety of her chamber she lost no time in communicating her plan to Concha. Her companion listened with quiet and smiling approval.

'We have the opportunity now, Doña Elena. The rest is up to us.'

Elena nodded, feeling anticipation rising. For the first time since entering this house she felt real hope. She was more than ready for the coming adventure. Goodness alone knew what her unwitting accomplice was going to say when he found out; she would cross that bridge later. All that mattered now was escape and she knew exactly how it was to be done.

Chapter Four

The following morning Elena rose before dawn and dressed for her role. Surveying herself in the mirror afterwards she couldn't repress a smile. Her aunts would have a fit if they could see her now, her figure shamelessly displayed by the masculine attire. It felt good though, comfortable and familiar after the restrictions of female clothing. She checked the priming of her pistol and then thrust the weapon into her belt beside her knife. The smaller blade slid into her boot. Then she sat down on the edge of the bed to wait, turning over in her mind every last detail of the plan.

Minutes crawled by like hours until three discreet taps on the door announced Concha's return. Quickly Elena unlocked the door and let her in.

'Well?'

'The horses are ready and waiting, Doña Elena. I've packed the saddlebags with a change of clothes and a few other necessities. I couldn't risk taking too much out of the house with me. We'll have to buy provisions later.'

Elena nodded. 'Did you meet any of the other servants?'

'No, but they will be stirring soon. We need to make haste.'

'You've done well. Get changed now while I find out what's happening.'

Concha nodded and began to strip off her gown. Elena went to the door and, after listening carefully, opened it a crack. From the end of the corridor she could just make out the murmur of men's voices. Then a door opened further down the passageway.

'Is that everything?'

'Aye, my lord. Groom's bringing t'horses round directly. I'll take these bags down now.'

A few moments later the English servant went past carrying saddlebags. Elena frowned; she had mistakenly assumed that Lord Henry would continue his journey by coach but of course it was quicker to ride. Easier too, given the state of the roads. She had no leisure to consider the implications because, as the servant disappeared from view, his master hove into sight and he was unmistakably dressed for riding. Elena's heartbeat quickened. She could only hope he would forgive what she was about to do. When he had gone she turned back to Concha.

'Now.'

The two women left the room and, closing the door silently after them, hurried along the passage to the chamber so recently vacated. Once inside they locked the door after them. Concha dragged the sheets off the bed. While she tied them together Elena went to the window and peered out. Then she breathed a sigh of relief. The lane below was deserted. Just now all attention would be on the front of the house from whence Lord Henry was leaving. Her aunts had said their farewells the previous evening and Don Fernando and Don Esteban never rose before ten. Her uncle would likely be the only one abroad because courtesy demanded he be present to see his guest depart. With a pounding heart she turned to her companion.

'Come on, Concha. It's now or never.'

They fastened one end of the makeshift rope to the central mullion and flung the rest out of the window. It snaked away down the wall and stopped a few feet clear of the bottom. Elena climbed over the sill and then, taking a firm grip on the sheet, began her descent. It was only a short distance to jump at the end and then she was standing in the lane. Moments later Concha joined her. They exchanged grins and then, together, they ran.

Another two minutes brought them to the waiting horses. Of necessity they had to keep to a steady pace until they were clear of the city and Elena had to resist the urge to look over her shoulder every five minutes. There was no reason to fear pursuit just yet. With luck it would be hours before their flight was discovered. Enquiries would reveal that they were seen heading west, but once clear of Madrid they would circle round and turn south instead. After that they would have to ride fast. Fortunately they were well used to that. If they could throw off their pursuers for long enough her family would likely wash their hands of the whole business. She and Concha would go to England. It was going to be a long and dangerous journey but, if things turned out as she'd planned, they wouldn't have to do it alone.

Harry and Jack made good progress over the course of the day and, by evening, had covered about twenty miles. It might have been more but they'd stopped at midday to rest the horses, and thereafter had deliberately slackened the pace. With so many miles to cover it made no sense to push their mounts too hard, especially not in the heat of the day. Harry was glad it was not yet summer so the midday heat would not be too fierce.

They made their camp by a stream, and having attended to the animals' needs, turned to their own. Don Manuel had been generous in providing them with provisions so they wouldn't need to concern themselves with that for a while. Afterwards they could stop off en route to restock, even hunt if necessary.

'Did you ever visit Seville before, my lord?'

'No, but I understand it's a beautiful city.'

'I heard that too. It'll be interesting to find out.' Jack smiled wryly. 'T'army didn't allow time for much sightseeing.'

'No, it didn't.'

'When I left Spain after t'war I never thought as how I'd be back one day.'

'Nor I.'

'Strange how things work out, isn't it?'

Harry sighed. 'Very strange. If there is a divine plan I'm damned if I know what it is.'

'Well, I suppose if we don't want local bandits to be part of t'plan we'd best keep a watch. I'll take first one if you want to get some sleep, my lord.'

'Very well. You can wake me at...' Harry broke off, listening intently. Then he looked at his companion. 'Do you hear it?'

'Aye, my lord. Riders, coming this way.'

'They could be harmless, but keep your rifle handy until we find out.'

Harry scanned the road, staring intently into the gathering twilight. While banditry was rife he would have expected to be further from the city before experiencing any such problems. Most likely the two horsemen were just travellers like themselves.

'They're slowing down,' said Jack. 'Must've smelled t'smoke from our fire.'

'Probably.'

The horses came into view round a bend in the road. There were only two. Harry let out the breath he had been holding.

'Not a serious problem, I think.'

'Aye, they may just ride on, my lord.'

'Perhaps. Best to be sure though.'

'As you say.'

However, as they drew nearer the riders turned off the road and approached the camp. Harry frowned.

'Wait. Do they look familiar to you?'

'Funny you should say that, my lord. I was just thinking t'same th…' Jack broke off. Then as the riders reined in his eyes widened. 'Blood and sand! What in hell's name are they doing here?'

Being temporarily robbed of speech, Harry vouchsafed no reply. He thought he knew the answer already, and the ramifications were deeply disturbing. Mingled with that was another sensation that he didn't want to examine too closely.

'Looks like a mort o' trouble, my lord.'

Harry found his voice. 'Indeed.'

As far as he could see, trouble didn't begin to cover it. Reading his expression correctly, Jack nodded.

'Best take a firm line wi' 'em, I reckon.'

'Absolutely.'

Harry watched as the two women dismounted and then, grim-faced, went to meet them.

Elena handed her horse's reins to Concha and, taking a deep breath, watched the advancing figure. When she had plotted the details of their escape from Madrid her imagination had conveniently glossed over this scene. In those hopeful plans Lord Henry was most sympathetic and immediately acceded to her request. Now that the reality was upon her, she felt far less confident. In the first place Lord Henry looked distinctly forbidding, and, in the second, much larger than she remembered. His servant was no weakling either. He would do what his master ordered. She licked dry lips. What if his master decided to take her straight back? What if she had been entirely mistaken in him? Sweat started on the palms of her hands.

Further speculation was impossible because he was in front of her now, every last intimidating inch of him. Under the weight of that penetrating gaze any coherent thought became difficult. It swept her from head to toe, creating a *frisson* that was only partly to do with fear. Then it returned to her face and remained there. He came straight to the point.

'You've run away.'

'Yes. I'm sorry to spring this on you, my lord, but I had no choice.'

The grey eyes were steely. 'To spring what on me, exactly?'

Her heart pounded. 'Concha and I want to travel with you.' Seeing his expression she hurried on. 'We are both accomplished riders, we both know how to take care of ourselves and we're used to rough living.'

'I dare say. All the same…'

'We won't slow you down and we won't be a nuisance.'

'You cannot seriously imagine…'

'All we ask is the protection of your company until we reach England.'

'England! Now, look…'

'I have a married sister who lives in Hertfordshire. She will help us, only first we have to get there.'

'I'm not going to England, Elena, not for months yet.'

'Of course not. First we will help you to discover the truth about your brother. Then we will go.'

'Elena, you must see that it isn't possible.'

There it was again, the familiar use of her name,

yet it didn't seem in any way disrespectful on his lips. Rather it afforded a glimmer of hope.

'I will not go back, my lord.'

'I wasn't suggesting that you should, but nor is it fitting that you should attempt such a journey.'

'If you do not help us, then we shall go on alone and face what comes.'

'It's too dangerous. Quite apart from the vagaries of the weather and the numerous natural obstacles you are likely to encounter, the mountains are full of brigands.'

'It would be less dangerous with four,' she replied. 'Concha and I both shoot well.'

Harry felt winded, as though he had fallen from a great height and then landed between a rock and a hard place. Desperately he tried to marshal his thoughts. Elena wouldn't go back and he didn't blame her for it, but neither could he let her go on alone. Every masculine instinct forbade it. Yet the implications of their going on together were fraught with difficulty too. No matter what she said to the contrary, he would be responsible for the two women. It was a burden of care he could do without. Besides, his track record in that area was abysmal. Had he not already failed the woman who had trusted him most? Had he not also failed the man who had been his best friend? Their trust in him had been misplaced and both were dead. His jaw tightened. If he abandoned Elena and Concha now he would be adding two more to that score because they would likely perish before they ever saw Seville, never mind

England. Conscience dictated that he couldn't let that happen.

'All right. You travel with us, but it will be on the condition that you take orders from me.'

'Of course.'

'I mean it, Elena. All our lives may depend on it.'

She nodded. 'Very well.'

'You will take your turn to keep watch, gather wood for the fire and cook when necessary. You will also look after your own mounts. Is that understood?'

Her expression was the epitome of meekness. 'Clearly, my lord.'

'Good.'

'I'll help Concha unsaddle our horses, then.' She turned away and then paused, glancing back over her shoulder. 'Thank you. You won't regret this, I swear it.'

Harry wished he could believe that.

As the two women led the horses away, Jack came to stand beside his master, regarding the scene quizzically.

'They're not leaving right way, then, my lord?'

'They're not leaving at all.'

Jack stared at him. 'Does that mean what I think it does?'

'Yes.'

'Er, right.'

Harry's eyes glinted. 'You have some difficulty with that, perhaps?'

'Oh, no, my lord, none at all.'

Chapter Five

Elena lay on her back looking up at the stars. For the first time in weeks she felt a real sense of optimism and contentment. She and Concha would get to England and they would have a future. Life was looking better than it had for a long time. They were going to have to tread warily around Lord Henry Montague for a while though. As she had hoped, he had done the gentlemanly thing. In that respect she had not mistaken her man. All the same it was clear that he wasn't overjoyed about having two women along. No doubt he feared they would be a burden. He would learn the error of such thoughts in due course. She smiled to herself in the darkness.

Now that his face had imposed itself on her mind she was in no hurry to dismiss it. He was unlike any man she had ever met and he aroused her curiosity. Although he had told her a little about his home and his family there was so much more she would have liked to know. Was he married? Was there a wife waiting for him in England? It seemed likely. Such a man could have his pick of all the noble ladies in the land, but he did not seem to be a womaniser. His heart would not be easily won, but the woman who succeeded in doing that would have it for ever. She sighed. Once she had dreamed of something similar but the dream was ashes now. Her former betrothed might have had one of the oldest and most respected names in Spain but he had turned out to have feet of clay as well. With hindsight she suspected he could never have made her happy no matter how prestigious their marriage. Happiness now was not concerned with such things, only with reaching England and finding some pleasant spot where she might live in peace.

Harry leaned against a tree, listening, but apart from the gentle chirring of cicadas and the occasional rustling sound that betrayed a small animal in the grass, he heard nothing to disturb him. Having relieved Jack of the watch some time ago he could have expected a lengthy period of tedium. As it was he had plenty to occupy his mind. When he had set out for Spain he had anticipated difficulties, but nothing of this magnitude. All his concerns were centred on the past; never in a thousand years would he have imagined the advent of Elena Ruiz or the thoughts her presence would evoke. Since Badajoz his contact with women had been restricted to polite social intercourse and that by choice. All thoughts of romance were gone along with Belén. War lent intensity to love; since the future was uncertain there was always a sense of wanting to make the most of the present. At the same time was the hope that there would be a future, a home, a family. They'd made so many plans…

A twig snapped behind him, jerking him out of thought. He swung round, pointing the rifle in the direction of the sound. Then a familiar figure stepped out of the darkness.

'Elena. What are you doing here?'

'I have come to relieve you of the watch, of course.'

'Oh.' For a second or two he was completely taken aback. Then, as the recollection of their earlier conversation returned, he felt a twinge of guilt. Temporary consternation had caused him to speak rather more harshly than he'd intended. Besides, leaving a woman alone in open country in the middle of the night went right against the grain. 'There's no need.'

'I think there is.'

'We can discuss it tomorrow. You must be tired. You've had a long ride today.'

'So have you,' she replied. 'Besides, we made an agreement, did we not?'

'Well, yes, but…'

'Then I think we should start as we mean to go on.'

For a moment he was silent, then reluctantly nodded. 'Very well.'

'Concha will take over from me later.'

In spite of himself he smiled. 'You seem to be well organised.'

'I have always found it helpful. Then everyone knows where they stand.'

'Yes, quite.' He paused. 'I'll leave you to it, then.'

'Goodnight, my lord.'

He turned to go, then checked mid-stride. 'Since we're going to be spending a lot of time together we can dispense with formalities. My name is Harry.'

With that he left her. For a moment Elena stood staring after him, then smiled to herself.

'Goodnight, Harry,' she murmured.

On his return to camp Harry rolled himself in his blanket and settled down to sleep. However, in spite of fatigue it proved elusive. The thought of Elena alone in the darkness didn't help, but it was clear she wasn't going to be dissuaded. She'd been part of a *guerrilla* group for two years so he knew he could trust her with the job. The ground rules had just been established: she and Concha were not expecting any preferential treatment. They were comrades-in-arms and nothing more. It was undoubtedly the right decision. If this new-formed partnership was to succeed there could be no suggestion of flirtation or anything untoward. It would be better for all concerned if he continued to think of Elena as a nun. Better and safer. He sighed. If only she'd looked the part it would be easier. As it was, the nun had beauty enough to waken the dead and was disarmingly easy to talk to. No matter how he looked at it, the future seemed beset with difficulty.

They broke camp early the next day to make the most of the cool morning hours. Harry eased his horse alongside Elena's, eyeing it critically.

'Is that beast from your uncle's stable by any chance?' he asked.

'No, it would have been too risky. Concha purchased them from a livery stable. She made the owner an offer he couldn't refuse.'

'I'll wager he was delighted.'

She laughed. 'They're not exactly bloodstock, are they? But then good looks aren't everything.'

'True enough.' The horse was no longer uppermost in his mind; rather it was the way that laughter lit her face. It suited her. He thought he'd like to see her laugh more often. He couldn't help noticing either that her current attire suited her very well too, confirming all his earlier notions about her figure. Nor did he miss the pistol in her belt.

'I assume that isn't for decoration.'

'You assume correctly.'

'Where did you learn to shoot?'

'My father taught me. He thought it an essential part of my education.' Elena gave him a sideways glance. 'How do you come to speak Spanish so well?'

'I spent many years in your country during the war.'

'In the diplomatic service?'

'In the army.'

She felt a sudden knot of tension in her stomach. 'I see.' Framing her next words carefully she went on, 'You must have been involved in a lot of actions.'

'Enough to last me a lifetime.'

'War leaves a bitter legacy, does it not?'

The words were an uncanny echo of a former conversation, one that Harry would have preferred to forget.

'It's something I choose not to dwell on,' he said.

She nodded. 'Probably most of those who lived through it feel the same. Yet life can never be as it was before.'

'We do the best we can.'

'My sister has been lucky—Dolores, I mean. She has a good man and, now, three children.'

'Her husband is English, I collect.'

'Yes. He was a soldier too, a gentleman of means but not of high birth. They met at the start of the war. There was opposition to the match—Dolores was intended for a wealthy Spanish nobleman—but she wore our father down eventually. Our aunts never forgave either of them, of course.'

'That doesn't entirely surprise me.'

'Are you married?'

'No. I once hoped to be, but my fiancée died in the war.'

It was out almost before he'd realised, but then her question had caught him unawares. The answer awakened a host of painful memories. His jaw tightened. Belén had died because he'd failed her. If he'd followed his instinct and married her at once he could have taken her away and she would have been safe. The consequences of that decision haunted him still.

Elena surveyed him with quiet sympathy. 'I'm so sorry.'

'So am I.'

She would have liked to know more but it was clearly dangerous ground and she had no wish to alienate him. He must have been very much in love. Indeed, it seemed he still grieved for the woman he had lost. She was aware of a sensation very like envy. Her betrothed had never cared like that, had not cared at all, in fact—only she hadn't discovered it until she needed him most. The memory was bitter and she pushed it away. Harry Montague's lady had been lucky in that respect at least.

'My father died in the war.'

'Your uncle mentioned the fact.' As soon as the words were out he cursed mentally. He hadn't meant to reveal any part of that private after-dinner conversation.

Elena kept her voice level. 'Did he relate the circumstances?'

Harry hesitated, but decided it was pointless to lie. 'Briefly, yes.'

'I see.' Although it was a difficult subject she was rather relieved that her uncle had been frank with him about her past. It would save further explanations. 'Well, after what happened I could not stay in Badajoz.'

His heart leapt towards his throat. 'Badajoz?'

'Yes. My family home was there. Did not my uncle tell you that?'

'No, he said only that it was soldiers who performed the outrage. I assumed they were French.'

'Atrocities were not confined to any one military group,' she replied. 'It was British soldiers who ran amok in Badajoz and it was they who… Well, you know what happened.'

Harry shut his eyes for a moment to regain his equilibrium. He knew what had happened all right. Murder had stalked the streets then.

'What occurred there is a matter of everlasting shame to my country,' he replied.

'I imagine you can understand why my family were so keen for me to enter a convent.'

'Their view is not one I share.'

'That is fortunate for me and I'm grateful.'

'I wasn't seeking your gratitude.'

'You have it all the same.' She shot him a sideways look. 'I must apologise for embroiling you in my problems but in truth I could think of no other way out.'

'I hope you won't come to regret your decision. The journey is going to be long and hard.'

'But the company is good.'

'I'm glad that you think so.' He could only hope she wouldn't be disillusioned. Fortunately she knew relatively little about him and he wasn't about to enlighten her further.

'You would not have come on such a journey without a servant whom you trusted.'

Harry nodded. 'You're quite right. Jack Hawkes and I know each other well.'

'He is a family retainer?'

'Not exactly. He was once a member of my company. We served together during the war.'

'And then you employed him afterwards.'

'Just so.'

'Had he no family, then?'

'None that he knows of. The company was his family in the end.'

She nodded. 'I can understand that. War creates a bond between men.'

It was an echo of his own former thought and he regarded her in surprise. 'You speak knowledgeably.'

'I have spent some time among fighting men.'

Curiosity increased. 'The *guerrilla* force your uncle mentioned?'

'That's right. Does it shock you?'

'I own to surprise. It's not the role I would immediately have associated with you.'

'It was that or the convent.'

'But were you not engaged to be married?'

'My betrothed broke off our engagement.'

Harry was conscious of having strayed onto dangerous ground. He sensed the hurt beneath the level tone and felt awkward. Clearly these were personal matters which he had no right to probe.

'More fool him,' he replied.

The words carried no discernible trace of irony. Elena eyed him askance, momentarily taken aback. At the same time the memory she had tried to suppress resurfaced. It ought not to have hurt any more, and she was disconcerted to discover that it did. With an effort she kept her tone neutral.

'It would have shamed him to marry me.'

'Why? You had been through a dreadful experience and you did what you thought you had to afterwards.'

'Yes, but I was dishonoured all the same. He was

very polite but he made it quite clear that marriage was out of the question.' She lifted her chin. 'I realised then that he felt nothing for me at all.'

The scene was still horribly vivid, the details etched on her memory. The Barilla family estate was outside the city, but Jose had come to find Elena when news of the rioting troops reached him. His shock on seeing the destruction they had wreaked was plain, but it was as nothing when he understood what had happened to her father, and to the female members of the household. Elena had been so relieved to see him that she hadn't considered what might lie beneath his evident abhorrence. More than anything she wanted him to take her in his arms, to make her feel safe. However, on entering the vandalised *salón* where she waited, he left a yard of space between them and made no attempt to close the gap.

'I should have been here to protect you,' he said.

'They would have killed you, Jose.'

'Better that than such dishonour.'

'The dishonour is not yours,' she replied. 'It belongs to those who committed the deed.'

'Yet the taint can never be expunged.' He let out a long breath. 'I imagine that you intend to follow your sisters to the convent.'

Elena frowned. 'Why should you imagine that?'

He stared at her. 'But surely, after what has happened there can be no other choice.'

A cold lump settled deeper in her stomach. 'No other choice?'

'You must see that we cannot marry now. It is impossible.'

'Is it?'

'Elena, there may be consequences to the events that took place here.'

'You mean I may have conceived a child.'

He winced. 'It is a possibility. You must know that.'

'I will know soon enough.' She paused. 'And if there is not a child?'

He shook his head. 'After such a violation I cannot consider… I have my family to think of. You must see that.'

'I do see. I think I'm truly seeing for the first time.'

He ignored the implication and stolidly maintained the calm, reasonable tone. 'The wisest course for you now is to enter a convent. You have become soiled goods. No man of good family can marry you after what has happened.'

Elena felt as though she had been turned to stone. It couldn't be happening. This stranger could not be Jose; he only looked like him. She wanted to shake him, to scream, to weep, to plead with him not to abandon her but she did none of those things, knowing that it would be useless. Gathering the shredded remains of pride she lifted her chin.

'You're right, of course. I was foolish to think anything else.'

He nodded. 'I wish it had been otherwise, Elena, from the bottom of my heart.'

'Your heart? If you possess one at all it was never mine.'

'Elena, I…'

'Go, Jose. Just go.'

For a moment he looked as though he were about to answer but then thought better of it. Instead he had turned away and walked out of her life for good….

'He felt nothing for me,' she repeated.

Harry regarded her steadily. 'In that case you were well rid of him.'

'So I think, now.'

He hesitated, but the urge to know overcame reticence. 'Were you in love with him?'

'I thought I was. He was young, handsome, wealthy, educated, amusing—all the things a young woman could want in a suitor.' She smiled wryly. 'I see now that I was in love with the idea of him. Of course I was younger then and very naive. It never occurred to me to look beneath the superficial charm. I accepted it all at face value.'

'We've all done that at some point in our lives.'

'It is painful to discover that the idol has feet of clay.'

'There must have been other admirers since.'

Her expression grew cool. 'I have not sought them.'

Again he could have kicked himself. 'Forgive me. That was confoundedly tactless. It's just that a woman like you would always excite admiration.'

'My time was spent planning ambushes and fighting. Romance played no part in it.'

'I didn't mean to imply anything untoward.' He paused. 'You might have got yourself killed.'

'At the time I didn't care. But, as it turned out, I never suffered any serious injury. It was as though I bore a charmed life.'

'I'm glad of it.'

Again the tone was sincere. Moreover, he was not critical of her actions and nor was he judgemental. After the opprobrium she had suffered of late it was a pleasant and unexpected change. But then he was unexpected in so many ways. It occurred to her to wonder then what might have happened if she had met such a man when she was younger, before the war had changed her life for ever. For a brief instant she had a glimpse of something that was beyond all former dreams of romance. It was followed by a sensation of sadness and loss. Her throat tightened. Such happiness as that was afforded to few, and it certainly didn't include her.

They stopped at midday to rest their mounts and then, having eaten and taken a short siesta, resumed their journey. It was late afternoon when they heard other horses approaching, a large group riding fast. Elena's stomach lurched and she darted a look at Concha. The other woman's face revealed the same misgivings. Jack Hawkes looked at his master.

'Should we pull off t'road and let 'em pass, my lord?'

'Yes, and let's hope that passing is their intention.'

Jack glanced at the women. 'Do you think it might be…'

'I don't know but I expect we're about to find out.'

They had no sooner reined aside than the oncoming group swept around the bend. Harry counted a dozen riders; depressing odds if they were local brigands. His jaw tightened. The leading horsemen saw them and he heard a shout. There could be no doubt now that they were the target. The thunder of hooves came closer. His hand moved towards the Baker rifle in the saddle boot, then paused. Had he and Jack been alone he wouldn't have hesitated, but the women's presence made him reluctant to draw fire.

'What do you want to do, my lord?'

'Nothing, yet,' he replied.

Before they could say more, the oncoming riders were upon them. In moments the little group was surrounded and a dozen pistols trained in their direction. Judging from their stony expressions, the bearers would very much have liked to use the weapons and clearly wouldn't hesitate if given the order. Then, through the swirling dust, Harry recognised the man who led them. Don Manuel reined in a few yards away.

'Did you really think to get away with this, my lord?' He glowered at Elena. 'Or you either?'

Elena's stomach wallowed. This was rapidly assuming the proportions of a nightmare. She had miscalculated badly to assume that her uncle would wash his hands of her, and now innocent people were caught up in her botched plan. She directed an agonised glance at Harry but he failed to see it: his attention was focused squarely on her uncle.

'I can explain, *señor.*'

Don Manuel regarded him with cold contempt. 'I'm not interested in your explanation. I welcomed you in good faith and gave you all possible assistance. In return you have betrayed my hospitality in the basest way possible, and you have brought dishonour to my house.'

'I understand why you might think so, but the situation is not what it seems.'

'The situation is perfectly clear, my lord. I can only lament that a man of your rank and birth should have stooped to such subterfuge.'

Harry held on to his temper. 'There was no subterfuge here.'

'Do not compound your crime with falsehood.'

'I resent both those suggestions, *señor.*'

'You resent? It is *I* who am the injured party here and *you* who have violated my trust.'

Unable to remain silent any longer, Elena interjected. 'No. He was not to blame.'

Don Manuel glared at her. 'Lies won't save him. He will learn what it means to besmirch the noble name of Urbieta.'

'What do you mean to do?'

'He and his treacherous henchman will hang from yonder tree. When it is done you will be delivered directly to the convent and your name will never be mentioned in my house again.' Don Manuel turned to his servants. 'Bind these men.'

She stared at him in appalled disbelief. However, it

became horribly clear that her uncle meant every word. Under his flinty gaze, four of his men dismounted and advanced on Harry and Jack. Despite strong resistance, they were dragged from their horses and manhandled across the intervening space to be brought before their judge. Sick with dread now Elena flung herself off her own mount and ran to stand with them.

'They are innocent. They had no knowledge of my intended escape. I used their departure to cover my own. It was only later when they were embarked upon their journey that Concha and I came up with them.'

The maid nodded. 'It is true, *señor*.'

Don Manual directed a quelling glance her way. 'Silence, wench! You are as complicit as the rest and you will be punished accordingly. Were you a man I'd have you hanged. As it is you may count yourself fortunate to be let off with a flogging.'

Concha paled but she did not lower her gaze.

'She was obeying my orders,' said Elena. 'No blame attaches to her either. If your anger must fall on someone, let it fall on me. Lord Henry did not wish to take us along with him but he would not abandon us either. He had no choice but to do what he did.'

'He should have brought you back at once.'

'I did not wish to return and he would not force me to do so.'

'I can well imagine he would not. No doubt he had other plans for a slut such as you.'

A muscle jumped in Harry's jaw. 'You are insulting, *señor*. I will not permit such imputations to be made.'

'Can you deny that it was part of your scheme?'

'I certainly do deny it. My intention was to escort the lady to England in accordance with her wishes, and that is all.'

Elena glanced at Harry and then met her uncle's gaze. 'He's telling the truth.'

'He *is*, *señor*,' said Concha, 'though you flog me for saying so.'

Don Manuel scowled at them but made no immediate reply. Elena's heart pounded in her breast.

'The fault is mine, Uncle. I swear this on my parents' graves.'

'Even if Lord Henry was not the instigator of the plan,' said Don Manuel, 'he has been instrumental in bringing dishonour to the family name.'

Harry's eyes glinted. 'If you seek satisfaction, *señor*, you may have it.'

'No,' said Elena. 'I would not have any bloodshed on my account.'

'Have no fear. I would not sully my blade in so sordid a matter,' replied her uncle. 'Yet this dishonour must be expunged.' He fixed Harry with a gimlet stare. 'If your intentions are honourable as you claim, my lord, then you will prove it.'

'How may I do so?'

'By taking my niece to wife. You shall marry her this very day. If not I shall have you and your servant hanged and she will go to the cloister.'

The pronouncement was met with dumbfounded silence. Elena's cheeks went paper-white.

'Uncle, this is not…'

'Enough! Which is it to be, my lord?'

Harry knew there was only one possible answer now and he gave it.

Chapter Six

It was a matter of some five miles to the nearest town, a journey undertaken at a pace that precluded any opportunity for speech. Once or twice Elena glanced Harry's way but he continued to look resolutely ahead of him, his expression like stone. Shocked beyond measure by her uncle's decision and appalled by the consequences of her actions, she found coherent thought almost impossible. All she could see just then was looming disaster. Once she had eagerly anticipated marriage and all that it entailed. Of course, back then, the agreement would have been entered into by mutual consent and in all honour; now she was soiled goods to be offloaded because it suited her uncle's purpose. One way or another he meant to be rid of her. Her wishes didn't enter into it, or those of her intended bridegroom.

As she thought about Harry her stomach churned. How disgusted and angry he must be at this moment. He hadn't wanted any part of her scheme but had been too gentlemanly to abandon her. By heaven, he must be wishing he had though. And when the knot was tied and she was completely in his power, what revenge might he take then? The memory of Badajoz returned with leering drunken faces and men obscenely unbuttoned, hands tearing her clothing, holding her down while they did their will.... She shuddered. Was it all about to happen again? From her limited experience of him, Harry did not seem to be the brutal type but, even so, as her husband he would expect his will to be met. Elena swallowed hard.

In an alarmingly short time the cavalcade arrived at the town and pulled up in the plaza in front of the church. Half a dozen men detained Jack and Concha; the remainder hustled Elena and Harry inside. Hearing the intrusion a startled priest paused by the altar.

'Mass is not for another hour.'

Don Manuel fixed him with a steely gazc. 'We are not here for the mass, but to see these two married.'

'That is not possible. Perhaps tomorrow...'

A fat leather purse landed on the floor at his feet, the jingle of coin seeming loud in the still air.

'Marry them,' said Don Manuel.

The pricst hesitated and licked dry lips. Then he nodded. 'As you wish.'

Elena's heart thumped against her ribs and she closed her eyes, willing that she might wake up. White-faced, she glanced at the man beside her. This time he saw it and returned her gaze. His face was impassive but the expression in the grey eyes was unmistakable. Good heavens, he was furious. How he must despise her now.

She shivered inwardly. Mingled with dread was a deep sadness that she had forfeited whatever small regard he might once have had for her. At that moment she would almost have preferred to be in a convent cell.

At the priest's command they knelt. Harry was scarcely aware of the droning voice, only of roiling emotion. Elena had correctly read the fury uppermost in his mind but she had entirely mistaken its direction. For a moment or two he indulged a savage fantasy involving a dull blade and Don Manuel's vital organs. Underlying that were very different feelings.

He threw a covert glance at the woman beside him. He hadn't missed the expression of abject terror in her eyes just now; by rights she should have fallen into a fit of hysterics. Most women would have done so long since. But then Elena wasn't most women. She'd had the courage to face her uncle's wrath and to take responsibility for her actions, to exonerate everyone else. But for that determined intervention he and Jack would almost certainly be swinging from a tree by now. She had been subjected to public insult and humiliation into the bargain, another bone he'd like to pick with her uncle. As for this present outrage…

'…do you take this woman to be your lawful wedded wife?'

The priest's voice brought him back to reality with a jolt. Taking a deep breath Harry made his reply. A short time later he heard the corresponding affirmation from Elena.

'Do you have the ring?'

Harry looked blankly at the priest for a moment and then, as his brain caught up, realised he'd got nothing of the kind or indeed anything that would serve. In consequence it looked as though Elena's humiliation wasn't over yet. He took a deep breath.

'I regret…'

Don Manuel cut him off. 'It is here.'

From his jacket pocket he produced a fine gold band and placed it on the open bible. Harry stared at it in astonishment. Where the devil had the man got that from? Borrowed it from one of his entourage, perhaps? However, when he picked it up, it was immediately evident that so small a ring could never have belonged to any of the brawny thugs who had accompanied Don Manuel. It slid easily onto Elena's slender finger though, almost as if it had been intended for the purpose. Suspicion took root. He shot a swift glance at the don and saw the faint cold smile on his lips. Implication became certainty and Harry understood then that this had been the intention from the outset. *If ever I need a favour I will know where to come.* When he discovered Elena had fled, her uncle had taken a shrewd guess at her plan and laid his own accordingly. On discovering his guess to be correct, he'd baited the trap and drawn them in. They'd fallen for it hook, line and sinker! In that moment Harry didn't know what he wanted most: to shoot the old fox, to run him through or to strangle him with his bare hands.

Elena sensed the sudden increased tension in the man beside her. His anger was almost palpable now. She swallowed hard, not daring to look at him, too keenly aware of the enormity of what she had done. Instead she looked down at the ring on her hand. It felt like an alien presence but it bound them fast, like the promises they had just made. For one irrational moment she thought that, if they had been compelled to wed years ago, then their chance of happiness would surely have been as good as anyone else's on entering the married state. As it was…

'I now pronounce you husband and wife.' The priest's face assumed an unctuous smile. 'You may kiss the bride.'

Her heartbeat accelerated. She saw Harry turn towards her and then his gaze met hers, only now the grey eyes revealed nothing of the thoughts behind. His face came closer and she closed her eyes, felt his lips brush hers, a sudden intimacy that intensified the fluttering sensation in the pit of her stomach. It should have been repellent but it was not. Rather it revived something in her that she had thought long lost. Then it was over. When she opened her eyes again he had drawn back. She saw him rise and extend a hand to her. Trembling she took it. Strong warm fingers closed over hers and squeezed gently, a gesture that was both reassuring and unexpected.

Wordlessly she allowed herself to be led from the church. After the close confines of the building with the musty smells of dust and stale incense, fresh air was a blessed relief. She took several deep breaths to steady herself. Then she became aware of the rest of her uncle's entourage waiting a little way off, and with them Concha and Jack, both grim-faced. Harry paused and, retaining his hold on her hand, turned to face her uncle. For a moment they faced each other in silence. Then Don Manuel spoke.

'I bid you both farewell. We shall not meet again.'

'You are quite correct,' replied Harry. 'We shall not.'

The don strolled across to the horses and, retrieving his own, remounted. As the rest of his servants followed suit he glanced once more at the newly wed couple. Then he turned his horse's head and rode away with his men.

For a moment the quartet in front of the church watched them go. Then several more moments passed in awkward silence. Offering congratulations to the newly married couple didn't seem appropriate in the circumstances and yet, in the light of what had just happened, all other topics seemed irrelevant. It was Harry who eventually solved the dilemma.

'It's getting late. We'll find an inn and stay there tonight. Jack, why don't you and Concha go and seek out somewhere suitable?'

Clearly relieved at having something to do, Jack nodded. 'Right away, my lord.'

He and Concha exchanged glances and then hurried off. Elena watched them depart and then turned to Harry.

'I don't know how I can begin to apologise to you.'

He surveyed her steadily. 'It is not you who should apologise.'

'I dragged you into this business and, but for me, you would still be a free man.'

'But for you I might have been a dead man.'

'You are generous.'

'It's the truth,' he replied, though remembering the don's cold smile he knew that superintending this marriage had always been the man's intention.

'Your life has been turned upside down because of my folly.'

'You did what you felt you had to do at the time. Would you rather have gone to the convent?'

She shook her head. 'Never that.'

'Things could be much worse, then.'

'They are bad enough, I think.'

'You do yourself too much disservice.' His gaze held hers. 'I know that from now on I shall be the subject of much envy among my fellow men.'

She could detect no trace of irony in his tone or any note of disdain. It intensified her guilt. In many ways it would have been easier if he had given voice to his anger and berated her soundly. This quiet and gentlemanly conduct was unnerving. Was he waiting for a less public place in which to vent his wrath? After all, he could do anything he liked now. Officially she had become his property. As the ramifications of that loomed large her unease increased.

Fortunately Jack returned a few minutes later with the intelligence that suitable accommodation had been secured.

'It's not t'finest inn I've ever seen, my lord, but it's clean and seems to be well-run.'

Harry smiled faintly. 'Good. At least we can look forward to a decent meal and a comfortable bed, then.'

Elena's stomach lurched.

The inn was just as Jack had described it: unpretentious but clean and well-run. The food, though equally unpretentious, was good, home-cooked fare. At any other time Elena would have enjoyed it. As it was, she had no idea what she ate that evening. All she could think of was the man sitting opposite, the man who was now her husband. Apart from one brief interlude in the library at her uncle's house, this was the first time she had been alone with him. Once she would not have found that a displeasing prospect. Now it filled her with dread.

They were sharing a private dining room but, since the food required their attention, conversation was minimal. Elena's appetite had fled but she forced herself to eat, taking her time, trying not to think about what must inevitably come. Several times she shot a glance at her companion but his face gave nothing away. Nor did his appetite seem in any way diminished by recent events. She watched him put away a bowl of soup and a manchet of bread, a generous portion of *pastel de puerros* and then follow it up with *patatas bravas* and a *bistec* that must have come from the largest steer in all of Spain. Moreover, he ate it with ease. How could he be so calm when her stomach was in knots? She took another drink of wine to steady herself. She noticed that he drank sparingly, consuming only two glasses of wine over the entire meal. He intended to keep a clear head, then. That thought was no more reassuring than the rest. Unable to bear her own thoughts she grasped at distraction.

'I take it we shall resume our journey tomorrow.' She was surprised to discover how steady her voice sounded.

'Yes. I need to be in Seville as soon as may be.'

'Have you been there before?'

'No.'

'Nor I but I've heard it's a fine city.'

'So I believe. When my business is concluded we might explore it if you wish.'

'I'd like that.'

To her ears the conversation sounded stilted, but it was better than silence. Nor was he unwilling to follow her lead and thus the conversation remained safely on neutral ground until the meal was done.

She saw him lean back in his chair, stretching his legs in front of him, to all appearances quite relaxed. He poured a little more wine and sipped it slowly, surveying her steadily. Under that quiet scrutiny she felt more than ever aware of her appearance. In the years since Badajoz her masculine attire had been a useful defence in many ways. When she had dwelt among the *guerrilla* force she had carried herself with the same show of outward confidence she saw in the men around her, adopted the same faintly arrogant swagger in her stride and looked them straight in the eye when she spoke to them. Such stratagems had served her well, being as they were the antithesis of everything feminine. Now, a part of her regretted the gowns she had left behind in Madrid. To be found so lacking by this English lord was mortifying. How far removed she must be from his notions of ideal womanhood. Perhaps the closest she had come was during those brief hours in Madrid when she had at least looked like a woman. Once or twice she had thought there was admiration in his regard, but it was so fleeting she couldn't be sure. A Spaniard would have made it plain; Englishmen on the other hand concealed their feelings behind a barrier of cool reserve. Of course, if he thought her attractive that would be downright dangerous. It was like being caught in a cleft stick.

In fact, she would have been startled to know what was going through the mind of the English lord just then. It had not escaped him that Elena had barely eaten anything this evening or that her unease was almost tangible, and he thought he had a pretty shrewd idea as to the reason. She might put a brave face on things but underneath she was terrified. Her vulnerability had never been more evident. Nor had her beauty which was rendered all the more artless by her present attire.

For the first time full realisation began to sink in that this lovely and exotic creature was now his wife, that she belonged to him. It created a gamut of emotions, not least of which was guilt. He hadn't looked at another woman since Belén and nor had he wished to. The society beauties in London had no power to attract him: compared to her they had seemed cold and colourless, lacking the inner fire that she had possessed in such measure. The same fire he glimpsed in Elena. In her it was contained, he might even have said suppressed. It excited his imagination and aroused his curiosity, as that brief chaste kiss had aroused him earlier—an effect that had been quite unexpected. It put paid to all thought of the nun.

He tossed back the rest of his wine and, pushing the chair back, stood up. Then he held out his hand.

'Come, my lady. It's time to retire.'

Somehow Elena got to her feet. Her heart was thumping so hard she felt sure he must hear it. Obediently she placed her hand in his, felt the pressure of his fingers on hers. Their touch seemed to burn now. He led her to the door and thence to the upper floor where their bedchamber was situated. He paused on the threshold to let her precede him, then closed the door behind them. The room was spacious though sparsely furnished, and dominated by the large bed opposite. Elena shivered, her gaze travelling thence to the man standing just feet away. He had always been physically impressive but now he seemed bigger than ever. Moreover, that lithe frame was powerfully muscled. Her strength would be no match at all for his; he could compel her to do whatever he liked. Her mouth dried. She had not even the right to refuse. As her husband his authority was absolute.

In stomach-churning silence she waited. He looked

so calm and self-assured, but then how could he not when circumstances were so clearly stacked in his favour? He surveyed her steadily for a moment.

'It has been a long day and there's another one ahead of us tomorrow. Let's get some rest, shall we?'

She stared at him dumbfounded, torn between disbelief and hope.

'Besides,' he went on, 'I think we both need a little time to come to terms with what happened today.'

The tone was gentle, even kind, but suggestive of more beneath. For perhaps the tenth time that day she wished she could read him better. She watched him shrug off his coat and toss it over the back of a chair. Neck cloth and shirt followed to reveal a hard-muscled torso. She drew a sharp breath, her gaze drawn to the line of dark hair that led her eye to the narrow waist and lean flanks below it. He sat down to remove his boots. Having done so, he reached for the fastenings of his breeches. Confused and uncertain, Elena turned away and reluctantly began to remove her own jacket and boots. Behind her she heard a faint creaking sound as he climbed into bed.

Hoping her voice wouldn't shake, she said, 'I'll douse the candle.'

She suited the action to the words and the room was immediately plunged into darkness. Under its protective shade she hurriedly removed her breeches. Then, clad only in her shirt, she padded across to the bed and, groping for the edge, slid gingerly beneath the covers. She lay very still, hardly daring to breathe, every nerve stretched taut with awareness of the man beside her. The bed shifted under his weight as he turned towards her. Elena tensed, closing her eyes, feeling his warmth down the length of her body, waiting for the inevitable invasion of hands and limbs. It didn't come. Instead she felt the light pressure of his hand against her cheek. It lingered a moment in a light and gentle caress. Then she heard his voice.

'Goodnight. Sleep well, my lady.'

The hand withdrew and the bed shifted again and he turned away from her onto his side. Heart hammering she stammered out a response. He made no further reply. She listened intently, but after a few minutes heard only the soft sound of rhythmic breathing. Slowly she let herself relax a little, hardly able to credit that he really didn't intend to make any demands on her. The thought occurred then that he might not wish to; he had not chosen her any more than she had chosen him. Yet his boldness in undressing before her suggested a man quite at ease with women and with his own body. Tears prickled behind her eyelids and she swallowed hard, wondering if she would ever feel at ease with her own body again.

Harry stared into the darkness, trying not to think about the semi-naked beauty just inches away. Temptation whispered in his head that she was his wife now. All he had to do was claim what was already his. The thought sent a wave of heat to his loins. Determinedly he ignored it. Elena was his in name only and he could hardly suppose she would welcome intimacy with him. He had not missed her unease or her embarrassment just now. The use of force was out of the question. No man worthy of the name would use his strength in that way. Besides, there was the matter of Badajoz to take into account.

It still informed his nightmares on occasion. What would be her response on discovering that he had been one of that infamous army? He had not taken any part in the violence, but he had been a British soldier nonetheless. Would she make any distinction between him and the men who killed her father? And if she knew how he had failed Belén what would be her reaction then? Would she ever wish to give herself to such a man?

He took a deep breath. It was too early even to think of those things. To do so was to be disloyal as well as unreliable. Belén's image was still vivid, the ache of loss still present. It was wrong to think lustfully of another woman. He and Elena needed time to talk, to get to know each other better. At some point, when the time was right, he would tell her about Badajoz, and about Belén. Then they would decide where they wanted to go from there. In the interim he needed to focus on the reason for coming to Spain in the first place.

Chapter Seven

For a second or two after Elena woke the next morning she couldn't remember where she was. Then, gradually, the details came back. Turning her head she looked for the man who had lain beside her last night but the bed was empty. She pushed herself up on one elbow and looked around. Her gaze fell on the tall figure a few feet away by the washstand. He was dressed now in shirt, breeches and boots and was currently shaving. Glancing her way he smiled.

'Good morning. I trust you slept well.'

'I… Yes, thank you.' In fact, it had taken her a long time to fall asleep last night but she wasn't about to say so. 'What time is it?'

'A little before seven.'

Elena began to feel guilty. 'You should have woken me before. I know you wanted to be away early.'

'An hour or so will make little difference. Besides, you looked so peaceful I didn't like to disturb you.'

Had he been watching her, then? The thought brought

warm colour to her face. The knowledge that she was going to have to get up and dress in front of him did nothing for her equilibrium. Although she was still wearing her shirt the fabric only reached the tops of her thighs revealing everything else. She bit her lip. Fortunately Harry turned away and resumed his task so Elena seized her chance. Sliding out of bed she hurried across the room to find her breeches. They were still in the middle of the floor where she'd left them last night. Hurriedly she grabbed them and began to pull them on. Once she darted a look towards Harry but he seemed oblivious. Breathing a sigh of relief she continued her task. Feeling slightly less vulnerable now she pulled on her boots and began to rummage in her saddlebag for a comb. Her hair must resemble a bird's nest by now. Sinking on to the chair nearby, she turned her attention to rectifying the matter. It took some time to tease out the small tangles so that the fine teeth slid through the glossy curls. When at last she was satisfied she tied her hair back with a ribbon and reached for her jacket.

By the washstand Harry finished shaving and dried his face with a towel. For the first time, Elena noticed the mirror on the wall above the washstand, and then, given her present position, belatedly grasped the implications. How much had he seen? However, he made no remark on the subject and nothing could have been more innocent than his expression. Perhaps she was being oversensitive. All the same, the thought that he might have seen her half-clothed made her feel suddenly warmer. To cover her embarrassment she busied herself repacking her saddlebags.

Harry laid the towel aside and finished dressing. Once he glanced at Elena but she seemed not to notice. Schooling his expression to neutrality, he tried not to think about the vision in the mirror; she really did have the most wonderful legs. Beautiful hair too, waist length, blue-black and glossy as a rook's ring. Hair that made a man long to touch it. He pulled himself up short knowing that he had no right to think along those lines. He could not offer her his heart and without that what remained was lust. To follow such an inclination would be contemptible. With a determined effort he turned his mind to other things.

'Are you ready for some breakfast, Elena?'

'That sounds good.' It surprised her to discover how good. Having eaten little the previous evening she was hungry now.

They went down together. The *patròn* plied them with ham and eggs and fresh bread. It was delicious and Elena did full justice to the meal. Harry watched in quiet amusement, privately relieved to see her eat well. The nervousness he had seen last night was gone, and that pleased him too. The thought of any woman fearing him was distasteful, but in this case it was downright painful. He made no attempt to hurry her or reveal any impatience at the delay; as he had told her, an hour or two would make little difference.

Thus it was nearer to nine before they eventually set out again. The horses seemed to have benefitted from their unscheduled stop at the inn and stepped out eagerly. Seeing Harry engaged in quiet conversation with Jack, Concha eased her mount alongside Elena's horse, regarding her mistress with a critical eye.

'Are you all right? I was so worried I hardly slept last night.'

'I assure you I am quite well.'

'I'm glad to hear it.' Concha bit her lip. 'I never anticipated such a move by your uncle.'

'Nor I. He outmanoeuvred us all.'

'He knew you would not refuse.'

'I underestimated him and no mistake.'

Concha hesitated. 'The Englishman did not hurt you?'

'No, he did not.'

'Thanks be to God.'

'He didn't touch me.'

'What!' Recovering herself quickly, the maid lowered her voice again. 'You mean he didn't even try to...'

'That's right.'

'But that's...that's...'

'Unheard of?'

'Well, yes.' Concha paused. 'Have you ever heard of such a thing before?'

Elena shook her head. 'In truth I have never met a man quite like this one.'

'He's English. One must take that into consideration.'

'There is that, of course, but given the circumstances his reaction is not so surprising.'

'Isn't it?'

'He was compelled to this match as well.'

'He didn't resist very strenuously though, did he?'

'My uncle left no room for argument.'

'If you ask me, your husband was not as unwilling as you seem to think. I saw how he looked at you before.'

'He looked at me with respect.'

'There was a lot more than just respect in his eyes,' said Concha.

'You're mistaken. His manner was always correct to a fault.'

'More like a man keeping himself on a tight rein. Of course, he did think then that you were going to be a nun.'

'But for him I would have been.'

'Do you regret the decision?'

The question caught her unawares but it took less than a second for Elena to know the answer.

'No, I don't regret it. How could I?'

'So you are not entirely indifferent to him.'

'I think it would be hard to feel indifferent to him. He is a good man.' It was an evasion and Elena knew it, but she could not have explained her feelings just then since she hardly knew what they were herself.

Concha made no reply but smiled quietly.

They stopped at midday to rest the horses and then broke out provisions for themselves. Elena, relaxing on a sun-warmed rock, thought that bread and cheese and sausage had never tasted so good. Perhaps it was something to do with the open space around her, or the blue vault overhead, or the scent of pine resin from the trees, or just knowing that at last she was free of pursuit, that her uncle no longer had any authority over her. That reposed in the hands of a very different kind of man. She glanced in Harry's direction. Currently munching on a hunk of bread, he looked relaxed and entirely untroubled. Did he share her anxieties about the future? That last was something yet to be discussed. The advent of their marriage was still too new and too strange to permit such things. Besides, he might have had plans of his own which had been entirely overset. When he had spoken of their needing time to adjust he had hit the nail on the head.

She finished eating and strolled towards the stream that ran among the rocks a few yards off. The water was cool and delicious, the sound restful. It was pleasant here and she felt more at ease than ever she had in the city. Here the noise and the bustle and the stench seemed a million miles away. She bent to scoop more water and then looked up quickly as a shadow fell across her. Harry stepped into her line of vision.

'The water looks good.'

'It is.'

'Then I shall follow your example.'

He came to join her, bending down to cup a drink in his hand. For so tall a man he moved with almost feline grace. She watched him covertly, taking in the chiselled profile of his face, the dark hair above the curve of his ear, the breadth of his shoulders beneath the fabric of his coat. His hands were large and strong yet unmistakably those of a gentleman. She knew their touch already, albeit briefly. The recollection created unwonted sensations, like his presence beside her now. To cover her awkwardness she took refuge in conversation.

'How long will it take us to reach Seville, do you think?'

'Without delays, between three and four weeks.' He smiled faintly. 'Of course, that is an optimistic reckoning.'

'You think we shall run into problems?'

'I hope not, but it's best to be prepared.'

'That is what Juan Montera used to say.'

'Juan Montera?'

'The leader of the *guerrilla* group that I rode with.'

'Ah.'

Mentally Elena cursed her tongue. She had not meant to allude to that time but it had come out anyway. She eyed him warily.

'Does it displease you that I should speak about such things?'

'No. Tell me if you wish to.' The tone was kind and quietly encouraging. Suiting action to words he sat down and waited, making no attempt to probe even though she knew there must be many questions in his head concerning her past.

'Montera was a farmer, until the French came and murdered his family, destroyed his crops and burned his village to the ground. They killed all who tried to resist. The survivors fled to the hills. Montera had some education and was intelligent besides. He took control, uniting the fugitives and shaping a fighting force to strike back against the enemy.'

Harry nodded. 'Such things happened across the whole country.'

'As the French depredations increased, the numbers of the *guerrilla* group increased too. There were several women among them. Montera had no prejudice in that respect. If a woman was prepared to fight the French he was prepared to let her.' She smiled faintly. 'I think he was a man ahead of his time there.'

'That's one way of looking at it, I suppose.'

'Do you disapprove?'

'I cannot like the idea of women standing fire, but in this instance I have no right to pronounce on the matter. Were the situation here to be repeated in England, I have no doubt that there would be women aplenty who would take up muskets and pistols to defend their own.'

'The French were foolish. They left people with nothing to lose, and men with nothing to lose are truly dangerous,' she replied. 'Montera understood this very well and used it to good effect.'

Harry paused, framing his next words carefully. 'It sounds as if you respected this man.'

'I did. He was a clever strategist. He also knew the area like the back of his hand so that his force could strike and retreat before the enemy even knew what had hit them. Montera always made sure of his escape routes too.'

'An able commander by all accounts.'

'And wise enough to listen to what others had to

say before making a final decision. Even women had a voice in his camp.'

His curiosity was whetted now. 'He seems to have been a remarkable man.'

'In many ways he was, but then war brings out unsuspected qualities in people, does it not?'

'Indeed.'

'I could already shoot accurately, but with the *guerrillas* I learned how to fight as well, how to kill a man silently, how to plant booby traps or lay an ambush. It stood me in good stead.'

Harry regarded her askance. 'Remind me never to make you angry.'

She returned a wry smile. 'It is all very shocking, is it not? Yet it is part of who I am now.'

'It is part of who you were then,' he replied. 'What happens from now on is for you to decide.'

Her pulse quickened a little. 'The past is not so easy to let go of, however much we might wish to do so.'

Silently he acknowledged the truth of this. The words he had spoken to her held good for him too, and for the first time he caught sight of a different future from the insular, work-orientated one he had envisaged. It was a tantalising vision. At the same time he felt guilty for even entertaining it.

'No,' he said. 'It isn't easy.'

Elena eyed him curiously, sensing layers beneath those words. She wanted to know more, to understand exactly what he meant by them, but before she could say anything else he got to his feet.

'We should move on. I want to cover some more miles before we stop this evening.'

Clearly the conversation was over for now. Feeling slightly cheated, she nodded and made to rise, then checked to see the outstretched hand. For a brief moment she hesitated but then her own went to meet it. That strong clasp sent a shock along her skin. He drew her easily to her feet. Having done that he made no attempt to retain his hold and she was free. The sensation should have been relief but it felt oddly like disappointment. In confusion she averted her gaze. Together they rejoined the others.

Chapter Eight

When they made camp that evening Elena and Concha tended their horses and then set about collecting wood for the fire. When they had amassed a suitable pile Concha laid the base and then took out tinder and flint from the leather pouch on her belt. Within a short space of time she had the fire started.

Jack, who had been watching quietly, nodded approval. 'You've done that before, haven't you?'

'Once or twice,' said Concha.

Elena grinned and handed her some more sticks.

'Can you use that pistol an' all?' he continued.

Concha glanced up and met his eye. 'With perfect accuracy.'

'Oh, aye? Shot many men, have you?'

The scepticism in his tone was not lost on his audience. The two women exchanged glances.

'Yes,' replied Concha, 'but not nearly enough of you.'

Jack grinned. 'Frenchies, I'll be bound.'

'Frenchmen, of course, though nationality does not

always govern the choice of target. I'd be just as willing to shoot an annoying Englishman.'

Harry's eyes gleamed. 'You'd best take heed, Jack, if you want to keep a whole skin.'

'Aye, my lord. I'm trembling in me boots here.'

'Nice boots too,' replied Concha. 'If anything untoward were to happen to you, I'd get a good price for those.'

Elena turned away to hide welling laughter. 'I'll go and fetch some water.'

'Let me help you.' Harry picked up the spare pan. 'A mug of tea wouldn't go amiss just now.'

The stream was only a short distance away and the pan wasn't heavy, but Elena made no demur for the thought of his company was not displeasing.

'I think Jack may have met his match there,' he observed when they were out of earshot.

'Don't be in any doubt about it. I've never seen Concha bested.'

'Is her nature really so warlike?'

'No more than mine, but we can defend ourselves when we have to.'

'That role falls to me now,' he replied.

She shot a look his way but his expression was perfectly serious. The notion sat oddly with her.

'It may take some time to adjust to that idea.'

'Is it not a husband's first duty to protect his wife from harm?'

'So tradition has it.'

'Well, then.' He paused. 'Will you trust me so far?'

'I trusted a man once before but on that occasion my trust was misplaced.'

'He has much to answer for, but I hope to restore your faith in our sex.'

'That may take some time.' It was an understatement: she wondered if she would ever be able to trust in that way again. While she felt an instinctive liking for Harry and he had behaved in a gentlemanly fashion thus far, would he stand by her *in extremis*? Would she be able to rely on him or would he too prove to have feet of clay?

'No matter. We have plenty of that, and I know how to be patient.'

His gaze met hers and held it. There was no discernible trace of arrogance or mockery, only quiet certainty, and it sent a tremor through her that had nothing to do with fear.

Later, after they had eaten and Jack had gone to take first watch, the others turned in. Elena was weary now. Quite apart from the day's ride, she had slept little the previous night. Of course, there had been considerable distraction then even though her fears came to nothing. It would be some time before she and Harry shared a chamber again and it was unlikely he'd initiate any kind of intimacy while they were on the road. She was safe enough for the time being.

Over the next few days the little group of travellers settled into a routine. Harry soon discovered that his marriage to Elena had not altered the original *modus vi-*

vendi within the group as a whole: she and Concha still undertook their share of the chores with good grace, they took their turns on watch and neither of them complained about cold rations, long days in the saddle or hard ground at night. Both rode well and were knowledgeable about the care of horses. He never had to remind them of anything. Thus far the arrangement was working out better than he could have hoped. It seemed he wasn't the only one to think so since Jack had privately confided that he thought both ladies regular troopers.

'I've not heard one complaint so far,' he went on, 'which same does surprise me, being as how they're women an' all.'

'Men do their share of complaining,' replied Harry. 'Remember Private Digby?'

'Couldn't ever forget t'cove, my lord. Blighter could've moaned for England.'

'Actually I think he did.'

Jack nodded. 'It were a relief to all concerned when he finally stopped a bullet at Talavera. I expect he's still complaining to t'devil about it now.'

'Very likely.'

'T'ladies could teach him a thing or two about fortitude, eh, my lord?'

'Yes, they certainly…' Harry broke off as a flash of light caught his eye on the hillside ahead. 'Did you see that?'

'Aye, my lord. Sunlight on metal. Musket barrel?'

Harry reined in. 'My thought exactly.'

It seemed they weren't alone in noticing the phenomenon. Elena pulled up beside Harry. 'Bandits do you think?'

'Quite possibly.'

'What do you want to do?'

Before he had time to answer a shot whined past his ear. Harry swore under his breath.

'Take cover among those rocks.'

They needed no urging, nor did they show any signs of panic, reacting much as trained soldiers would have done. In less than half a minute they had reached shelter, dismounted and armed themselves. They were only just in time as more lead shot whined past and ricocheted off stone. It was followed by shouts and a thunder of hooves.

'Here they come,' muttered Concha.

Elena checked the priming of her pistol. 'We'll give a good account of ourselves anyway.'

Squinting round the edge of the sheltering rock she saw ten horsemen hurtle down the slope and thence along the dirt road towards them. Even from a distance there was no mistaking who the riders were.

'Bandits, definitely,' said Jack.

Concha nodded. 'Idiots too, if they think to cross such a large area of open ground unscathed.'

'Quite right,' said Harry. 'Let's take advantage of their stupidity, shall we?'

He lined up his rifle and squeezed off a shot. Almost simultaneously Jack's gun spoke. Two of the oncoming riders fell.

'Not bad,' said Concha.

While the others reloaded Elena took aim. A man cried out, swaying in the saddle and clutching his shoulder. Harry glanced her way and smiled.

'Well done.'

'You also,' she replied.

Concha levelled her pistol and fired, bringing down the leading horse. It fell like a stone, catapulting its rider over its head and causing others to swerve around it. Hurriedly she reloaded while Harry and Jack opened fire. Elena heard cries of pain. She ignored it, knowing that sentiment had no place here. If they were captured the best they could expect was to be robbed of everything. In the worst-case scenario... Cold-eyed, she fired and reloaded, her hands moving automatically and with practiced ease. Then she took a deep breath, took aim again. The riders were closer now and thus easier targets. Concha was right, she thought. They were not competent strategists. Montera certainly wouldn't have let himself get caught in the open like that. She smiled grimly, picked her target and fired. A man clutched his chest and toppled sideways, dead before he hit the ground.

And then, without warning, the remaining riders veered away. For a second or two the significance escaped her. Then she heard Concha's voice.

'They're running! The cowards are running!'

Jack grinned. 'They got more than they bargained for, I'll warrant.'

Elena leaned back against the rock and let out the breath she had unconsciously been holding.

'Are you all right?'

She opened her eyes to see Harry. 'Yes, quite all right, I thank you.'

'That was good shooting. Well done.'

The words cheered her immeasurably, like the hand squeezing her arm. She smiled wryly. 'You weren't so bad yourself from what I could see.'

He returned the smile. 'High praise.'

'No, just the truth.'

Before he could say more, Jack intervened. 'The question is whether they've gone for good or just to fetch reinforcements.'

Harry nodded. 'I think we should leave while we can.'

No one needed telling twice. They remounted and rode fast. Elena urged her horse to a gallop, leaning low over its neck, glancing back from time to time, half expecting to see a larger group of riders behind. The road was empty. Even after several miles there was still no sign of pursuit.

'Maybe just a small group of opportunists, after all, my lord,' said Jack when at length they pulled up to rest their blowing horses.

'Maybe,' replied Harry. 'All the same, we'll ride on for a while.'

Once again no one made the least demur, wanting to put as much distance between them and the scene of the attack as possible. Even though the immediate danger was over Elena still felt the residual thrill coursing through her veins. It had been that way when she and Concha had ridden with Montera's men. The habit was hard to break.

It was dusk before they eventually stopped. There were still no signs of pursuit but he wasn't prepared to take chances.

'We'll exercise caution until we're sure,' he said. 'No fire tonight and we'll double the watch just in case.'

'Right you are, my lord.' Jack looked at Concha. 'Do you take t'first one wi' me, then, lass?'

She returned a cool and level gaze. 'As you wish—lad.'

Elena caught Harry's eye and saw the gleam of amusement there. It drew an answering smile from her. Bone-weary now but exhilarated too, it felt as though something in her had awoken after a long sleep. It wasn't that she relished being attacked by brigands, but rather that the brush with danger made her feel more alive than she had for a long time. Perhaps the present company had something to do with that as well. In any adventure it was important to know that, in a tight spot, one could rely on one's companions. She'd had no doubts whatever about Concha, but today the two men had proved their worth once more. They were cool-headed, swift to act and prepared to be ruthless when required.

'Can I offer you something to eat?'

Harry's voice drew her from her reverie. 'Oh, yes. I thank you. What is on the menu this evening?'

'Bread and cheese.'

'Bread and cheese sound divine.'

'You are easily pleased, my lady.'

'I am hungry, my lord, and have eaten far worse.'

He grinned and, having handed her a ration of food, sat down to eat with her. 'You and Concha handled yourselves well today. Seasoned soldiers could not have done better.'

His praise created a little glow of warmth deep inside. 'I suppose we are what you might call seasoned *guerrillas*.'

'An apt description. You certainly took those robbers in your stride.'

'It's not the first time we have met their kind. Concha and I were once taken prisoner by El Lobo.'

'I have heard of him. An ugly customer by all accounts.'

'The accounts were true.'

'How did you fall into his clutches?'

Elena hesitated, regarding him speculatively, wondering whether he would be shocked if she told him the story. On the other hand he already knew a lot of shocking things about her, so perhaps one more wouldn't make much difference now.

'We had been out hunting in the hills with a small group of companions. We shot a deer and were returning to camp when, by ill chance, we ran into some of El Lobo's men. I think they were as surprised as we. Unfortunately there were far more of them than there were of us, and so we were captured and taken to his headquarters. It was a remote hill village that had been abandoned by the inhabitants in the early part of the war.'

'There were quite a few of those around by the time the French had finished.' He made a vague gesture with his hand. 'Forgive me, I'm interrupting.'

'El Lobo demanded to know where Montera's hide-out was but none of us was prepared to tell. So then our captors entertained themselves by beating one of our companions half to death. Still he wouldn't talk so El Lobo shot him, as an example. We knew it wouldn't be long before he killed the rest—the men anyway.' She hesitated. 'He announced that he had a very different plan for Concha and me.'

Harry's eyes grew steely. 'I think I can guess what that was.'

She nodded. 'We knew there was nothing to lose by attempting to escape. So, while he and his men drank, we pretended to seduce the guard of the hut where we were confined. It wasn't hard.'

'I almost pity him.'

'When we'd eliminated him we smashed the lamp and set fire to the building as we left to create a diversion.'

'An effective stratagem, I imagine.'

'It was. While all attention was on the fire we released our friends. We also discovered that the room next door to their prison was piled high with weapons and ammunition stolen from the French. There were also several barrels of gunpowder.'

'Let me guess. You set a fuse.'

'Correct.'

'A longish fuse, I hope.'

'Long enough to let us get clear.' She smiled reminiscently. 'The explosion was huge—the biggest I ever saw, and deafening. It demolished the entire building and half a dozen near it. Debris was flung over a wide area. There were massive casualties among the robbers.'

'I have no doubt of that.'

'One of the victims was El Lobo himself— impaled through the chest by a huge splinter of wood.'

'I don't suppose that grieved you too much.'

'It didn't grieve me at all.'

'How did you get away?'

'In the confusion we stole some horses and set the rest free. Then we rode fast.'

Harry shook his head, torn between astonishment and admiration. 'I'll wager you did.'

'I'm afraid I have shocked you again.'

'The shocking thing is that women should be forced to such extremities as a consequence of war.'

It wasn't what she had been expecting at all and she eyed him curiously. 'No matter what you learn about my past you never judge me, do you?'

'I have no right to judge you,' he replied.

'You have secrets of your own, perhaps?'

Harry avoided her gaze. 'Who does not have secrets about the past?'

'Is yours about Belén?'

He flinched as though stung. 'That need not concern you.'

'Forgive me. I should not have said that. It was only...'

'Only what?'

'It doesn't matter. Forget it please.'

Harry got to his feet. 'Since we're on the next watch we should try and get a little rest now. Excuse me.'

She stared after him in stunned silence, mentally kicking herself. When she had asked the question it had never occurred to her that he might resent it so fiercely. With hindsight she realised how impertinent it must have sounded. What made it worse was the knowledge that she had inadvertently touched a sore place with him. She bit her lip. How could she have been so foolish as to think his tolerance extended so far?

Harry shook out his bedroll with unwonted vigour and then climbed in. Despite his weariness though, sleep eluded him. Anger continued to smoulder too, only now it was directed inwards. Being unprepared for her question he had snarled at Elena like an injured wolf. And in truth it had been a defensive response, albeit a churlish one. She had been open with him, after all. He sighed. He had never discussed the subject of Belén with anyone: he'd never told his family about their engagement, even Ross and Giles didn't know about it. It wasn't because he had anything to hide—although her birth was not of the highest her family was respectable. He hadn't intended it to be a secret but events had overtaken him so fast he'd never had time to communicate the matter to his own relations. By the time he could there was nothing that he wished to communicate. He never spoke of it to anyone. Only Jack knew the truth. And then, out of the blue, Elena had unwittingly touched the wound and he'd bitten her head off. She'd tried to apologise and he hadn't even listened. What must she be thinking now?

At some point amid these reflections he must have dozed off because the next thing he knew was Jack's hand on his shoulder, gently shaking him. Like most military men he came to at once, alert and ready for action. Hefting his rifle he glanced towards Elena and saw her get up. She paused only to exchange a few quiet words with Concha and then came to join him.

'Ready?' he asked.

She nodded and they set off, taking up their position atop a small knoll hard by. Although it wasn't particularly high, it afforded a good view of the countryside around. In this respect they were aided by the light of the waxing moon. Elena listened intently but the only sounds were the cicadas and, once or twice, an owl. Nothing else stirred.

Finding a convenient boulder she sat down in its shadow so that she was out of sight. If anyone were to approach they would be on top of her before they became aware of her presence. She saw Harry take up a position a few yards off. However, she made no attempt at conversation, guessing it wouldn't be welcome. In any case she had no wish to get her head bitten off again.

Instead she let her gaze range over the hills whose tops were now silvered by the moonlight. Overhead a million stars filled a velvet sky and the air was scented with wild thyme. It was a romantic scene. She sighed, wondering what on earth had put that thought in her head. There was nothing remotely romantic about the situation: she had been foisted off on a man who had unwittingly become embroiled in her family's sordid affairs, and she had now added insult to injury. Glancing across the intervening space she looked at Harry but his attention was firmly fixed on the land in front of him. No doubt about it, he was still angry. It saddened her to know that she had offended him; his opinion mattered rather more than she had expected. However, the fear of another rebuff held her silent.

A shooting star flashed a trail of radiance across the hcavens and she caught her breath, smiling in spite of herself. Then she heard Harry's voice, quiet on the night air.

'You saw it too.'

Her pulse quickened a little. 'Yes. This is an ideal place.'

'Far from ideal from your point of view, I imagine,' he replied. 'You must be wishing me at Jericho. I can only apologise for my foul temper.'

'Well, I should not have asked so impertinent a question and I'm sorry for it.'

'Forget it. It doesn't matter.'

Elena strongly suspected that it did, but she wasn't

about to reject the offered olive branch. 'All right. Let's just pretend it didn't happen.'

'Yes, let's.'

Hearing him fall in so readily with the suggestion, she wondered then what other pretences they would have to maintain in this relationship: the pretence that he was content to be married to her; the pretence that he wasn't still in love with another woman? Yet she could hardly criticise him when she had not faced and conquered her own demons. What future could there be for them if they did not confront the past?

Chapter Nine

There was no further sign of the bandits who had attacked them so it seemed most probable that it had been a chance encounter with a small band of marauders. The countryside was full of them, men whom war had dispossessed or made desperate. As he and his companions continued on their journcy, Harry could only hope that they wouldn't meet any more. They had been lucky last timc. If the robber group had been larger it would have been a different story. Had it been only himself and Jack he would have been less concerned: having women along altered his view substantially, even if the women concerned were able to shoot remarkably well. Elena's account of their adventure with El Lobo only served to underline this. While Harry applauded her courage and resilience, he was more aware than ever of her vulnerability.

Since the shared watch their relationship had, superficially at least, settled back into its former pattern of mutual civility. Yet, underneath that, he was aware of a fundamental shift. Even though he had apologised, he knew that he had ducked the issue. The habit of silence had become ingrained. The very mention of Belén was a trigger to close up like a clam. *Let's pretend it didn't happen.* How those words had haunted him in the hours since. By glossing over the matter in that way Elena had only been trying to keep the peace, but her openness with him suggested that she would have welcomed reciprocal honesty. Now that his temper had cooled he realised that her question was never intended to be impertinent, only to open a dialogue between them. A necessary dialogue, he now admitted. No relationship could survive if it were based on pretence.

He also knew that, one day, they would have a deeper relationship. She was his wife and nothing would change that. It behoved them to make the best of the situation. After all, many marriages were based on mutual respect. There was no reason why they shouldn't have a future together, even if it wasn't the one either of them would have chosen. Eventually they were going to have to talk and he would have to tell her the truth. He had no idea what might happen after that, but more than anything else he dreaded her contempt. After what he'd done, or rather failed to do, how could any woman think him worthy of her affection?

That evening they camped by the side of a small lake. Since water was an important consideration for both horses and humans, Harry had planned his route accordingly, making use of the maps Don Manuel had provided. Small streams or springs served their turn and supplied what was essential, but the thought of being able to bathe for the first time in days was very appealing. It seemed he wasn't the only one to think so.

'A swim would be very agreeable,' said Elena, when the subject was first broached. 'But if you and Jack wish to go first Concha and I will prepare things here.'

Harry grinned. 'A generous offer. However, I believe the rule is ladies first.'

'Very well. We accept.'

He reached into his saddlebag. 'Here. You might want this.'

'What is it?'

'A bar of soap.' He placed in in her hand, closing her fingers around it. 'Don't lose it. It's the only one I have.'

The effect of that casual touch was disturbing. She summoned a smile. 'I'll guard it with my life.'

'See you do. The penalty for failure is severe.'

Although she caught the gleam in the grey eyes her pulse quickened. She had no idea what he might be capable of—in fun or earnest.

'I'm not going to ask.'

'What a pity.'

Elena's cheeks grew a shade warmer. This gentle teasing was more difficult to deal with and, more disturbingly still, part of her wanted to push this a little further. Not so long ago she would have avoided any kind of flirtatious behaviour with a man; now the temptation was strong. With a sense of shock she realised that fear had been replaced by something very like suppressed excitement. It was definitely time to leave.

'We won't take too long.'

'No hurry. The lake will still be there.'

Leaving the two men to perform the remaining chores, she and Concha took themselves off. They walked a little way from the camp and found a curve in the shoreline which provided a secluded little cove and complete privacy. They lost no time in stripping off and wading in. The water was cold but wonderfully refreshing.

Concha submerged herself completely and came up grinning. '*Madre de Dios*, this is good. I have dreamed of bathing for days now.'

'I also. Dust and horse sweat are not ideal perfumes.'

'Better than the reek of incense though.'

Elena laughed. 'When you put it like that all objection begins to fade.'

They scrubbed themselves vigorously and took the opportunity to wash their hair as well. Then, at length, they climbed out and sat on a sun-warmed rock to dry off.

Elena smiled to herself, imagining her aunts' expressions if they could see her now. Their disapproval was an irrelevance, of course. It was as though they belonged to a past life. She could well imagine their reactions on learning of her marriage. From now on she would be *persona non grata*. Dolores was the only family she had left. That was a reunion to look forward to. In the meantime, there was Harry. Even though they spent so much time together she still knew little about him. Just occasionally there would be a tantalising detail but they were few and far between and, more than ever, she found herself wanting to know.

By the time she and Concha had dressed and returned to camp, the fire was made and tea brewing. Then Jack broke out their rations.

'Simple fare again, but it'll take t'edge off hunger for a while.'

'Here.' Harry handed Elena a mug of tea. 'Something to wash it down with.'

As she reached for the mug his fingers brushed hers, an apparently inadvertent touch that caused her pulse to quicken. Assuming what she hoped would look like a casual smile she met his gaze.

'Thank you. It is most welcome.'

'I promise you a better supper when we reach the next town.'

'I look forward to it. In the meantime I have no objection to simple fare.'

He smiled wryly. 'That's just as well since there will be a lot more of it.'

Hawkes nodded. 'We've had far worse, mind. Army specialised in it. Flour full o' weevils and salt pork so rancid it climbed out o' t'barrel on its own.'

'Flour and pork?' said Concha. 'You were fortunate. Often we had to make do with cat or dog.'

'Nowt wrong wi' that. Quite tasty if it's cooked right.'

'Oh, we didn't have a fire to cook it.'

'A bit o' raw food never hurt anyone.'

'No, but a half-starved cat is not much between a hundred people.'

Hawkes raised an eyebrow. 'At least it were meat. Our men were reduced to boiling their boots to make soup.'

'Our men had no boots. When times were really hard they were forced to eat grass.'

'Grass! We'd have given anything for grass where we out in t'desert. It were a cause for celebration in t'company if someone found a scorpion to roast. There were no water either so we were forced to suck on rocks just to keep t'saliva flowing.'

'We did the same,' said Concha, 'after we'd scraped off the lichen with our teeth, of course.'

Harry grinned. A stifled choking sound to his right caused him to glance round. As he did so he caught his breath. Elena's face was alight with laughter. It suited her very well, he thought. Very well indeed. She needed to laugh more often. Leaning closer he murmured confidentially in her ear.

'I think those two are well-matched.'

'You're right, they are.'

'I also think Jack enjoys this.'

'So does she.'

'He likes a worthy sparring partner,' he replied.

His closeness set her tingling but not with fear. Rather the earlier sensation of suppressed excitement returned. If he leaned a little closer their lips would touch. It shocked her to realise that she wouldn't have minded if they had.

However, it seemed that such an idea had never crossed his mind because then he drew away again and resumed a companionable manner. Immediately she upbraided herself for refining too much on what was no more than a little light-heartedness.

In fact, Harry was annoyed with himself: he had not expected to feel such a power of attraction and had no idea how it had happened. Things were complicated enough without him making them worse. He would need to be more careful in future.

When they had eaten and the hour drew on, Elena excused herself from the company to take the first watch. From her earlier survey of the terrain she had mentally selected a rocky promontory for her vantage point. It offered concealment but, at the same time, would allow a clear view of the surrounding countryside and the shoreline of the lake. It was unlikely that anyone would get close without being seen or heard. However, the night was quiet. Since the incident with the brigand group they hadn't set eyes on anyone else. She settled herself down to wait.

It was perhaps half an hour later when she heard the sound of leather on stone somewhere off to her right. Immediately her hand tightened on the butt of her pistol. Casting a swift look around she saw a dark figure emerge from the trees onto the shoreline some fifty yards away. As he stepped from the shadows into the moonlight she recognised Harry at once. For a moment she wondered what he was doing there but when he removed his coat the intention became clear. He sat down to tug off his boots. Then the rest of his clothing followed to reveal the lithe, hard-muscled form beneath. It might have been threatening but it wasn't. Unable to look away now she watched him wade out into the water. Just as she had done earlier he scrubbed himself thoroughly from head to foot. Having done so, he soused himself and repeated the exercise. She thought he would climb out then but it seemed that was not his intention. Instead he swam away from shore, cleaving the moonlit water in long, clean strokes. He swam like a fish, the light lending a silvery sheen to the flesh of arm and shoulder and buttocks and for a moment she had the fanciful notion that she had unwittingly found a merman. It was undoubtedly voyeuristic but she could not have looked away if her life had depended on it.

He swam perhaps a hundred yards and then returned. This time he did wade ashore. Elena caught her breath. She had not thought until now that a man's body could be beautiful. It was also virile and dangerous but it was not in any way repellent, awakening thoughts that were both alarming and exciting and creating pooling warmth in the region of her pelvis. The sensation sent another flush of heat along her neck and into her face.

Unaware of the sensations he was causing, Harry dried himself on a linen towel and then, unhurriedly, began to dress himself again. Elena relaxed a little. As she did so her foot dislodged a small stone. It rolled over the edge of the rock, striking the one below it. The sound seemed horribly loud in the stillness. Horrified, she froze. Had he heard it? If so, he would investigate and discover her present position. Then he would realise that she must have been observing him all this time. The ramifications turned her hot all over. However, he gave no sign of having heard anything and with a sense of relief she saw him continue dressing. When he had done so, he bent to retrieve the soap and towel before heading back towards the campsite. She let out the breath she had been holding.

As he reached edge of the trees he paused and turned her way. 'Goodnight, Elena.'

The words, though quietly spoken, carried with ease in the silence. Moreover, she was certain that she heard a note of laughter too. Mortified by the implications, she could only be glad of the darkness which hid her burning cheeks.

Harry did not advert to the incident next morning and Elena took care to avoid his eye as they struck camp. In some ways the thought that he had found it amusing was worse than anger would have been. It was also difficult to look at him now and not remember what she had seen, or that he had wanted her to know he was aware of the fact. Perhaps there were limits to pretence, after all. And that had other implications.

These thoughts occupied her as they rode on. She was only distracted when her horse cast a shoe some ten miles further on.

'We'll find a farrier in the next town,' said Harry. 'Fortunately it isn't too far. We'll lead your horse with the others. You can get up behind me in the meantime.'

It was on the tip of her tongue to say that she could

just as well ride with Concha, but the words withered and died there. As Jack secured her horse to the pack saddle of one of the lead animals, Harry offered Elena his near-side stirrup. As she slid her foot into the iron he reached down a hand. She took it. An arm like steel propelled her effortlessly onto the horse's back. He glanced over his shoulder.

'All right?'

Elena assumed an expression of casual ease. 'Yes, I thank you.'

Harry nudged the horse with his heels and they set off. Since there was no other option she let her hands rest lightly on his waist, immediately aware of his warmth through the fabric of the jacket. Her vision strayed from the broad shoulders to his neck and the dark hair above his collar and thence to the strong line of his jaw.

'I'll check all the horses' feet when we get to town,' he said. 'It'll be as good an opportunity as any to replace any worn shoes.'

With an effort she found her voice. 'Good idea.'

'While the farrier is sorting that out, we can all have a decent meal.'

'It will be most welcome.'

His lips quirked. 'Yes. Cheese and chorizo are all very well but a change won't come amiss.'

'Were you thinking about a large beefsteak by any chance?'

He laughed. 'Am I so transparent?'

'Where food is concerned men are not so hard to read.'

'Indeed.'

'I have never yet seen a man who was not mellowed by a good meal and a bottle of wine.'

'Do I need mellowing, then?' he asked.

'It would benefit us all, I think.'

'A tactful answer.'

'A truthful one,' she replied.

'You have always been truthful, have you not?'

'I try to be.'

'I shall strive to follow your example.'

'That would seem to imply that you have not been truthful. I find that hard to believe.'

'I'm flattered. However, it is possible...if not to lie, then to evade the truth.'

Her heart beat a little faster. 'Sometimes evasion is a form of defence. It is easier to hide behind it than to speak of what is painful.'

'No one wants to revisit such things.'

'Perhaps not, but if they remain hidden they can fester and cause deeper harm.'

He returned a non-committal grunt and then lapsed into silence. Elena did not care to push the subject any further for fear of alienating him. However, the seed was sown now and she could only hope it might take root.

They reached the town about an hour later, and found the main street and plaza decorated with bunting and lanterns.

'A party, perhaps?' said Jack.

'A local fiesta,' replied Concha.

Elena smiled. 'It must be. It has been so long since I had anything to do with one that I had almost forgotten they existed.'

'And I.'

'Perhaps we could join in. It might be fun.' As soon as the words were spoken she felt a twinge of guilt and looked anxiously at Harry. 'Of course, you may have other plans, my lord.'

He looked at the hopeful faces around him and smiled faintly. 'Perhaps we might join in, after we've seen to the horses.'

Enquiry led them to the farrier without much difficulty, but a check of the horses' feet revealed half a dozen shoes that needed replacing. By the time the work was complete Harry calculated it would be late afternoon.

'There's not much point in setting out again at dusk. We might just as well remain here tonight. Let's find an inn.'

Elena felt her heart skip a beat. Part of that was due to the thought of attending the fiesta but mostly because an inn meant that she would share his bed again tonight.

Chapter Ten

The fiesta would not start until the middle of the evening so there was plenty of time to enjoy a meal beforehand. Hot, home-cooked food was something they all relished. A hearty soup and a loaf of bread were followed by a plate full of *chuletas de cordero* with a side dish of *alcachofas con judías verdes.* Dessert was *arroz con leche* and a selection of fruits. They washed it all down with a jug of rich red Tempranillo.

For the first time since embarking on this adventure, Elena wished that it had been possible to change out of breeches and boots. Unfortunately all her gowns had been left behind in Madrid. The best she had been able to manage was to wash her face and hands and comb her hair. Harry had made no comment or revealed by so much as a raised eyebrow that he found her appearance lacking, and she was grateful for it. All the same the thought persisted that she would have liked to wear a more feminine costume this evening. She didn't examine the reasons beyond the fact that they were about to attend a party.

As dusk closed in and the first stars appeared, the local people came out in force. It seemed to Elena that all the generations were represented. Excited children ran about chattering and laughing while the adults talked and strolled beneath the trees in the plaza. Lanterns suspended from the branches lent the whole scene a fairy-tale atmosphere. There was music and wine, and the air was redolent of roasting meat and wood smoke. Later there would be dancing and fireworks.

Elena threw a sideways glance at the man beside her, wondering if he liked to dance. More and more she wished she were wearing something more suited to the occasion. Intercepting that look Harry smiled faintly.

'You have something on your mind?'

'Is it so obvious?'

'Your face often speaks before you do.'

'In that case I should make a wretched politician and a worse card player.'

'I fear you would.' He paused. 'However, you still haven't answered the question.'

Under that searching gaze she felt suddenly self-conscious. 'I was just thinking how long it has been since I last attended a celebration like this. I didn't realise that I had missed it.'

'The fiesta is an integral part of Spanish culture,' he replied. 'A very vibrant part too. How could you not miss it?'

'Do you enjoy such things?'

'In truth I did not get much chance to enjoy them. Duty kept getting in the way. Occasionally I was lucky though.'

'That's good. What is it that you say in your country about the consequences of always working and never taking time off?'

'All work and no play makes Jack a dull boy.'

'That's it.' She grinned. 'But I think you were never dull.'

'I hope not. Besides, it would be impossible to be dull in your company.'

She could not detect the least irony in his expression. On the contrary she saw something there that was remarkably like admiration.

'Would you like a cup of wine?' He gestured towards the tables that had been set up outside a small tavern.

'Why not?'

She turned to look at Concha. However, the maid shook her head. 'If you don't mind, Doña Elena, I want to look around a little more.'

'Just as you like.'

'I'll stay with her, my lady,' said Jack, 'an' see as all's well like.'

Concha gave him a haughty look. 'I am quite capable of looking after myself, Englishman.'

'Aye, I know that. It's t'other folk I'm worried about.'

She sighed. 'Very well, since you insist I suppose there's no help for it.'

'That's right, but I'll bear it as best I can.' He made an elaborate gesture with his arm. 'Shall we?'

Concha lifted her chin and muttered something under her breath as she walked past him. Jack grinned broadly and set off in her wake.

Elena laughed. 'You know, I suspect that she rather likes him.'

'You think so?' said Harry. 'I was rather under the impression that she did not.'

'She hasn't hit him or shot him. It's a positive sign.'

His lips twitched. 'You haven't hit or shot me. Am I to take that the same way?'

'You may take it as a sign of respect.'

'Respect—how very reassuring.' He poured wine into horn cups and, having handed her one, raised his own. 'Here's to continued respect.'

Elena sensed that more lay beneath those words but she drank anyway. The wine was deep red and deliciously mellow. She suspected it was also quite potent. When combined with the present company it was a heady and dangerous mix.

For a while they sat in companionable silence watching the people pass by. In spite of all that had happened she felt oddly content. Perhaps the secret was not to think too far ahead and just live in the moment.

'Do you not miss your home?' she asked.

'Sometimes. What concerns me more is to see justice done.'

'Towards the new claimant to the title?'

'If the boy really is my brother's child, then yes.'

'Do you find the claim credible?'

'The lady in question—Alicia—is pretty enough, and

genteel. Her birth is respectable, if not noble. I could envisage Jamie falling in love with such a woman.'

'It was a wartime romance, no?'

'Apparently so.'

'To lose her husband so soon after marriage must have been a terrible shock for the lady. To be left alone like that with a young child cannot have been easy.'

'I don't suppose it was.'

'No doubt she will be relieved when the matter is settled,' said Elena. 'I am sure that you will find the answers you seek when we reach Seville.'

'I hope so. It would be something to put an end to all the uncertainty.' Harry toyed with his cup. 'A talk with Garrido and Sanchez should do that. Then we can all move on.'

'How will your family respond when they find out that you are married?' she asked.

'With some surprise, I expect.'

'An understatement if ever I heard one.'

He smiled faintly. 'You need not be concerned. They will welcome you into the fold.'

'You seem very certain of that. I am a foreigner, after all.'

'Such considerations would not weigh with them. Besides, your birth and education are as good as theirs and your wit better than most.'

She returned the smile. 'I have often thought that I should like to see England. My sister has told me a lot about it.'

'I hope you won't be disappointed.'

'Does it really rain as much as she says?'

'Our climate is renowned. It's why England is known as a green and pleasant land.'

'Dolores says that your lower classes are more prosperous and better educated than their Spanish counterparts. That they play a game called cricket in which they mingle with noblemen.'

'True enough. Sport tends to dissolve class barriers—for a while anyway. The finest batsman I ever saw was a village blacksmith.'

'Such a blurring of social boundaries would not happen here.'

'I imagine not.'

What Elena might have said next was unknown because Jack and Concha returned just then, both in apparently good humour.

'The dancing is about to start,' said Concha.

Elena smiled wryly. 'Will they let us join in, do you think?'

'I wasn't going to ask for permission.'

Jack grinned. 'Aye, well, saves 'em t'embarrassment of a refusal, eh?'

'From that I infer you use the same stratagem.' Concha paused, her expression speculative. 'Do Englishmen know how to dance?'

'Some do, I reckon, but I regret to say that in my case it were never a strong suit.'

'Then it's time that you learned.'

'I were thinking more of watching from here like.'

'You learn best by doing, not watching. Come.' Concha extended her hand imperiously.

He threw a look of mute appeal towards his master. Harry shook his head.

'When a lady has made up her mind argument is fruitless.'

'I swear life were never this hard in t'army.' As he caught sight of Concha's expression Jack threw up his hands in a gesture of surrender. 'All right. No need for bloodshed. I'll come quietly.'

As he and Concha went off to join the dancers Harry looked at Elena.

'Shall we join them?'

She smiled. 'Why not?'

The music and the wine on their own would have been sufficient to make her smilc, but when combined with the presence of a handsome and charismatic partner they took enjoyment to another level. In spite of being a tall man Harry was a graceful dancer. Moreover he seemed familiar with most of the steps. She wondered who had taught him. Belén, perhaps? Determinedly she pushed the thought away, unwilling to spoil the evening with another impertinent question. Instead she gave herself up to the music.

Harry smiled. 'You know I had a suspicion you'd dance well. I was right.'

'You don't do so badly yourself.'

'Thank you.'

'I just wish I were more suitably attired for the occasion.'

'Clothes don't make the dancer,' he replied. 'Besides, most of the women here would be prepared to kill for your figure.'

The warm colour deepened in her cheeks. 'I'm flattered you should think so.'

'It wasn't flattery.'

The expression in the grey eyes set her heart to beating a little faster. Did he find her attractive, then? He'd shown little sign of it and she could hardly ask. Yet the thought that he might was pleasing rather than not, like the touch of his hand when the dance brought them together. It filled her with sensations she had not experienced for years and had not thought to have again.

Eventually they retired to rest awhile and presently were joined by Jack and Concha. Then they talked and drank more wine. Conversation flowed just as smoothly amid joking and laughter. It seemed to Elena that this was what Harry had meant when he spoke about the dissolution of class barriers. Her uncle would never have countenanced this for a moment. Yet it seemed right and natural somehow. On the surface of it they were an ill-assorted group whom circumstances had thrown together, yet it worked. When she spoke to Harry of respect she had meant it. She was also fast coming to like Jack Hawkes too. When things got tough he too could be relied upon to do his part.

A series of explosions drew her out of thought and she looked round quickly. A spray of coloured stars filled the sky. The fireworks had started. Realising that there wasn't the least danger, she settled back again to watch.

Her reaction had not gone unobserved and Harry smiled. This evening she had been more relaxed than he had ever seen her, more animated too, in conversation and in laughter. He had always thought her a beautiful girl but tonight it was as though some invisible restraint had been cast off. The atmosphere had touched a chord in her and, aided by the wine perhaps, had brought out the natural exuberance and sense of fun that she usually kept hidden. It was damnably alluring. She was damnably alluring, even dressed in men's clothing. Much as he'd tried to ignore the thought it refused to be banished. Just then he would have given a great deal to see her in the red gown she had worn on the evening when first they had met. For a moment he indulged the fantasy, and then mentally removed the gown altogether. The result was a coil of tension in the region of his groin. He suppressed it ruthlessly. By rights he ought not to be thinking in those terms. However, he was forced to acknowledge now that he did want it to happen. Just when that change had occurred he was unable to say; he only knew it had.

Eventually, as the hour grew late, they made their way back to the inn. Elena felt weary now but also exhilarated and pleasantly tipsy. When Harry offered her his arm she took it; somehow it seemed a natural thing to do now. They strolled in companionable silence; then he glanced her way.

'Did you enjoy yourself this evening?'

'More than I have for a long time. And you?'

'Equally,' he replied.

'I'm glad my horse cast that shoe.'

'I cannot say I'm sorry either. I did not think this journey would be so enjoyable.'

'You are kind.'

'No, just truthful.' He stopped and drew her round to face him. 'You must stop thinking of yourself as some kind of encumbrance.'

'I wish I could.'

'You have no reason to feel guilty and nor would I have you do so.'

Although his face was in shadow, she heard the sincerity in his voice. He was much closer now, his face only inches from hers, his hands resting lightly on her shoulders. Her breathing quickened. Could she trust him? She wanted to, but…

He bent his head and she felt his lips brush hers, a gentle touch that sent a charge the length of her body. Doubt receded. Involuntarily she swayed towards him, feeling his arms around her shoulders pressing her closer. The kiss, though gentle still, became a little deeper and now coaxing too, until her mouth yielded to his. The taste of wine on his tongue was headier by far than any she had drunk and it was dangerously arousing, like his warmth and the musky scent of his skin. Memory removed his clothing. Imagination pressed his nakedness to hers. Her whole body quivered in response to the thought.

Harry felt the tremor and recognised it at once. It

was tempting to pursue this and give ardour free rein. Yet instinct counselled patience. Elena was apparently not repelled by his advances but she'd had quite a lot to drink this evening. Was it attraction she felt or was it the wine talking? He resolved then that when their marriage was consummated it would be when she was sober and knew exactly what she was doing. Besides, deferred gratification was always stronger. If she really did want him, then waiting would only intensify desire.

He drew back. 'Forgive me. I shouldn't have done that.'

'There's no need...I mean, it wasn't...' She broke off, floundering.

'It's all right. You don't have to explain.' He took her hand in his. 'Come. It's getting late and we have an early start.'

They walked the remaining distance in silence. Elena was glad of the darkness now that hid her embarrassment and confusion. What must he think of her? She had permitted that kiss, had wanted that kiss. What she hadn't expected was her own response. He had clearly misinterpreted it as fear. Yet just then she had no idea how to explain. And if she tried might he not take that as an invitation to further intimacies? For the first time she wondered what it might be like to give herself to him, a thought that titillated and terrified at the same time. At some point it was going to happen, that much was inevitable. He was her husband, after all, and his patience wouldn't last for ever.

Yet when they returned to their room at the inn he

made no attempt to touch her, merely undressed and climbed into bed. Elena stripped off her jacket and boots, then blew out the candle before removing her breeches. In spite of his apparent absence of embarrassment she still lacked the confidence to undress in front of him. Hurriedly she slid into bed and drew the covers over her. Then she heard his voice in the darkness.

'Goodnight, sweetheart. Sleep well.'

The mattress moved as he turned away from her on to his side. Elena's throat tightened and for no apparent reason she wanted to weep.

Chapter Eleven

Towards the end of that week as they descended onto the open plain, the air became sultry and oppressive. By late afternoon dark thunderheads were massing on the horizon. Harry eyed them with misgivings.

'I'd like to find shelter before that lot arrives.'

Jack nodded. 'Aye, my lord. It would be best.'

They rode for another couple of miles but the only sign of habitation was a lone farmhouse in the middle distance. By then the sky was darkening rapidly and the wind picking up. Harry made his decision.

'We'll head for the farm.'

By the time they reached it the first drops of rain began to fall. However, the place looked unprepossessing. The farmhouse itself was rambling and dilapidated with a sagging pantile roof. Elena could see two small windows, now shuttered, and a door made from stout oak planks. In front of it a few scrawny chickens scratched in the dirt. At one end was a midden.

Adjacent to it were a small byre and a pigsty. Opposite those on the other side of the farmyard was an old barn.

As they approached the property two large and half-starved dogs set up a frenzy of barking and brought the farmer out to investigate. He silenced the dogs with an oath and then came to look at his visitors. A short and burly individual of middle years, his swarthy face was stubbled with several days' growth of beard. Small dark eyes regarded the newcomers suspiciously.

'What do you want here?'

'Shelter from the storm,' replied Harry.

'Better you find an inn.'

'There is no inn close enough.'

'My house cannot accommodate so large a group.'

Harry kept his tone level. 'The barn, then. We'll pay, of course.' He tossed over a coin.

The man caught it, examining it closely. His eyes widened a little and then he smiled, revealing stained and uneven teeth amongst which were prominent gaps. 'This way, *señor*.'

They followed him across the yard and waited while he dragged open the door. Then he gestured for them to enter. The barn, though old, was well-maintained and smelled of hay and grain and horses. In the gloom Elena could make out half a dozen stalls, though only two were occupied, currently by heavy draught horses. In one corner were several feed bins, various barrels and a small pile of sacks filled with corn. At the far end a ladder led up to what looked like a hay loft.

'You can sleep up there,' continued their host. 'In

the meantime there are stalls for your horses and hay and grain besides.'

Harry nodded. 'We also require food ourselves.'

'That will cost extra.'

'Naturally. What do you have?'

'Tortilla. Jamón.'

'All right.' Harry held up another coin. 'We want bread and wine as well.'

The man's eyes glinted. 'As you wish.'

'We want the food as soon as may be.'

The farmer grunted assent and with that he left them and hurried off towards the farmhouse. Outside the rain fell faster.

'A real charmer,' said Jack.

'We have shelter and food,' replied Concha. 'We can survive without the charm.'

'True enough.'

Harry looked at the others. 'Let's see to the horses, shall we?'

By the time they had unsaddled and rubbed them down the rain was falling in earnest. Elena could only feel relieved to have found shelter for the night. It might not be a palace but it would keep them dry. While the men went to fetch hay, she and Concha measured out a ration of grain for each horse.

They had just finished when the farmer returned. He carried a lantern which he hung on a nail by the door. With him were two younger men, in their late teens or early twenties perhaps. Seeing an undoubted resemblance to the farmer, Elena guessed that they were his sons. One carried a large tray, the other a jug and some horn cups. At their father's instruction they set their respective burdens down on a couple of the larger barrels. Then they turned to survey the newcomers. They glanced at Harry and Jack but their gaze lingered on the two women. Seeing those hot, lascivious looks Elena felt her neck prickle.

Their host smiled unctuously. 'See, here is your meal. I hope you will enjoy it.'

'I'm sure we shall,' replied Harry.

'If you require anything more, be sure to let me know.'

'We'll do that,' said Jack.

The farmer's gaze flicked his way and for a moment the two men regarded each other steadily. The farmer was first to look away.

'We'll leave you to it, then.'

He turned towards his sons and then jerked his head towards the door. Then all three trooped out. Beyond the door was a grey curtain of rain. Elena shivered and turned away.

'Let's eat, shall we?'

'Good idea.' Harry smiled. 'Pull up a barrel.'

In fact, the food, though simple, was surprisingly good. As they ate the rain intensified and thunder rumbled in the distance. Elena was thankful to be indoors, no matter how humble the accommodation. Quite apart from the misery of being soaked through there was the added risk of lightning strikes. This open countryside would offer no protection at all, as Harry was no doubt aware. They had been lucky. They might be sitting on barrels and eating from wooden platters but it was a lot better than the alternative.

Harry's voice reclaimed her attention. 'It looks like the hay loft tonight. Shall you mind too much?'

'I shan't mind at all,' she replied with perfect truth. 'Anything is better than trying to sleep on sodden ground during a storm.'

'Yet I think few ladies would view the prospect of a barn with equanimity.'

'Soft living makes one spoilt. A few nights in the open restores an appreciation of the comforts taken for granted before.'

'I think you're right.'

'We rarely appreciate what we have until it's taken away.'

'True.'

That succinct reply made her suddenly aware that they were skirting dangerous ground. Happily for her peace of mind, Jack intervened.

'Nowt wrong wi' a barn, especially on a night such as this. Where I come from there's plenty o' folk'd be glad o' such accommodation.'

'Where *do* you come from?' asked Concha.

'Leeds,' he replied. 'It's in Yorkshire.'

'Your family is there?'

'Never had a family that I can recall. I were left outside t'workhouse door apparently. I grew up in t'same establishment.'

'This is a charitable institution, no?'

'In a manner o' speaking.' He smiled wryly. 'You get a roof over your head and you don't starve—not quite anyway.'

'Do you get help to find a trade?'

'Aye. When I were ten I were set to work in a woollen mill. Hours were long and t'work were dangerous, to say nowt o' t'din. I hated it. Another lad and I tried to run away only we were caught.'

'They brought you back?'

'Aye, they did that. Then they shaved our heads and flogged t'pair of us before all t'others to serve as a warning like.'

The others stared at him, appalled, not least for the matter-of-fact tone with which the tale was delivered. However, it was at variance with the look in his eyes which suggested emotion usually kept hidden. None of them had the least doubt that what they were hearing now was the truth.

'So I bided me time after that. Made out as I'd learned me lesson like, and knuckled under. Then, when I were fifteen I ran away again, and that time I didn't get caught.'

'Where did you go?' asked Concha.

'London, 'cos I knew it'd be easy to disappear there. I found work in a livery stable. Lad had been dismissed only t'week before, see, and they were short-handed. So I got t'job. It were hard work and it didn't pay much, but it were a sight better than t'mill.'

'So you remained there until you joined the army, no?'

'Joining t'army were t'furthest thing from me mind

then. Working wi' the horses were all right but I wanted to earn better money so I found a new job as a doorman in a gambling den. It were a shady sort o' place and it attracted a similar clientele for t'most part. It were also run by a crook so t'profits to be made were pretty big.'

'You mean he cheated?'

'Aye, he did. Got away wi' it too—for a while. Then one night a young cove came in and lost a lot o' money. He swore t'cards were marked, which same they were, o'course. He were drunk and angry and eventually I were ordered to throw him out. We had a bit of a tussle, but he came off worse and eventually I got rid of him.'

'But not for good.'

'Turned out his father were a lord and he tipped off t'authorities. Next night t'place were raided. Everyone concerned wi' it were arrested. Being as t'plaintiff were a lord's son, t'judge sentenced us all to hang.'

Concha paled. 'But you did not cheat the man. You only removed him from the premises on someone else's orders.'

'That made no odds and so I ended up in t'Fleet along wi' t'rest. Anyway, day before sentence were due to be carried out, a recruiting sergeant turned up at t'gaol. Seems army were short o' men. Anyhow, we were given a choice: take t'king's shilling or hang.'

'You were fortunate.'

'Aye, I was, though to be honest it didn't seem like that at first. After a while though I got a taste for army life and it weren't so bad.'

'You survived.'

'That I did, so I can't complain really.'

Elena wondered how he could speak so matter-of-factly about so hard a life. In comparison her upbringing had been one of unvarying comfort and ease. She'd had parents who loved her; she'd been given an education, food, clothing and every advantage. In that respect she'd been so much luckier than most. If the war hadn't come along she'd have been married to a nobleman and would have continued to live a life of luxury, quite unaware of how precarious existence could be. The war had provided a different kind of education and it had changed everything.

She wasn't alone in feeling sobered. Harry had listened in thoughtful silence too. Although he knew something of Jack's past he'd had no idea of the earlier details of the man's life, until now. It reinforced his own sense of how fortunate he'd been. Born into a life of privilege and plenty, he'd always taken it for granted. As he grew older he began to realise that other people lived very differently, but, until he'd joined the army, he had never encountered the reality at close quarters. At first he was horrified by the ignorance, coarseness and brutality he'd encountered among the rank and file, but acquaintance with Jack Hawkes had given him a deeper insight into why they were like it. Many of the regular soldiers were gaol fodder but most of them were not bad men. Jack was proof enough of that. Harry wasn't at all sure that he could have dealt with such adversity with that level of courage and determination.

They finished their meal and Elena collected the platters and cups and returned them to the tray. Then Jack got his feet.

'I'll take first watch tonight, my lord, if you'd like.'

Harry nodded. 'Concha, you'll join him. Elena and I will relieve you later.'

She experienced a momentary surprise but said nothing. Doubtless he had his reasons for doubling up on the watch. Jack didn't argue either.

'You're thinking what I'm thinking, then.'

'I expect so,' said Harry.

Elena intercepted the glance that passed between the two men. 'You expect trouble from our hosts?'

'Let's just say that it doesn't pay to get complacent,' replied Harry.

'You're right. It doesn't.'

'Regard it as a precaution only. In the meantime, let's get some rest.'

Elena nodded and went to investigate the hay loft. It was essentially a platform under the rafters and was reached by a ladder. However, though primitive, the place smelled sweet enough and the bed would at least be soft. After all, she had slept in far worse.

Having laid out the bedroll she removed her jacket and used it to improvise a pillow. Then she tugged off her boots and lay down, settling herself comfortably. A few minutes later Harry joined her. In the confined space his presence seemed even more imposing. Covertly she watched as he spread his blanket and then removed his own coat before stretching out beside her. However, he made no move in her direction. There had been no repetition of the brief intimate moment they had shared after the fiesta, and it occurred to her that it might well have been the wine talking that night. Once he was completely sober perhaps he found the thought of her less pleasing. No matter how much time had passed since the events in Badajoz, she was still soiled goods.

She closed her eyes, listening to the rain drumming on the roof, each particle of her being attuned to the man beside her. Her lips still bore the imprint of his kiss, her flesh remembered his touch. In those fleeting moments he had made her feel truly alive. What might he make her feel if she surrendered herself completely? If he took her, if he made her his, might not the evils of the past be expunged? Might she not become a real woman again? It was the first time such a possibility had suggested itself. It was also the first time since Badajoz that a man had made her feel that way. If only she could find that degree of trust within herself…

At some point during these musings she must have dozed off because the next thing she knew was a hand on her shoulder gently rousing her. Rather groggily she propped herself on one elbow and then, in the soft lamplight, met Harry's gaze.

He smiled faintly. 'Time to relieve the others.'

'Already? What o'clock is it?'

'Just before one.'

'Right.'

With an effort she shook off weariness and dragged on her boots and coat. Then she followed him down the ladder. It was still raining and thunder rumbled intermittently. The air temperature had fallen too, and she shivered a little, missing her snug bed in the hay.

Thrusting her pistol into her waistband, she took up her position and settled down to wait. The barn was quiet save for the occasional rustling of straw in the horses' stalls and the rattle of a halter chain. The only illumination was a pool of the soft radiance around the lantern which sat on a barrel top by the far wall. In the relative gloom of her position she could easily discern the dark shape that was Harry but, although he was only feet away, his expression was in shadow. He made no attempt at speech and she did not care to intrude on his private thoughts. All the same he was a solid and reassuring presence.

They had been there about an hour when Elena heard the sound of water splash outside. It was louder than the rain, rather as though someone had inadvertently stepped into a puddle, and followed by a muffled curse. She straightened, listening intently, feeling the hairs stir on the back of her neck. Silently she edged closer to Harry.

'Did you hear it?' she murmured.

'Yes. They're coming. Rouse…'

Before he had time to say more the barn door scraped softly open. Both of them flattened themselves against the wall, pistols in hand. In the gloom they saw three dark figures creep in. The intruders paused then, evidently listening. Hearing nothing untoward they advanced slowly. They had reached the middle of the barn when Harry stepped out of concealment behind them.

'Stop where you are unless you plan to die.'

The three turned swiftly. Elena heard a snarled oath, saw Harry dodge something that flew past his shoulder and then caught a soft thud as a knife bit into wood. He levelled his pistol and fired. Someone cried out and fell. Daggers raised, the other two intruders launched themselves at Harry. In one smooth movement Elena raised her pistol and fired. The target stopped in his tracks, arms outflung, and keeled over. Somewhere beyond she glimpsed movement at the rear of the barn. Then Harry and the third assailant went down together, the knife swaying between them.

Harry swore softly as a clawing hand groped for his eyes. A reek of foetid breath hit him full in the face as a swarthy and stubbled visage drew close to his own, the lips drawn back in a feral snarl. The blade inched closer to his throat. Increasing his grip he forced the point away and rolled, landing a punch under the man's ribs. He heard his assailant grunt but his grip on the dagger never altered. With a supreme effort Harry tightened his grip and slowly forced his arm upwards towards his opponent's neck. The man's eyes widened and he launched a rain of desperate blows with his free hand but the point of the blade came inexorably closer. The point pierced flesh. As the blade slid deeper it was followed by a muffled choking noise. The punches ceased and the man stopped struggling. Then slowly he sagged and lay still. Breathing hard, Harry staggered to his feet.

Elena felt a surge of relief wash through her. 'Are you all right?'

He gave her a wry smile. 'Thanks to you I am. That was quick thinking.'

'I didn't have time to think about it. Luckily, at that range, it was impossible to miss.'

'If they'd stopped when I told them they'd still be alive.'

'They made their choice,' she replied. 'They'd have killed us without a second thought and robbed our corpses afterwards.'

Jack and Concha came to join them.

'The world's well rid o' t'scum, my lady.'

Concha nodded. 'We dealt honestly with them and they repaid us with treachery. I have met their kind many times before.'

Elena looked at Harry. 'What now?'

'We need to find out if there are any more of them. Jack and I will check the house. You and Concha stay here.'

'Be careful.'

'Depend on it.'

The two men went out into the darkness. While they were gone Elena reloaded her pistol, hoping she wasn't going to need it again that night. It seemed the hope would be realised: when the men returned they reported the house empty. Relief replaced anxiety. However, no one felt remotely inclined to sleep now so they sat and waited for dawn.

By then the rain had stopped, though the air was chill and damp. Harry and Jack found some spades and dug three graves behind the barn. Then they carried the bodies out and buried them. When it was done they rejoined Elena and Concha, who were waiting with the horses, and all four rode away.

They rode in silence for the most part, each lost in their own thoughts. However, each of them wanted to put as many miles as possible between themselves and the sinister farm before they stopped again. Elena was weary now and guessed the others felt the same. Now that the drama was over, the incident left a bitter taste. She could only feel thankful that none of them had been hurt. Had they not been so vigilant it would have been they who were lying in shallow graves now.

'Are you all right?'

She looked round to see that Harry had brought his mount alongside. His face registered quiet concern.

'Yes. I'm just a bit tired, that's all.'

'It's hardly to be wondered at,' he replied. 'Let's hope my next choice of accommodation is a vast improvement.'

'You were not to blame. You did what you thought right at the time.'

'But for your presence of mind I'd certainly be dead now. I owe you a great deal.'

'Should not a wife defend her husband?'

He smiled ruefully. 'The roles are usually reversed.'

'But then it is not usual to be under attack by a band of cut-throats.'

'No, but it sits awkwardly with me all the same. I must try to do better in future.'

'I have no complaint to make.' She paused. 'Besides, you saved me from the convent.'

'Are you saying that the honours are even now?'

'No, for I still consider mine the greater debt.'

Something in her expression caused his heart to beat a little faster. 'You must not talk of indebtedness, Elena. I do not think of our relationship in those terms.'

She wanted to ask how he did regard it but bit the words back. It was another impertinent question and would almost certainly annoy him. Moreover, they were both tired and she had no wish to quarrel. Instead she changed the subject.

'Will we reach Seville soon, do you think?'

'Yes, quite soon. Another week at most.'

'I'm looking forward to that.'

'So am I,' he replied. That was the absolute truth. He wanted to be able to stop exposing her to danger and reckless adventure, especially when he was such a dismal failure as a protector. That realisation only intensified his guilt.

Their conversation also remained on his mind for some time. Elena had shown courage and presence of mind, and never at any time had she treated him to a fit of feminine hysterics. In fact, he thought that she had more spirit and more nerve than many men he'd met. She was remarkable in so many ways. She was also beautiful. After losing Belén he'd been certain that he'd never marry, that no other woman could make him feel as she had done. He had never anticipated rediscovering that kind of magnetic attraction, but now it was impossible to deny that he did feel it. That brief stolen kiss with Elena had only intensified his desire. It was so tempting to give it rein and the opportunity had been there. It would have been easy. He could have taken her, could have made her his in fact as well as in name. He grimaced. Even if Elena was willing to give herself to him what would be her reaction when eventually she learned the truth? It could only be delayed so long, but at some point she would find out and it would be better if it didn't happen in a casual conversation with someone else. Once they returned to England the likelihood of a chance revelation increased substantially. He was going to have to deal with the matter before then. In the meantime he needed to concentrate on the business in hand.

Chapter Twelve

They reached Seville without further incident some five days later, and put up at the Posada del Sol, one of the recommendations on Don Manuel's list. Elena wasn't in the least sorry for the change. After they had eaten and rested, Concha went out to find them some more suitable clothing. It was one thing to sport masculine dress while they were out in the sticks, but quite another here in the city. Elena was hopeful of seeing at least some of the sights once Harry had undertaken his own business affairs. To do that, she had to look respectable.

The first thing she did was to request a bath. Then she stripped off her travel-stained garments and sank into the hot water with a blissful sigh. She scrubbed herself thoroughly with scented soap and washed her hair. It was good to be clean again and to smell of flowers instead of horses and leather. She smiled wryly, thinking that she'd hardly fitted the mould of a newly married woman when she didn't even look feminine.

Masculine clothing was practical and comfortable for travel but she was looking forward to a change now.

Concha had returned with various purchases which included a couple of figured muslin gowns, a shawl and a straw bonnet. 'They are perhaps not in the first stare of fashion but they may serve until we can locate a dressmaker,' she observed.

'They will do very well,' said Elena. 'The material is pretty.'

'So I thought.'

The gowns were a reasonably good fit and, surveying herself in the glass later, Elena was satisfied.

'At least I can step out of the room now without attracting undue attention,' she observed.

The maid grinned. 'You will always attract attention, Doña Elena.' She surveyed her handiwork critically. 'It looks well.'

'I wish I could say the same for my hands. They look terrible.'

'Not so terrible. A rest from work and a little cream will work wonders.'

'I haven't used hand cream since we left Madrid.'

'You will soon recover the habit.'

'I need to if I am to resume the role of a lady.' Elena sighed. Such things hadn't mattered before but the advent of Harry had changed all that. Now she needed all the help she could get.

'If you don't mind, I would like to take a leaf out of your book and make myself more respectable,' said Concha.

'Of course. I need to speak to His Lordship in any case.'

'He is in the private parlour.'

Harry, who had also bathed and changed sometime earlier, had been reading a newspaper but glanced up as the door opened. Seeing Elena he got to his feet at once. His gaze swept her from head to toe but could find no fault. The sprigged muslin gown was simple and pretty and exquisitely feminine. Dark curls framed her face and were caught up behind in a simple knot. The effect was both artless and alluring. Realising he was staring, he recollected himself quickly.

'You look wonderful.'

'Thank you. It feels good to wear a dress again.'

'You should make a habit of it.'

'Indeed I hope to.'

He gestured to a chair. 'Please.' When she had settled herself comfortably he continued, 'I am glad you are come since I wished to speak with you about my next line of enquiry.'

'I imagine that means a visit to Señor Garrido.'

'Just so. It is my intention to call upon him this afternoon.'

'Then I wish you all good fortune.'

'I thank you.' He paused. 'I just hope that all the effort to get here will not have been in vain.'

'Why should it?'

'In truth I'm afraid of raising my hopes too high lest they should be dashed.'

She regarded him sympathetically. 'I can understand

that but, all the same, I think your fears are groundless. If Señor Garrido can help, then I'm convinced he will, especially when he learns how important a matter it is.'

'Well, there's only way to find out.' He surveyed her steadily. 'I'd be glad if you would remain here in the meantime since I shall want to speak with you on my return.'

'As you wish.'

'I hope not to be too long. Can you find some means of amusement until I get back?'

'I'm quietly confident.'

'Good.' He possessed himself of her hand and raised it to his lips. *'Hasta entonces.'*

With that he smiled and departed. Elena stared after him, aware of a strange sensation of loss and the warm imprint of his kiss on her skin.

Harry found the address with no difficulty. It was a large house in a respectable part of the city, evidently the property of a man of some consequence. By good fortune Garrido was at home and, on receipt of Harry's card, had him shown into the study at once.

Pablo Garrido was in his mid-forties. Although only of average height his compact frame suggested strength. Like most Spaniards he was dark, though grey hair was evident among the black. His clean-shaven face was angular, though not ill-favoured, and commanded by a pair of piercing brown eyes. He received his guest courteously and, having invited him to sit, asked to know how he might be of service.

As Harry summarised, Garrido listened intently and without interruption. His gaze never left Harry's face. At length, when he had concluded, Garrido nodded.

'I did indeed meet your brother, my lord. A most intelligent man and an excellent operative in every way. His loss was deeply regretted in many quarters.'

'Never more so than by his family.'

'Of course, especially in the light of what you tell me.'

'It is imperative that I establish the truth about my brother's death. The law in England requires it. To obtain the proof I require I must find Xavier Sanchez.'

'Yes, I can see that. However, I have not set eyes on the man for some time.'

'Do you know where he may be found?'

'No, but I can make enquiries.'

Harry experienced a surge of excitement but reined it in hard. 'I'd be most obliged.'

Garrido nodded. 'I'll do what I can. If you will give me your direction I'll send word when I know more.'

When Harry returned to the inn, he lost no time in seeking out Elena. He found her still in the parlour engaged in reading the newspaper he had left there. She looked up eagerly as he entered, and he saw her smile. It was a warm, unforced expression and it caused his heart to beat a little faster. Telling himself not to refine on it, he closed the door.

'What news?' she asked.

As he communicated what he had learned, she listened carefully.

'It sounds hopeful,' she said when at length he had done.

'Yes, though I'm not counting my chickens.'

'I'm sure all will yet be well.'

He smiled. 'In the interim we have time to spare. Would you like to take a look around? I believe Seville has some fine sights.'

An answering smile lit her face. 'I should like it very much.'

'The cathedral and the Giralda are very near. Perhaps we should start with those.'

'Oh, yes. Let's.'

He offered his arm. 'Come, then.'

They strolled along the street in companionable silence. Although Elena looked about with interest, every part of her being was alive to the man beside her. It occurred to her also that this was the first time they had ever done this. Of course, their relationship had lacked any kind of courtship and, hitherto, they had always been in the company of others. This was a pleasurable change.

Then they turned the corner and for a moment everything was driven from her mind except for the towering edifice in front of them.

'Oh, my.'

The Gothic cathedral of Santa María de la Sede was breathtaking. Elena stared at it incredulously.

'Oh, Harry, it's magnificent. I'd always been told that it was, but it's not the same as seeing for oneself.'

He smiled. 'Indeed not.'

'My father told me that it is one of the largest churches ever built.'

'He was quite right.'

'He said it took more than a hundred years to construct, and it has the longest nave in the world.'

'So I believe.'

She craned her neck, gazing at the intricately carved frontage and soaring tower above, wondering at the skill that wrought it. 'The ancient builders were certainly masters of their art.'

'Yes, they were.' He paused. 'Shall we look inside?'

For a second she hesitated, then nodded. 'Why not?'

If she had thought the outside impressive, the interior with its elegant pillars and vaulted ceiling and glory of stained glass was even more awe-inspiring. And that, she reflected, was the point. This building was not just about architectural splendour; it was about power and control. A control she had so narrowly escaped. Of course it wasn't possible for a woman to escape some form of control. Society would not countenance such a thing. She glanced at the man beside her. He wore his power lightly but, ultimately, she was still subject to his will. Yet of the two choices she knew whose authority she preferred.

Sensing her preoccupation Harry regarded her covertly. He thought he could guess at some of her thoughts and wondered if it had been entirely tactful to bring her here.

'Are you all right, Elena?'

'Perfectly.'

'Only you seemed a little uneasy.'

'This is the first time in years that I have voluntarily entered a church,' she replied. 'I have not done so since Badajoz.'

'I'm sorry. I didn't think.'

'It's all right. I'm glad to have the chance to see this. Besides, faith is not a prerequisite for the appreciation of architecture.'

'True.'

Again she wondered if she had shocked him with such an impious remark. However, she did not see disapproval in his face and nor had he rebuked her. Her former betrothed most certainly would have done. He had observed all the outward forms of Christianity but never translated his faith to the earthly plane. The tolerance she saw in Harry had been entirely lacking in Jose.

They strolled on, pausing occasionally to admire the marvellously carved tombs and to look into the small side chapels.

'There seem to be lots of these, don't there?' said Harry after a while.

'About eighty, according to my father.'

'What!' The exclamation drew disapproving glances from those nearest. He lowered his voice. 'How many sins is it possible to commit?'

'It depends whom one asks. My aunts are authorities on the subject of other people's sins.'

'Your aunts are confounded bores. It grieves me to speak harshly of your relations, but in their case I'm willing to make an exception.'

Elena grinned. 'I won't take offence.'

'Indeed I hope not.'

'I feel sure that your family is not boring.'

'Boredom is not a word I associate with the name of Montague. In fact, there's rarely a dull moment.' Harry sighed. 'I dream of dull moments sometimes.'

Elena laughed. 'Be careful what you wish for.'

'Do you fear that the wish may come true, then?'

'I doubt whether I will ever be bored in your company, my lord.'

'I'm flattered—I think.'

Elena gave him a sidelong glance in which mischief and amusement were mingled in equal measure. It was also unwittingly beguiling and, ordinarily, would have met with a fitting response. As it was, he had to remind himself that they were in a church.

It was another hour before they stepped out into the sunshine again. The light seemed dazzling after the relative gloom inside the cathedral. Harry paused and turned to Elena.

'Where to now?' he asked.

She looked around, taking in the various possibilities. Then she pointed to the Giralda. 'Up there.'

A former minaret from the mosque that had once

stood on the site of the cathedral, the bell tower took its name from the weathervane on the top.

'I'm game if you are,' he replied. Then, catching the look in her eye, added ruefully, 'All right. That was a stupid comment. I should know better by now.'

Elena grinned and slipped her arm through his. Then they strolled across to the tower. It had no stairs; instead a series of carefully inclined ramps led to the top. At the halfway point they paused for breath.

'Apparently the muezzin used to ride up here,' she said.

'I don't blame him when he had to do this five times a day.'

'Well, I suppose the horse was fit anyway.'

He laughed. 'Yes, I imagine it was. This tower is higher than the one in Babel.'

She reached out and took his hand. 'Come on, not far now.'

Harry groaned in mock despair but allowed himself to be led nevertheless. Her spontaneous gesture had not gone unnoticed; it was the first time that she had made such an overture towards him and it created a strange sensation in his breast. Moreover, her hand felt right in his, as though it belonged there.

They climbed on up the final ramps. By the time they reached the viewing gallery at the top they were breathing hard. However, the views repaid the effort and, since they were alone, they had leisure to admire them undisturbed. Elena leaned on the edge of the parapet, looking out towards the Alcázar.

'I expected Seville to be fine but it is far better than I expected,' she said. 'Does England have sights as fine as this?'

'When we go to London, I'll take you to see Westminster Abbey and St Paul's Cathedral. They're both impressive in their different ways.'

'I'll look forward to that.'

'Shall you not be sad to leave Spain?'

She turned to face him. 'In some ways, but it is also tied to things I'd like to forget.'

'It was never my intention to return,' he admitted. 'Had it not been for Jamie's demise I might never have done so.'

'You could hardly be blamed for your reluctance when the memories were so painful.'

'Not all of them were painful. I had some good friends and even in the army it was possible to have fun occasionally. And of course there was Belén...'

Elena's heartbeat quickened but she remained silent, waiting.

'Her father was a doctor, a gentleman for whom I had the highest respect. One day one of my comrades was injured and it was too far to get him back to camp for the surgeon so we sought a doctor in the nearest town. That's when I met Belén.' He smiled faintly. 'She was acting as an assistant to her father. I'd never seen anyone quite like her.'

'She must have been very beautiful.'

'In truth she was, and yet, oddly, it was her hands I noticed first. They were unmistakably those of a lady yet they were so deft and gentle in tending my friend's wound. It was after they'd patched him up that I began to look at the woman. Does that sound ludicrous?'

'No. Under the circumstances it makes perfect sense.'

'My friend had lost a lot of blood so they put him in their spare room until he was well enough to travel. I went to the house every day. The more I saw of Belén the more strongly I was attracted to her. She was not only pretty but also well-educated. We talked about all manner of things. She had a keen sense of humour too, and a strong spirit. It didn't take me long to fall completely under her spell and to know that I wanted her to be my wife.'

Elena's stomach knotted. 'And so you spoke to her father.'

'Yes. He could tell which way the wind was blowing and he had no objection to make. I wanted us to marry at once, but Belén particularly wished us to wait a little to allow certain members of her family to attend the wedding. It was only a matter of a fortnight and so I agreed.' He took a deep breath. 'In the interim the town came under attack, people were killed, businesses looted and many properties set alight, including the house where Belén and her father were living.'

Elena paled. 'And they didn't get out.'

'The building burned like a torch and they were trapped on an upper floor.'

'Madre de Dios.'

'By the time I got there the place was an inferno. I

tried to get in but the heat was too great. Minutes later the whole interior collapsed.'

'I'm so sorry.'

'I should have taken her away while I had the chance.'

'It's easy to be wise after the event.'

'She trusted me and yet, when she needed me most, I failed her.'

'You must not think like that. You were not to blame for what happened.'

'And yet I cannot rid myself of guilt. When I think of the terror she must have felt before she died…' He made a vague gesture with his hand. 'The crowning irony was that I survived the war. For a long time I wished that I had not.'

'Your death would not have changed anything, Harry.'

'I know it, but I'd cheerfully have settled for oblivion.' His gaze met and held hers. 'You are not the only one who has stayed out of churches, my sweet.'

The implications resonated deeply and she had no difficulty in empathising with him. What kind of God permitted such things to happen? Not one with whom she had any affinity. Nor it seemed did the man beside her. Their conversation raised other questions too, that required an answer. Yet for the first time she feared to ask.

'It is not easy to come to terms with the loss of those we love.'

'No, it isn't, but there is no use in clinging to the

past. Eventually one has to let go and start to look ahead instead.'

'Yet the scars remain, do they not?'

'Yes, they remain with us, but they also fade with time.' He paused. 'After what happened I never expected to share my life with another human being, but fate took a hand in that. I'm glad it did.'

Her heart missed a beat. 'Are you?'

'I am daily more reconciled to my fate.' He watched her closely. 'Are you?'

'I would like us to have a future, Harry.'

'There is no reason why we should not.'

'Except that I am no true wife to you. I'm sorry...' She broke off awkwardly.

He took her gently by the shoulders. 'I told you once that there was no hurry. That has not changed. When the time is right it will happen.'

'Does the thought of me not disgust you?'

'No, why on earth should it?'

Before she could reply they heard the sound of voices from below announcing the arrival of more visitors. Harry sighed. He would very much have liked to continue the conversation but clearly that wasn't going to be possible for a while.

'Have you seen enough?' When she nodded he went on, 'Let us go down, then.'

The descent was much easier and fifteen minutes later they were out in the open air again. By tacit consent they walked slowly towards the Alcázar, stopping briefly to let a carriage pass. It was a handsome equipage drawn by a pair of beautiful chestnut horses. As it passed, Elena glimpsed a crest on the door, although she did not recognise it, or the livery of the footman who rode on the step behind.

The vehicle had barely gone fifty yards before it came to an abrupt halt. The window was lowered and a man leaned out. He scrutinised them keenly for a moment and then his face lit in a beaming smile.

'Is it possible?'

Elena looked quizzically at her companion. 'A friend of yours, by any chance?'

'He does look familiar I have to say.'

'But you don't recognise him.'

'Not immediately,' he admitted.

The carriage door opened and a man got out. Then he strode towards them. As he drew near his smile widened.

'Harry Montague! I knew I was not mistaken.'

Recovering his wits and his memory, Harry returned the smile. 'Villanueva! Of all people. This is a pleasant surprise.'

The two men shook hands warmly. Elena regarded the newcomer with interest. He was of an age with Harry and almost the same height. The face with its neat moustache and goatee beard was also strikingly handsome. His dress proclaimed him a nobleman. Harry performed the introductions.

'May I present the Conde de Villanueva. Conde, this is my wife, Elena.'

The conde's dark gaze swept her from head to foot,

registering admiration. 'An honour, my lady.' He smiled. 'Your husband is a fortunate man.'

'I know it,' said Harry.

'It has been a long time, my friend. Too long.'

'Yes, it has.'

'May I ask what good fortune brings you to Sevilla?'

'A matter of business.'

'Do you stay long?'

'I'm really not sure. Some days at least.'

'That is excellent. My wife and I are holding a ball on Wednesday to celebrate our wedding anniversary. We would be honoured if you were able to attend.'

Elena knew Harry would decline. As he had said, they were here on business, and besides, all her gowns were in Madrid. She hadn't anything suitable to wear and not enough time to have anything made. It was an impossible situation.

'We'd be delighted, wouldn't we, my dear?'

For a moment she couldn't believe that she'd heard aright. Then, recollecting her manners, she summoned a gracious smile. 'I can't think of anything I'd like more.'

The conde beamed. 'That's settled, then. Here is my card—the direction is on it. I regret that I cannot stay to talk further but I am on my way to an appointment.'

'Don't let us delay you,' said Harry.

'Until Wednesday, then.'

With that the conde left them and a few moments later the carriage rolled away. 'That was unexpected,' said Harry. 'I haven't seen him since the end of the war.'

'How did you meet him?'

'By chance. He was an officer in the Spanish army and his men fought various actions in support of the British. He was a capable leader and a brave fighter.'

'He obviously remembered you.'

'I can recall him mentioning Andalucia, but not that his home was in Seville. It's a happy accident at all events.'

'Is it?'

'He's pleasant enough company. Besides, now you have a ball to look forward to.'

'I'd look forward to it a lot more if my gowns were not in Madrid.'

'Heavens, I'd forgotten that.' He looked thoughtful. 'We have a little time though, so I'm sure something can be contrived.'

Elena wished she could share his optimism.

Chapter Thirteen

In fact, Harry was as good as his word and, having made enquiries, took her to visit a reputable dress-maker. When patterns and fabrics had been discussed and Elena's figure measured, the question of a delivery date arose. She opened her mouth to apologise for the short notice but Harry was before her.

'My wife requires the gown on Wednesday afternoon. Kindly see that it is delivered to our lodgings.' He gave the woman the direction and tossed a purse of coins onto the table. 'Here is a little something on account. You will get the rest when the gown is finished.'

Elena blinked. She had never heard him sound so peremptory or so arrogant. His present mien fitted the words too, so that he looked and sounded liked the archetype of a haughty Spanish hidalgo. Nevertheless, it did not fail in achieving the desired effect. The dress-maker stared at the purse and then bestowed on him a fawning smile.

'I thank you, Your Excellency. Certainly the dress will be ready on Wednesday afternoon.'

'I'm quite sure of it,' he replied.

The woman ushered them to the door with all ceremony and then bade them an almost reverent farewell. With that they left the premises.

Elena stared at her companion, torn between incredulity and amusement. 'That was outrageous.'

His expression was unrepentant. 'It was intended to be.'

'I'd like to ask how much was in that purse but I'm afraid you wouldn't tell me.'

'I'm afraid you'd be right.'

'It is kind of you to do this. I appreciate it.'

'Did you think I would let you go to the ball in rags, Cinderella?'

She laughed. 'Perhaps not. All the same it was a generous gesture.'

'Should not a husband buy his wife a gown?'

'It's a new thought for me. Up to now I've had to purchase my own.'

'Do you think you might grow accustomed to the idea?'

'I really believe I might.'

As there was no word from Garrido they spent the next two days exploring the city. Harry was an entertaining companion and Elena enjoyed his company. Indeed when she was with him it was hard to be aware of anyone else. He put himself completely at her disposal, a novelty for one who had until lately been so self-reliant. He was also quietly attentive to her every need. It was the first time in her adult life that a man had ever made her feel as if she mattered, and she found it an oddly agreeable sensation. In many ways it was a deferred courtship. He encouraged her to talk and listened carefully to what was said but was never censorious. It was surprisingly easy to confide in him. He made no demands or any attempt to initiate intimacy and when he did touch her, to offer his arm or to point something out for her attention or to put a hand in the small of her back and guide her gently through a doorway, it seemed natural and right. His nearness was exciting but never threatening and she relaxed and enjoyed being with him. The thought of the forthcoming ball filled her with pleasant anticipation since it would be the first time they had attended such a function together.

They had returned from a walk along the banks of the Guadalquivir when a message arrived for Harry. He opened it hurriedly and scanned the contents.

'It's from Garrido. He asks me to call upon him. Would you mind if I left you for a while?'

'Not at all. Of course you must go.'

'I shan't be too long.'

'I'll still be here,' she replied. 'And, Harry…good luck.'

'Thank you. I'm rather hoping for some luck myself.'

When he arrived at Garrido's house he was admitted at once. His host rose to meet him with a smile.

'You are prompt, my lord.'

'It is a matter of considerable importance. I can do no other.'

Garrido bade him be seated and then poured two glasses of amontillado. He handed one to his guest and sat down in the chair opposite.

'Since last we spoke I have made enquiries among my acquaintance in the service,' he said. 'From them I have news of Xavier Sanchez.'

Harry drew a deep breath, dreading to ask the question but knowing he must. 'Is he still alive?'

'Oh, yes, very much so.' Garrido smiled. 'Alive and currently living in Cádiz.'

Harry's heart beat a little faster now. 'Do you have his direction?'

His host reached into his coat pocket and took out a folded sheet of paper. 'It is written here.'

Harry took it and glanced at the contents, struggling to repress emotion. The last piece of the puzzle was in his hand. All he had to do now was make use of the information and he would get the proof he sought. He would actually speak to the man who was with Jamie at the end. For a moment it was hard to speak.

'I cannot thank you enough for your help in this matter, not only on my account but on behalf of my family too.'

'I am very glad that I was able to help.'

'Is Sanchez also retired from the service now?'

Garrido smiled faintly. 'No, but then he is much younger than I.'

'Is Cádiz his home town?'

'Again, no. He comes from Valladolid, I believe.'

'Then he is in Cádiz on business,' said Harry.

'I imagine so.'

'I hope I shall not miss him.'

'My understanding is that he'll be there awhile yet.'

'That's good to hear.' Harry's mind was already moving ahead. 'Besides, it is not so far to Cádiz.'

'Will you leave at once?'

'No. My wife and I have a social obligation to attend to first.'

Garrido looked genuinely surprised. 'Your wife is with you as well?'

'That's right.'

'It is a long and hard journey from Madrid. Most women would hesitate to undertake it.'

'She is not like most women,' said Harry.

'Indeed not. She must be remarkable.'

'Yes, she is.' As he said it Harry recognised the words for truth. 'All the same she is glad to have a few days' break in town.'

'I can imagine.' Garrido smiled. 'Pray convey my respects to the lady.'

'I'll do that.'

Harry rose from his chair and the two men shook hands warmly.

'If ever you return to Sevilla I hope you will call upon me,' said Garrido.

'I'll make a point of it, *señor*.'

With that Harry took his leave. He barely noticed the

journey back; his mind was elsewhere. He wanted to tell Elena his news. Even though he'd been gone barely an hour he realised he'd missed her. Already she had become so much a part of everyday life that it was hard to recall a time when she hadn't been there. Now that he thought about it the years since Belén had been a void that he'd tried to fill with work and the dreary social round. Somehow, without his being aware of it, the void was gone and with it all sense of dreariness. There hadn't been a dull day since first he met Elena.

She was waiting for him in the private parlour and rose eagerly to meet him, her expression both anxious and hopeful at once.

'Well?'

He handed her the sheet of paper that Garrido had given him earlier. She took it and scanned the contents, then gave him a quizzical look. Harry grinned.

'It's Xavier Sanchez's direction.'

For a moment she stared at him; then her face lit in a dazzling smile. 'Oh, Harry, that's wonderful.' Impulsively she crossed the intervening space and hugged him. 'I'm so pleased for you.'

He lifted her off the floor and swung her round. 'Isn't it marvellous? I never hoped for so much.'

'Cádiz is not that far.'

'You're right.' He gave her a resounding kiss and set her down. 'It is not above eighty miles. With luck we can be there in a week.'

Feeling a little breathless now and keenly aware of

the hands still spanning her waist, she tried to concentrate.

'Do you want to leave straight away? I mean, we can forgo the ball if you'd rather. I'm sure the conde would understand.'

'By no means. This news should be celebrated.'

'I think it should.'

He looked into her face and his expression became more intense. Then, slowly, he bent closer and his mouth met hers in a gentler and altogether more intimate embrace. Elena leaned towards him, sliding her arms round his neck. His hold tightened and he drew her against him, seeking her response. Instinctively her mouth opened beneath his, her tongue flirting lightly with his.

A familiar heat flared in his groin. It shocked him to realise just how badly he wanted her; wanted to undress her, take her to bed and make love to her all afternoon. Imagination only increased desire and heightened arousal.

With a real effort of will he drew back knowing he couldn't afford to take this any further; that to do so would undo everything he had achieved over the past few weeks. Elena wasn't ready for a display of unbridled passion. She needed tenderness and patience. Besides, he had no right to make her his when he hadn't yet told her the whole truth. He felt ashamed of his reticence now. She was beginning to trust him without having any idea of what she was really doing. Once again the knowledge of her vulnerability only enhanced his guilt. There was only one right course of action now.

Elena felt him draw away mentally as well as physically, but her dominant emotion was disappointment rather than relief. His kiss filled her with new and wonderful sensations and she had not wanted him to stop. On the contrary her imagination had supplied a series of images that were decidedly titillating. However, it seemed that Harry wasn't yet prepared to take things to a different level. He had denied feeling disgust about her past, and part of him did desire her, she was sure of that, but he couldn't bring himself to go beyond the occasional kiss. What astonished her most of all was that she did want him to, that she wanted to trust him.

'Elena, there's something I need to tell you.'

His voice drew her out of her reverie. 'Oh?'

Her bright, expectant gaze made him feel worse. Most of all he dreaded the altered expression in her eyes that he knew must follow this conversation.

'You might want to sit down.'

Somewhat bemused now she settled herself in a chair nearby. 'Harry, what is it? Something you learned from Señor Garrido?'

'No.' He only wished it were that simple. 'It's nothing to do with that.'

'What, then?'

Before he could reply there was a knock at the door. Mentally stifling a curse he bade the caller enter. It was the *patrón* and he was bearing a bouquet of hothouse flowers.

'These were delivered a few minutes ago,' he explained.

'By whom?' demanded Harry.

'A servant brought them, *señor*. He said to tell you that they come with the compliments of the Conde and Condesa de Villanueva.'

'Indeed.'

'Sí, señor.' The *patrón* beamed. 'Where do you wish me to put them?'

Harry bit back the response that came first to mind. 'On the table.'

When the man had complied Harry dismissed him. Elena rose and went to examine the flowers.

'They're beautiful. What a very kind attention.'

'Yes, isn't it?'

Something in his voice jarred a little. 'Harry? Is something the matter?'

He summoned a smile. 'Of course not. And you're right. It is kind.'

Elena relaxed again. 'Do you know, I can't recall the last time I saw flowers like these. Is not the scent delicious?'

'It certainly is.'

He moved closer and surveyed the bouquet, privately wondering if the condesa even knew of its existence. All he could see in his mind's eye was the handsome face of his erstwhile colleague and the way in which he had looked at Elena before. The image caused an unexpected and unwonted emotion. That the man should take the further liberty of expressing his admiration in this way was breathtaking arrogance. He took a deep breath and mentally counted to ten. Then he felt ashamed of his response. It didn't matter. Why on earth was he overreacting to something so trivial? Let Elena enjoy the flowers.

She looked up. 'What was it you were going to tell me, before we were interrupted?'

'Nothing that won't keep,' he replied.

As soon as he'd said it he wished he hadn't. He needed to tell her the truth. Yet the moment had been lost and he felt rattled besides.

Elena regarded him quizzically. 'Are you sure?'

'Indeed.' He paused. 'Perhaps we should ask Concha to find a container for those flowers. Otherwise they'll wither.'

'Now you're changing the subject.'

For a few moments he was silent but under the weight of that steady gaze it was impossible to pretend. Elena was too perceptive to be easily deceived and he didn't want to deceive her in any case.

'It's something I've wanted to say but didn't know how.'

'I don't understand.'

'It concerns Belén, or rather the circumstances surrounding that tale.' He hesitated. 'What I've told you thus far is all true, but one detail is missing.'

'What detail?'

Harry steeled himself. 'The place where these events occurred was Badajoz.'

Elena was completely still, staring at him in appalled

disbelief. 'Badajoz?' Then the implications began to dawn. 'Then you must have been among the British troops who…'

'I was among the British troops who besieged the town, and afterwards I was among the officers who tried to stop the looting.'

Disbelief vied with slow-burning anger. 'Why did you not tell me this before?'

'I wanted to but somehow the right moment never came along.'

'The right moment?'

He sighed. 'I know. There never could be a right moment for such a disclosure.'

'Yet we have discussed this subject before. There were opportunities to tell me.'

'In truth I did not know how.'

'But now you do?' Her heart thumped unpleasantly hard. This man was her husband, the man she most wanted to trust. How could he have waited so long to tell her?

'If you are prepared to hear it,' he replied.

A part of her wanted to fling the suggestion back in his teeth, but, in a more rational area of her mind, she knew that she needed to hear him. All the same this dilatoriness hurt beyond measure.

'Very well.'

The icy tone was at distinct variance with the burning anger and hurt he saw in her eyes and he cursed his tardiness. He should have said something long ago. Perhaps if he had got it out into the open earlier they might have been better able to deal with it. From the start she had tried to be open with him, to face the things she knew to be difficult. Yet what had been his response? *Let's pretend it didn't happen.*

'I'm not going to make excuses, Elena. I should have told you.'

'So tell me.'

'When the siege was successful I thought the worst was over—until I saw our own troops run amok. It was as though we were not dealing with men any more but wild animals, made savage and uncontrollable by drink.'

Her eyes glittered. 'The British troops were indeed like wild animals.'

'They were impervious to command or reason. They even turned on their own officers.'

'So I heard.'

'Half a dozen were killed as a result, including one of my closest friends.'

'I'm sorry to hear it, but then many terrible deeds were done at that time.'

'It was the most shameful episode I ever witnessed.' He paused. 'Those men were a disgrace to their uniform and to their country. But you know this if anyone does.'

'Oh, yes, I know it,' she replied.

'I am truly sorry about your father, Elena. It was an unspeakable act.'

'Everything that happened to my family that night was unspeakable.'

Harry frowned. 'Others were killed too?'

'Concha's mother, Amparo—although some might say she was fortunate.'

'Fortunate?'

'You know what I mean. After all, my uncle told you what happened, did he not?'

'He did not mention Concha's mother. Nor do I see why her death should be regarded as fortunate.'

A dreadful suspicion began to take root in her mind. 'What exactly did he tell you?'

'That your father was murdered and that his death was the catalyst for your decision to join the *guerrillas*. In consequence your fiancé ended the engagement between you.'

'What?' Elena paled as the significance of that statement sank in, along with the extent of her uncle's duplicity. Clearly Harry had no idea of the truth. All this time she had fondly imagined that his forbearance about her past had been based on full knowledge. The ramifications of that misapprehension were so enormous that she could not see past them. She didn't know if there *was* a way past them.

'Did he leave something out?'

'Only the truth,' she replied.

Harry's gaze grew piercing. 'I think you'd better tell me, don't you?'

Elena's stomach knotted as anger mingled with dread. At the same time she knew this had to be faced even if the consequences meant disaster. There had been enough lies. 'All right, but I warn you, it isn't pleasant.'

'So I infer. Nevertheless, let's have it.'

'The British soldiers broke into our house and when my father tried to stop them they shot him. When Amparo went to his aid they shot her too.'

A muscle jumped in Harry's cheek but all the words he wanted to utter would have sounded like mere platitudes. Besides, Elena was no longer looking at him but inward, remembering.

'Then they came after the rest of us—my sisters and me, the women servants. We attempted to flee but it was too late.' She swallowed hard. 'We tried to fight them off but they were too many and too strong. They stripped us and then held us down while they took it in turn to have their will.'

Harry's face went white. 'Elcna, you don't have to…'

'I think I do. After all, we're being honest, no?'

He winced inwardly but made no reply.

'I don't know how long it went on,' she continued. 'It seemed like a lifetime. Eventually I lost consciousness. When I came round the soldiers were gone and so was everything of value in the house. The place looked as though a hurricane had swept through it. Every part of me hurt and I was covered in cuts and bruises, but I was alive. Miraculously my sisters had also survived, though at that point we wished that we had not.'

'I wish that I had been able to stop it,' he replied. 'I wish that there was something I could say now to take away your pain, but I know very well that there isn't.'

'Nothing can erase the pain of that memory, of seeing my sisters' despair and shame, of sharing those emotions.' She drew a long, shuddering breath. 'I remember that what I wanted most of all was to bathe, as though somehow I could wash away the memory along with the filth. I went to the well in the yard and pulled up bucket after bucket of water and scrubbed myself repeatedly, but it didn't seem to make much difference.'

Harry's gut knotted. He didn't know which was stronger, fury or contempt for the perpetrators of that outrage. At that moment he felt ashamed to be a man.

'My sisters' sole wish was to shun the world and retreat to a convent. Mine was to leave Badajoz and join the *guerrillas*. Since the war had found me I decided to confront it, but not as a victim this time—never again as a victim.' She paused. 'Concha was of the same mind. Since she had suffered the same degradation as I, she understood what I was doing and why.'

'Concha too?'

'None of the women in our house were spared that night,' she replied.

'Dear God.'

'After that, marriage was out of the question. Even if my betrothed had wished to honour the pledge, I could not have gone through with it. The very idea of a man touching me was anathema.' She smiled with unwonted bitterness. 'I shot the first one to try. It was just a crease to the arm, but it sufficed. After that the rest kept their distance.'

'I imagine they did.'

'For a long time I didn't care whether I lived or died so I volunteered for all the most dangerous missions.

I never got so much as a scratch.' She shook her head. 'The men came to believe I bore a charmed life and that any action I was involved in must be successful. They would go wherever I led them. As time went on though, the risks became more calculated. I knew I'd survived the worst and, at some point, without being aware of it, I must have decided that I wanted to go on living.'

'I'm glad you did.'

'After the war I retired to a small family estate in the country, thinking to live there quietly. Unfortunately my uncle got wind of it. He came to see me and to point out my duty.'

'The convent, I collect.'

'Just so. We had a fierce argument and he left. I thought that was the end of the matter, but he returned a week later with a large group of armed retainers.'

'I believe I met them.'

'Indeed you did.' Her jaw tightened. 'I protested as far as I could, but in the end I was compelled to go with him to Madrid. The rest you know.'

Harry felt winded. He couldn't begin to imagine the horror of what she had endured, or the kind of courage it must have required to get up and fight back. The very people who should have provided support had cast her out. Nor had her uncle paid any heed to her feelings when he'd compelled her to marry. It hadn't concerned him one iota that he was effectively forcing her into a stranger's bed. Marriage got her off his hands and lent the whole business a spurious respectability. Quite possibly the pious old hypocrite relished the thought of Elena being returned to a man's control and subjected to his will. Recalling his former lustful thoughts Harry was ashamed and sickened. Almost as bad was his failure to be honest with her.

For once Elena had no trouble reading his expression, and her heart sank. He was disgusted all right, and yet she could not regret telling him the truth. There had been enough pretence. Now he knew who she was and what she was. She could not blame him for his reaction, nor had she expected it to hurt quite as much.

'I should have told you about Badajoz,' he said.

'Yes, you should.'

'I wish that I had.'

'So do I. I also wish that my uncle had been frank with you.'

'It would have saved a lot of misunderstanding.'

'Well, at least we're no longer at cross-purposes.' She rose from her chair. 'If you would excuse me I think I'd like a little time to myself.'

'Of course.' He wasn't in the least surprised that she should wish to be out of his company for a while. The very thought must be unpalatable now. 'We'll talk later.'

His gaze followed her to the door. When it closed behind her what remained was a powerful sense of sadness and loss.

Chapter Fourteen

Elena didn't return to the chamber she shared with Harry. The thought was intolerable just then. Feeling a great need for fresh air and open space she made her way instead to the garden behind the inn. It was walled and, thanks to a number of fruit trees between it and the buildings, relatively private. Elena paced about for a while, trying and failing to collect her thoughts amid roiling emotion. Eventually she gave it up and flung herself down on a bench beneath a tall walnut tree.

Concha found her there some time later. Having looked in all the usual places and failed to find her mistress, she guessed that Elena might have gone outside. She always preferred to be outdoors, especially on so fine a day. However, one look at her face was enough to reveal that she hadn't just come out here for the sunshine. Concha sat down beside her, regarding her in concern.

'What is it, Doña Elena? What has happened?'

Elena drew in a shuddering breath. 'I told him the truth.'

'The truth?'

'About Badajoz.'

For a moment Concha was silent. Then, with careful and deliberate calm, she said, 'Everything?'

'Yes, everything.'

'Dios mio.'

'You think I'm mad.'

'I think you must have had your reasons.'

Elena shrugged. 'My uncle had already given him the bones of the story. I just related my version.'

'And he did not take it well.'

'He took it as one might expect.'

'I see.'

'He may have suspected before that I was soiled goods, now I have confirmed it.'

Concha regarded her with alarm. 'He has not repudiated your marriage?'

'No, but he could not conceal his disgust.' Elena sighed. 'Matters had been going on so well between us and now I've ruined everything.'

'What could have induced you to rake up the past?'

'Harry was there. At Badajoz. He told me.'

'What!'

'He was an officer in the British army. He took part in the siege but he was not among those who ran riot. He said he tried to stop them.'

'It may be so,' replied Concha. 'Unfortunately nothing short of cannon could have stopped that mob.'

Elena nodded. 'I know. It's just that I was shocked to learn that he had been involved at all. He should have told me.'

'Yes, he should but perhaps he feared to.'

'These are fearful subjects but it doesn't mean we should run away from them. Running away solves nothing. It has taken me long enough to learn that.'

'I know, and you're right, of course.'

'I was angry with him.'

'That's hardly surprising.'

'As soon as he mentioned the place it all came back and suddenly I wanted him to hear my version of events.'

'Well, that is understandable.'

'I wanted to shock him and I succeeded. I saw it in his face.'

'I'll wager you did.'

Elena sighed. 'We were not the only ones to suffer, Concha. He lost his fiancée. She burned to death when the looters set fire to the house.'

'*Madre de Dios*. What evil deeds were done then! But if His Lordship knows all this he will surely sympathise with your situation. He cannot blame you for something that was not your fault.'

'He did not blame me,' said Elena. 'Nor could he conceal his distaste. Perhaps I should have let sleeping dogs lie.'

'Sooner or later it was going to come out. If not it would only have festered between you like an abscess.'

'But now the poison is uncontained.'

'At least it has a chance to drain.'

'I hope it may.'

Concha regarded her shrewdly. 'You care for him, don't you?'

'Yes, I care for him, but I have to be able to trust him.'

'He made a mistake in not telling you about Badajoz before, but that does not mean he is untrustworthy.'

'There is such a thing as lying by omission.'

'I cannot believe he intended it thus. It contradicts all the rest of his behaviour towards you.' Concha eyed her steadily. 'I truly believe he cares for you.'

'I thought he did but now…'

'Badajoz is emotional gunpowder and he did not handle it wisely.'

Elena sighed. 'Perhaps I am the one who did not handle it wisely.'

'A frank discussion does not destroy true affection,' said Concha. 'If he is the man I believe him to be he will not think less of you for it.'

'I hope you're right.'

Concha looked thoughtful. 'You realise there is another witness to the events at Badajoz?'

'Another?'

'Jack Hawkes was in your husband's regiment.'

As the ramifications of that statement sank in Elena was suddenly still. 'Of course.'

'It is most likely that he knows what happened to his master at that time.'

'He may not wish to speak of it.'

'If you don't ask you'll never know, will you?'

Elena pondered the matter for some time. It was not quite as straightforward as Concha had suggested. For a start the emotion was too raw. Secondly, she didn't want to go behind Harry's back, and thirdly, if Jack had been told not to speak of the matter he would not break his master's confidence. In spite of Harry's admission she was sure there were other things he was not telling her. No doubt he had his reasons for that, but his reticence hurt. Possibly he had been too shocked by her revelations. Concha was right: he could have repudiated the marriage on such grounds. Most men would have. A wife was expected to be pure. What men did was one thing. Women's behaviour was quite another and society was swift to punish perceived transgressions. Her relatives were evidence enough of that. She had thought Harry different. Of course, she had believed he had known what she was before they married. Her uncle was much to blame in that. The truth was unpalatable but it had needed to come out. Until the whole business was out in the open they could not address it.

She knew that she did want a future with Harry, that she liked him more than any man she had ever met. With him she felt truly alive. She had thought that if any man could help her overcome the past it would be him, that perhaps in his bed all evil might be eradicated. However, even before this latest debacle he seemed to have no wish to pursue that side of their marriage. Once upon a time his restraint had been a source of relief. Now it was fast becoming a source of hurt. It also marked a fundamental shift in her thinking that had crept up unnoticed. This latest revelation turned everything on its head. She had no idea where they would go from here.

When they dined together that evening he made no reference to the earlier discussion. Conversation was restricted to neutral topics. His manners were polished and courteous in every way, but the ease they had shared before was missing. It hurt much more than downright coldness would have done. The only thing to do was to follow his lead so she took refuge in correctness. Her appetite had vanished, but for the sake of form she forced herself to eat a little. Eventually the strain became too great and, after a suitable interval, she pleaded fatigue and excused herself, saying she would retire early. He rose at once but made no comment other than to bid her a goodnight. Sick at heart Elena made her escape.

When she had gone Harry sank back into his chair and tossed back the remainder of his wine. As soon as she was gone he had wanted to call her back but had no idea what he might say if he did. His mind was still reeling. The magnitude of his error was colossal, but even worse was the knowledge of what Elena had suffered. Her pain and her vulnerability touched him more deeply than anything else could. It was his part to keep her from hurt, not add to it. Once again he was proving to be abysmal in the role of protector.

It was much later before he came to bed. Elena didn't stir. No doubt she had been asleep for hours, worn out by the vicissitudes of the day. He placed the candle down on the table across the room so that the light wouldn't fall directly onto the bed and possibly disturb her. Then he began to undress.

In fact, Elena was very far from sleep but, unwilling to reveal it, she remained still and kept her eyes closed. Even so her entire being was attuned to his presence. She heard him undress and felt the familiar movement of the mattress as he climbed in beside her. She held her breath, hoping that he might reach out for her, hold her, that there might be mutual forgiveness and things could go back to the way they were before. However, he made no move to touch her. She bit her lip, telling herself not to be stupid. Of course he wasn't going to touch her. Why would he? The thought must be anathema to him. She had handled everything so badly and now had no idea how to put it right. It crossed her mind to reach out and touch him, but she had never done such a thing before. Under ordinary circumstances it would have been a bold move, but after all that had passed between them might it not seem positively brazen? If he were to reject her she didn't think she could bear it. The very thought of such a humiliation made her cringe inside. Tears pricked her eyelids. She lacked the necessary courage; in fact, she was lacking as a wife in every respect. She wasn't a real woman. She would never be a real woman again.

As a consequence of the emotional upheaval the subject of the ball had been temporarily forgotten. It was resurrected the following afternoon when the gown was delivered. Elena eyed the box dispassionately.

'I wish to goodness there were some way of getting out of the engagement.'

Concha shook her head. 'I think you cannot, not without angering your husband further.'

'You're right. The only thing now is to put a brave face on the matter, but I never felt less like socialising in my life.'

'It's only for one night. Besides, it will provide a distraction.' Concha eyed the box on the table. 'Shall we have a look inside?'

'Why not?'

The maid removed the lid and then carefully pulled aside a layer of tissue paper. Then her eyes widened. 'Oh, my! This must have cost the earth.'

Almost reverently she lifted the dress from the box and unfolded it before holding it up for inspection. In spite of herself Elena could not refrain from uttering a gasp of delight.

'It's exquisite.'

Made of white silk jacquard it had puff sleeves and a low square neckline, with a fan of pleats below the bust. Below it the skirt fell away in smooth straight lines. Fine gold braid added the finishing touch to the bodice, caught in under the bosom and edging the neck and sleeves. It was a simple but elegant creation. Long gloves and a lace fan completed the ensemble along with a silken wrap.

'Try it on,' said Concha.

'All right.'

Elena took off her muslin dress and allowed Concha to help her into the ball gown. Then she crossed to the cheval glass, surveying her reflection critically. The woman who stared back was almost a stranger.

'I've had some pretty dresses in the past,' she said, 'but never anything as fine as this.'

'You look like a princess.'

'Thank you.' Elena turned, examining the gown from different angles. 'It does look well, doesn't it?'

'I think you will draw all eyes.'

There was only one pair of eyes that Elena wished to draw. Having made her a most generous gift, would Harry approve the result? There was only one way to find out. Her gaze met Concha's in the glass.

'I think I should start getting ready.'

The maid nodded. 'I've already requested hot water for your bath.'

When Elena had bathed she sat at the dressing table while her hair was arranged in a stylish knot. Soft curls framed her face. Two judiciously placed silver combs completed the effect. Then she applied a light touch of colour to her cheeks and lips before donning the gown. It fitted to perfection and, as she had envisaged, flattered the line of her figure and enhanced its curves. She turned this way and that before the mirror, studying the effect with a critical eye. Then she nodded.

'It looks well.'

Concha smiled. 'You look beautiful. You'll break a few hearts tonight, Doña Elena.'

Elena reflected sadly that there was only one heart that interested her now. Whether it was in her power to capture it was another matter. She slid her feet into white satin slippers and dabbed on some perfume before looping the fan over her wrist. Then she glanced at the clock.

'It's time to go.' She gave Concha's shoulder a gentle squeeze. 'I imagine we'll be late back so don't wait up.'

'Have a wonderful evening.'

'I'll do my best.'

With that Elena summoned up the remains of courage and went to the parlour to look for Harry.

Having a shrewd idea of the length and complexity of the female toilette on such occasions, Harry had tactfully organised a separate room in which to get ready for the ball. He had bathed and then shaved. In the meantime, Jack had performed wonders with creased clothing so that no wrinkle now marred the elegant costume. A critical look in the mirror confirmed that it would pass muster. Then, having readied himself, Harry retreated to the parlour to wait.

In a part of his mind he wondered whether he hadn't made a grave mistake in committing himself and Elena to this event. Yet, in spite of everything, he found himself looking forward to dancing with her. Whether she would feel the same was another matter. Since that fateful conversation they had been almost like strangers, behaving towards each other with cool civility. He didn't intend to let it become a habit.

Hearing the door open, he turned round, anticipating

Elena's arrival. What he hadn't anticipated was the effect it might have. In spite of the weeks they had been together it was like seeing her for the first time. For a moment or two he could only stare, and his tongue seemed to have lost contact with his brain. With an effort he recovered himself.

'You look stunning.' Immediately he thought the words sounded lame. She was gorgeous and he knew that every other man present tonight was going to think so too. For an instant Villanueva's image impinged on his thoughts. He pushed it aside. Others could look their fill, but she belonged to him. The realisation made him feel both proud and protective.

There could be no doubting the sincerity of his initial response to her entrance. Feeling a little more encouraged, Elena turned slowly to let him see the new gown to full advantage.

'The seamstress has done a fine job, no?'

'She certainly has.' He decided that every last penny of the cost had been worth it. 'Although I can't help feeling that you show off the gown to advantage rather than the other way around.'

'It's an improvement on breeches and boots, I think.'

'A vast improvement,' he agreed.

The admiration in his eyes created a glow of pleasure deep inside. Moreover, she was supremely conscious of how well formal evening dress became him, enhancing every line of that lithe and virile form. He looked every inch the nobleman he was. His attention was also deeply disconcerting.

To conceal her inner trepidation, Elena made to adjust her shawl. He stepped forward at once.

'Allow me.'

He draped the fabric carefully across her shoulders. As he did so his fingers brushed the bare skin at the back of her neck, a light and possibly unintended gesture that sent a *frisson* down her spine. Then he stepped back and offered her his arm.

'Shall we go?'

A hired carriage took them the short distance to the mansion of the Conde de Villanueva. Lights blazed in every window and the queue of vehicles outside proclaimed an event of some importance. Harry and Elena joined the line of guests waiting to greet their hosts. The conde greeted them warmly, his gaze lingering on Elena with undisguised admiration. He bestowed on her a dazzling smile.

'Welcome to my house. May I present my wife, the Condesa Maria?'

The condesa was a pretty, dark-haired lady with an elfin figure. She smiled at her guests and bade them welcome. Elena returned the smile.

'Thank you so much for the beautiful flowers. They were a delightful surprise.'

The condesa inclined her head graciously. 'You're most welcome.'

Harry registered this with wry amusement. Either his suspicions had been entirely without foundation or else Villanueva was a lot smarter than he'd given the man credit for.

The condesa introduced them to some of the other new arrivals. When the necessary courtesies had been observed, they made their way through the antechamber that adjoined the ballroom. Curious eyes followed their entrance.

'You seem to have created a stir, my sweet,' murmured Harry, 'but don't let it go to your head. The first two dances are mine.'

'If you say so, my lord.'

'I do say so. Furthermore, I'm prepared to back my claim against all comers.'

Elena raised an eyebrow. 'Well, I wouldn't wish to cause a scene.'

'Wars have been fought for less.'

The tone was light but the expression in his eyes implied rather more. The effect was to make her flesh tingle. She had no desire to dance with anyone else even though good manners would likely make that inescapable. As she looked around all the other men in the room seemed decidedly lacking in comparison. She had not missed the curious and covert looks that came their way. Already the women were whispering behind their fans. Of course, Harry was hard to miss, being a head taller than most of the Spaniards present. Only the conde came near to him in height and good looks. Unable to help herself, Elena found herself making comparisons. Villanueva knew he was attractive to women but, in spite of his polished manner, there was about him the innate arrogance and hauteur of the hidalgo class. Harry's birth was arguably better but he made no parade of it, nor did he trade on his good looks. He was also possessed of natural kindness and patience. Of the two men she knew with absolute certainty which one she preferred.

When the orchestra struck up, Harry claimed her hand for the first dance. It was a pavanne. The dance was slow and graceful, a measure from a bygone age, but then, she acknowledged, Spain was behindhand in such matters. She guessed it hadn't been danced in England for many years and it surprised her that Harry should know it. Yet clearly he did, and well too. So much surprised her about this man and continued to sharpen her curiosity too. As they moved through the steps his gaze never left her and, although it was impossible to read his thoughts, her entire being resonated with awareness of it. All else ceased to exist for her except for the man and the music. This was quite unlike the first time they danced together; it was more intimate and more disturbing. Did he feel the same? Did he feel anything for her at all, or was this the triumph of hope over experience?

When, at length, the pavanne ended it was replaced by a cotillion. The mood and tempo were different but it was still exhilarating to dance with him. She caught his eye and saw him smile, an unaffected and natural smile that sent a pulse of warmth through her body's core. She could see other women watching them and once or twice registered envy in their eyes. When she looked at the majority of men in the room it was easy to understand why.

Without her being aware of it Elena was attracting attention too, and when Harry led her from the floor they were greeted by their host and two or three others who wished for an introduction. Those were followed up by invitations for future dances. Harry resigned himself to the inevitable. Much as he would have liked to keep her to himself all evening, it would have been the height of bad manners. He watched in silent chagrin as she walked away with another man.

Villanueva read him accurately. 'That is the penalty of having a beautiful wife, my friend.'

'Well, you should know.'

The Spaniard grinned. 'I content myself with the knowledge that Maria will always be with me at the end of the evening.'

Harry reflected that he would be the one to take Elena home, a notion that sent his mind in distinctly pleasurable directions. With an effort he brought it back. It was too easy to daydream about his wife, fantasies that had no foundation in anything except wishful thinking. He summoned a casual smile.

'Won't you introduce me to some of your friends, Villanueva? It'll prevent me from harbouring jealous thoughts.'

His companion laughed. 'Gladly.'

The conde's guests admitted Harry very readily into their company. Quite apart from his imposing presence he aroused curiosity too, since English lords were not a common feature of polite society in Seville. His fluency in the language did him no disservice either, and he was soon engaged in conversation with a group of gentlemen at the far end of the room. From time to time he glanced towards the dancers. Judging from her smile Elena seemed to be enjoying herself. She had probably put him out of her mind. His jaw tightened and he turned away, trying to concentrate on what his companions were saying.

Elena curtsied to her last partner and left the floor. The room was hot now, the air heavy with the scent of beeswax and flowers and perfume. A cooling drink would be more than welcome. The vague memory of a punch bowl in the anteroom directed her steps that way. In fact, memory served her correctly and with a sense of relief she ladled some of the liquid into a cup and took a sip. It was delicious.

Opposite, an open door led onto a terrace. Elena glanced round but everyone else seemed engaged in conversation so taking advantage of the fact she slipped outside for a few moments. Although it was still officially spring, the evening air was pleasant. Seville had a different climate from Madrid and the northerly provinces. The sky was clear, a sickle moon hanging amid myriad stars. Pools of light from the ballroom windows illuminated the flower beds and part of the lawn below. The rest of the garden was in deep velvet shadow where the soft chirring of cicadas mingled with the sound of music drifting from the ballroom. She sipped her drink and relaxed a little, enjoying the fresh air.

'Out here all alone, my lady?'

Elena started and turned quickly. At first glance

the tall figure in the doorway might have been mistaken for Harry, but the voice belonged to the Conde de Villanueva. She was conscious of a stab of disappointment but recovered her composure quickly.

'I needed a little air. It's very warm indoors.'

He smiled and strolled across to join her. 'I was afraid you were not enjoying the party.'

'Oh, yes. I am enjoying it very much.'

'I'm glad to hear it. I'd be sorry to think otherwise.'

'The occasion seems to be a great success.'

'Your presence has added immeasurably to that.'

Elena pretended to misunderstand. 'It was kind of you to invite us. My husband was delighted to renew his acquaintance with you.'

'It was a delight for me too.' He regarded her keenly. 'What do you think of our Sevilla?'

'It's a fine city. I'm impressed with what I have seen so far.'

'I wish I could show you more.'

Nothing could have been pleasanter than his expression but something in that smooth tone caused the first stirring of unease. The words were ambiguous too, capable of a perfectly innocent interpretation or a very different one. For no apparent reason the hothouse bouquet came to mind, and with it connotations she didn't care for.

'I regret that we will be leaving very soon. My husband's business here is concluded.'

'What a pity.'

'Yes, isn't it?'

'Do you return to Madrid?'

'No. We're moving on to Cádiz.'

'It's a long and tiring journey, my lady.'

'I'm well used to travelling.'

He reached out and traced one finger lightly down her arm. 'Your husband should leave you here while he takes care of business. It would be my pleasure to offer the hospitality of my house.'

There could be no mistake now about the intent behind the smooth, purring tone. He was also standing just a little too close and he was between her and the door. Elena quashed an urge to flee, knowing instinctively that he would prevent it. Then there would be a scene with possibly unpleasant consequences. Somehow she was going to have to bluff her way out of this. She forced a smile.

'You are most kind.'

'I should like to be.'

Her skin prickled. 'My husband would not countenance such a separation and nor would I.'

'You are quite right, my dear,' said a voice behind them. 'I would not countenance it.'

Her heart leapt as she saw Harry in the doorway and relief washed over her with the force of a tidal bore.

He surveyed the little scene just a few seconds longer. His timing had been fortuitous. A few seconds later and Villanueva would undoubtedly have tried to kiss Elena. Harry's jaw tightened. Although he would very much have liked to floor the man he didn't want Elena subjected to the kind of scandal that would result.

Instead he advanced to join them. Nothing could have been more relaxed than his outward manner, nothing more amiable than his smile. However, on this occasion it stopped well short of his eyes.

'My wife remains at my side,' he said.

As he turned round, Villanueva's urbane smile didn't alter either. 'Well, I cannot blame you for that, my lord. All the same the offer remains if you change your mind.'

'You are the flower of courtesy,' replied Harry. 'However, I shall not change my mind.'

The conde's eyes glinted briefly; then he bowed. 'Well, then, I can only wish you a safe journey. Now, if you will excuse me, I will return to my other guests.'

As he walked away Elena shivered a little. Harry regarded her with concern.

'Are you all right, my dear?'

'Yes. Quite all right, I thank you.'

'Are you sure? You look a little pale.'

In truth the conde's advances had left her feeling shaken. He was undoubtedly an experienced womaniser, and now she wondered uneasily if he had sensed something about her that had led him to try his luck. Such men tended to be intuitive. He could not possibly know about her past but the incident left an unpleasant taste. It annoyed her that she had laid herself open to such attentions; she was clearly out of practice when it came to social functions like this one.

'It's my fault,' she replied. 'I should not have come

out here alone, only the room was so hot and I needed some air. I didn't think anyone would even notice.'

'You are entitled to take the air without being propositioned by a cur.'

She hugged herself defensively. 'Odious man.'

He frowned. 'He didn't try to…'

'Nothing like that, thank goodness.'

'As well for him that he did not.'

'What would you have done? Hit him?'

'No, killed him.'

Seeing his expression then she was left in no doubt that he meant it. The realisation sent a different kind of shiver down her spine.

Harry kept the lid on his ire. While the thought of any man making suggestive remarks to his wife was an affront, he was glad that he'd been able to nip the situation in the bud and so avoid a very public confrontation. Villanueva had evidently been of the same mind. Having been warned off he wouldn't try and renew his addresses to Elena.

'I'm sorry,' she said. 'I didn't mean to cause trouble.'

'You didn't create that situation. He did.' Harry put his arms around her. 'You have no need to apologise and no need to be afraid. He can't hurt you.'

The gentleness in his voice was like balm and she relaxed against him. 'It was his manner I found so disagreeable.'

He dropped a kiss on her hair. 'I won't let anyone hurt you again.'

She looked up quickly and her gaze met his. The intensity of that piercing look caused her pulse to quicken. Very slowly he bent closer until his lips brushed hers.

Harry checked a little then, suddenly afraid that, after all she had endured at the hands of men, such advances might not be welcome from him either.

She felt him hesitate and gently returned the kiss. Thus reassured, he drew her closer. Immediately, all thought of Villanueva was swept away by a flood of sensation in which chill was replaced by delicious, glowing warmth. The glow kindled to flame. Elena pressed closer, her body moulding itself to his, and the kiss became deeper. Now there was no fear, only increasing desire and she surrendered to it, giving herself up to the moment.

Harry restrained the urge to crush her in his arms and let his own desire have free rein. He had no wish to frighten or, worse, repel her. What mattered was that she should enjoy this and want more. Eventually he drew back, looking into her face.

'I think we should go back inside.' He smiled wryly. 'Otherwise I may lose what little self-control I have left.'

'That might cause a few raised eyebrows.'

'I fear it would do a lot more than that.'

The implications brought a rosy blush to her cheeks. At the same time it caused a surge of hope that he really did want her, after all. If they'd been alone… Her blush deepened. She had no idea where so bold a thought had come from and was only glad he couldn't read her mind just then.

Harry surveyed her appreciatively. 'Do you know how very lovely you are when you blush like that?'

Her neck and face grew hotter. His smile did nothing for her composure at all. 'You are enjoying this, aren't you?'

'You have no idea.' The tone was both mischievous and provocative.

'It's no use, my lord. I shall not rise to this teasing.'

'What a shame. I shall have to try harder.'

With that he took her back to the ballroom. If she had imagined he'd relinquish her hand, then she was mistaken. He kept a firm hold of it until the next measure struck up. Then he led her onto the floor. As they moved through the steps every look and touch achieved heightened significance and there could be no mistaking the look in his eyes. Her pulse quickened in response. At that moment desire outweighed fear and she found herself anticipating the time when they would be alone together.

Eventually the company retired from the ballroom and sat down to supper. Elena made polite conversation with those around her but in reality only one person interested her. It seemed she was not alone. Several women vied for Harry's attention with smiling faces and inviting looks in their eyes but, although he was courteous, their blandishments seemed to make no impression on him. More than once Elena intercepted envious glances and experienced a little thrill of pride that he was her husband. She knew that most of these women had married at the behest of their families and it appeared that not all were entirely satisfied with their lot. If Harry had shown the least bit of interest she guessed it would have been followed up with alacrity. The thought sat ill with her and she realised then that she had no wish to share him.

It was late when they eventually took their leave. Their host bade them farewell with a charming smile. The previous incident might never have happened, save that he held Elena's hand a little longer than was strictly necessary. She ignored it. He didn't matter and after this evening the chances were they wouldn't meet again. She wasn't at all sorry to see the last of him.

Harry handed her into the carriage and then climbed in after her. As the vehicle pulled away he settled back in his seat, surveying her steadily. 'Did you enjoy yourself this evening?'

'With the exception of the five minutes I spent with the conde, very much.'

'Good. I'm afraid you'll have to live on it for a while. We leave tomorrow.'

'The sooner we leave, the sooner you will meet Sanchez,' she replied, 'and that is why you came here in the first place.'

'The thought of more days on the road doesn't daunt you, then?'

'Not unduly.'

'You are forbearing. Most women would have objected most strenuously by now.' He smiled faintly. 'But then you are not most women, are you?'

She was unsure how to respond to that and he saw it.

'I meant that as a compliment, my dear. Very much so.'

Her heart beat a little faster. This evening their relationship was almost back to the way it had been before that charged conversation about Badajoz. Nor did she want that to change.

The inn was quiet when they returned and they made their way to their chamber unnoticed, save for a watchman at the door. Elena laid down her fan and gloves and reached for the buttons at the back of her gown but, being new and stiff, they resisted her efforts.

'Allow me.' He stepped behind her and unfastened them. However, he made no attempt to do anything else. Instead he began to remove his own clothing.

Elena slid the gown off and laid it carefully over a chair. Then she finished undressing to her chemise and sat down to undo her hair. Freed of combs and pins the mass of dark curls tumbled over her shoulders and down her back. She reached for a brush. The glossy strands leapt beneath the strokes.

Harry removed the last of his clothes and slid into bed, watching her. 'You have lovely hair.'

'Thank you. It has a will of its own though.'

He grinned. 'Like its owner.'

'Hmm. I'm not sure how to take that.'

'You may take it as a definite compliment.'

Something about his tone brought warm colour to her face. 'It does not bother you then that a woman should have a will of her own?'

'Far from it. The opposite would be unbearably insipid.'

'I think most men would disagree, but then you are not most men.'

He laughed softly. 'I mean to take that as a compliment.'

'So you should.'

'I'm flattered.'

'No, I meant it.'

'Then I'm honoured.'

Elena laid down the brush and crossed to the bed. He drew the coverlet down and watched her slide in beside him. This time he did not turn away. Instead he leaned closer and kissed her softly on the mouth. It brought a rush of heat into the core of her being. She turned towards him and the kiss became more persuasive. Strong warm hands rested on her waist and stroked gently, then moved across her back. The touch sent a charge along her flesh. He slid the chemise off her shoulder and kissed her naked skin, gradually moving lower until his mouth closed over the peak of her breast, lightly teasing the nipple to tautness. Elena caught her breath. The caress was erotic and it aroused sensations she had never dreamed existed. His hand moved to the place between her thighs and gently stroked. She gasped, arching against him, pressing closer until every inch of their bodies touched, feeling his arousal hard against her thigh.

Harry rolled, pressing her back against the bed, pinning her with his weight while his mouth sought hers. Elena tensed. Out of nowhere an old memory stirred and woke. Unable to move and scarcely able to breathe, her heart began to thump and she felt the first flutter of fear. As the kiss grew more ardent fear quickly became panic. She tore her mouth away from his, panting.

'No…no…please.'

Harry drew back a little. 'What is it, sweetheart?'

'I can't.' Her hands pushed against his breast. 'I'm sorry. I…I thought I could but I can't.'

'I'm not going to hurt you, Elena.'

She struggled harder. 'Please…let me go.'

Desire ebbed and he rolled aside, frowning. 'It's all right, sweetheart. Don't be afraid. Nothing's going to happen that you don't want.'

Her eyes filled with tears of shame. 'I'm sorry,' she whispered. 'I'm so sorry.'

'There's nothing to be sorry for.'

The gentleness in his tone was the final straw. The tears spilled over and then became sobs. Harry was appalled but he had sense enough not to try and stem the flow, guessing that it was long overdue. In that he was right. It was as though the wall of a dam had given way and the gathered mass of emotion behind had broken loose. He knew it was a necessary part of the healing process but he was quite unprepared for how much it hurt to hear it and to know himself the catalyst.

When eventually the tears were exhausted he found a handkerchief and gave it to her. Elena took it and rather shakily dried her face and blew her nose. She felt wrung out, as though every last ounce of energy had been drained out of her. She was also mortified.

'Harry, I…'

He put a finger to her lips and stopped the words there. 'It's all right. You don't have to say anything. What you need now is some sleep.'

Elena closed her eyes, waiting for her breathing and her pounding heartbeat to quieten and wondering how she was ever going to sleep again. What must he think of her? Shame and embarrassment obliterated everything else. She'd really thought she could put the past behind her, had wanted to, only to behave like a frigid little fool at the last. She squirmed inwardly. Harry had never given her reason not to trust him so why hadn't she? No answer presented itself, then or later.

Beside her, Harry stared into the darkness. He could still see the fear in her eyes, hear it in her voice. It cut deeply. He'd really thought that tonight they might overcome the last barrier to their married relationship. He had wanted that so badly, had thought she'd shared his hope. At first she had seemed to. He hadn't imagined that spark of passion or the building fire inside her. She was beautiful and sensual and she'd wanted him, all right—until the shadow of Badajoz returned. It was clear that she equated his attempted possession with what had happened there. He would rather have cut off his right arm than hurt her but she didn't trust him. His lip curled in self-mockery. Why should she trust him? Others had and they were dead. He heard a woman call his name, a desperate plea for help that never came. In his mind's eye he saw the image of the burning house and, silhouetted against the flames, half a dozen sinister forms clubbing a man to death with rifle butts while he looked on helplessly and did nothing.

He rolled over and sat on the edge of the bed with his head in his hands. The images continued to taunt him. Belén had offered him her love and discovered how poor a choice she had made. It seemed Elena was wiser. All hope of sleep had long since vanished so he rose quietly and dressed. Then, with a rueful backwards glance towards the figure on the bed, he left the room.

Elena heard him leave. Her throat tightened. She wanted to call him back, to beg him not to go, but what would be the point? There was no reason for him to stay.

Chapter Fifteen

Harry walked for a while without having any particular destination in mind, letting the cool air clear his head. The night was far advanced now and the sky beginning to lighten. Soon it would be dawn and the city would start to stir. Then they would be on their way. He wasn't sorry. Quite apart from anything else he wanted Elena well away from Villanueva, not because he didn't trust her but because he most emphatically didn't trust his former colleague. For all manner of reasons Seville had lost its attraction.

Since he had no immediate solutions to the difficulties besetting his marriage, he turned his mind to the forthcoming journey instead. Barring accidents, they could be in Cádiz inside a week. Then he would find Sanchez and get the proof he needed. After that everyone could move on. Perhaps when they reached England he and Elena would have a better chance of making their marriage work. Here in Spain there were too many reminders of the past.

By the time he returned to the inn he felt more focused and marginally more optimistic. Seeing that the servants were once more in evidence he ordered some breakfast and, having eaten, went to find Jack. Between them they made the necessary arrangement for supplies and provisions. As Jack went off to expedite the matter, Harry returned to the bedchamber. It was empty. He found Elena in the parlour with Concha. When he arrived the maid murmured an excuse and left them.

For the space of several heartbeats neither one spoke. Elena was dressed in breeches and boots once more. Her face was pale and there were smudges of shadow beneath her eyes but she was composed now. However, he read sadness in her dark gaze, and it tore at his heart for she had never seemed so achingly vulnerable. He wanted to take her in his arms and hold her awhile but he guessed the attention would not be welcome. Instead he broke the silence.

'Have you breakfasted? We need to depart very soon.'

'I'm quite ready.'

'Good. I'll collect my things and meet you outside in the yard, then.'

'Certainly.'

He reached the door and paused on the threshold. 'Has Concha taken your things down?'

'Yes, I believe so.'

'Is there anything you need before we leave?'

'No, I thank you, nothing.'

'Very well. I'll see you downstairs.'

As he turned away Elena let out the breath she had been holding. The stilted conversation was painful but it obviated the need for anything more personal. She had no idea what she could have said to amend the situation in any case. Clearly he hadn't wanted to revisit the subject either. His cool, controlled manner was a reproach in itself. Not that she could blame him for that. He'd asked for her trust last night and been rejected. What was he supposed to think? With a heavy heart she made her way down to where Jack and Concha waited with the horses.

The day was fine and it felt good to be on the road again. Elena could not regret leaving the city behind in spite of the comforts it offered. It held too many memories. Now at least they were focused on their original purpose and it gave them something else to think about. She wasn't sorry for that either.

For the majority of the morning she rode with Concha, since the two men seemed to have matters of their own to discuss. The women travelled in companionable silence which afforded leisure to look around. Since leaving the city they had been following the river valley where the surrounding countryside was green and fertile with orchards and fields of crops. The region had a look of quiet prosperity about it.

From time to time Elena found her gaze shifting involuntarily from the scenery to the man in front of her. Harry sat his mount with the casual ease of a born horseman, controlling the powerful animal with the lightest touch of hand and heel. He wore his power lightly in every respect. He was also heart-stoppingly handsome. The thought that she had thrown away the chance to make him hers was all the more poignant and painful.

When they stopped at midday he made no particular attempt to seek her out and when they did speak it was about practicalities only. Elena followed his lead. It was impossible to do anything else now. She had created the gulf between them and in the circumstances it was small wonder that he made no attempt to cross it. He had been more patient than any man she had ever met, but even his patience was not infinite. If she could not give him what he wanted, then might he not seek solace elsewhere eventually? The thought appalled her.

'Are you all right?'

Concha's voice brought her back to the present with a jolt. 'I'm just a little tired, that's all. We were back quite late last night.'

Although the maid didn't look entirely convinced she didn't pursue it. 'No doubt you'll make up for it tonight.'

'I'll volunteer for the first watch,' said Elena. 'That way I can sleep straight through afterwards.'

'Good idea.' Concha glanced around. 'This scenery is pleasing. It reminds me that we are drawing close to our goal now.'

'I know what you mean.'

'At one point I felt rather like that foolish knight in the story.'

'Don Quixote?'

'Yes. I used to wonder sometimes if we were tilting at windmills, but I'm sure now that we are not.'

'Sanchez is real enough,' said Elena. 'All we have to do is reach Cádiz.'

They resumed their journey shortly after this. Elena had been unconsciously hoping that Harry might ride alongside for a while, but they barely exchanged a dozen words all afternoon. Several times when she looked his way he seemed not to notice even though she was sure he had. It was becoming increasingly clear that he didn't want her company. She could well understand it, but it hurt all the same.

When next they made camp Elena took note of his preference and avoided him as far as she could. Initially it wasn't too difficult. There were the horses to tend to and when that was done she and Jack went off to collect firewood. It was a relief to be out of the way and Jack was much easier company. Between them they gathered a pile of small logs and some twigs for kindling. Then they started slowly back for camp.

Elena eyed her companion covertly, knowing now that there were questions she wanted answers to, answers about Badajoz and about Belén. This was the opportunity to find out. However, she felt apprehensive about his possible response. Not wishing to alienate him as well, she decided to test the water.

'May I ask you something, Jack?'

He surveyed her steadily. 'You may ask, my lady.'

She came straight to the point. 'You were at Badajoz with my husband, were you not?'

Jack's eyes registered momentary surprise but he was quick to recover. 'Aye, my lady, I were there all right. It were a bad business and no mistake.'

'The officers tried to prevent the men from looting, I believe.'

'That they did, and His Lordship among them, but they hadn't a chance. They were vastly outnumbered and t'men crazy wi' drink. They were prepared to kill anyone who got in their road.'

'I understand that they killed one of my husband's friends.'

Jack nodded. 'Captain Radcliffe. He were attempting to stop a group o' rioters from looting a shop. There were nigh on a dozen of 'em. They'd have fired on him only they'd already discharged their weapons and hadn't bothered to reload, so they used t'rifle butts instead. Clubbed him t'ground and kept on hitting him.'

'Merciful heavens.'

'His Lordship saw it and shot two o' t'beggars straight off. Then he waded in t'rest to try and help his friend, but t'rioters attacked him too. I shot a couple more of 'em and t'rest ran off swearing revenge. By t'time we got to him Captain Radcliffe were already dead. Murdering brutes'd stove his skull in.'

Elena paled. 'What happened then?'

'We managed to get away before t'scum came back wi' reinforcements. It weren't easy neither. My lord had a concussion and a couple o' nasty gashes to his head as bled like t'devil, but he got off lightly, all things considered. All t'same, he took Captain Radcliffe's death very hard. Blamed himself, even though there were nowt more he could have done.'

She digested this in silence and then made an intuitive leap. 'It was the same night that Belén died, wasn't it? That's why he couldn't save her.'

Jack's nodded. 'Aye, my lady. Happen if His Lordship hadn't stopped to help Captain Radcliffe he might have been able to rescue her. As it turned out, by t'time he'd come to properly and we'd made a detour round t'mob, her house were ablaze. Heat were that fierce you couldn't get within twenty yards. No one could've got in there. Even so I had t'devil's own job to stop him trying. So, in t'end, he lost 'em both and it's my belief he's never forgiven himself for it.'

Elena swallowed hard. It was worse than she'd imagined and it explained so much.

'I'm glad you told me. Thank you for speaking so frankly, Jack.'

He nodded. 'May I ask why you wanted to know, my lady?'

'My husband told me much of the story but he omitted the part about trying to help Captain Radcliffe. I just wanted to understand.'

'His Lordship were never one to boast. Nevertheless, what he did that night were brave by any standard. He knew he were outnumbered and he knew t'men were drunk an' dangerous, but he wouldn't leave his friend in t'lurch.'

'I can well believe that.'

'To my mind there were no better officer and no one I'd rather have wi' me in a fight.'

The camp came into view and Elena paused. 'I'd be grateful if you didn't mention this conversation to anyone, Jack.'

'I won't say owt, my lady.' He smiled wryly. 'Besides, if His Lordship knew I'd been praising his courage I'd never hear t'last of it.'

Elena could well believe that too. Harry would never boast of such things, or indeed speak of them at all.

They walked the last fifty yards in silence and, on reaching the campsite, dumped the firewood in a pile. Then, leaving Jack to light the fire, Elena went to fetch water for tea. The conversation had given her much to think about and her heart bled for Harry. She knew how it felt to lose those she loved and to be helpless to prevent it. After such an experience pain and guilt had a tendency to turn inward. Her answer had been to seek a quiet house in the country, his to throw himself into his work. Then fate had brought them together and offered another way. Harry had once told her that he saw no reason why they could not have a future together. Perhaps he too had glimpsed the possibility of happiness. It was her failure to trust him that destroyed that chance, a failure now bitterly regretted.

She returned with the water and set it to boil. Then she began to help Concha prepare some food. She avoided looking at Harry. It didn't go unnoticed.

'Is everything all right between the two of you?' asked Concha, *sotto voce.*

Elena was about to answer in the affirmative but the words wouldn't come. In any case it was a waste of time trying to pretend anything to Concha.

'Not really. In fact, it's about as bad as it could be. Not his fault either.'

'Do you want to tell me?'

'I'm not sure I can at present.'

Concha made no attempt to probe but merely continued to slice bread. 'You mean to apologise, then, for whatever it was that caused offence, no?'

'An apology will not suffice.'

'Oh. That bad.'

'Yes, that bad.'

'Well, even if apologising does not suffice, it's a start.'

'I'm not sure he'd even listen.'

'Is your relationship worth the effort of trying?'

There was only one answer to that and Elena knew it. Being at odds with Harry just made her feel wretched. All the same, she had no idea how to mend fences with him. Even knowing what he did of her past he had wanted to make her his wife anyway. He must be feeling very disillusioned to say the least.

Later, after they had eaten and begun to think about retiring for the night, she got up and checked the priming of her pistol.

'I'll take this watch.'

Harry frowned. 'You should get some rest, Elena. You had a late night last night.'

'So did you,' she replied.

'I don't want you falling asleep at your post.'

'I won't fall asleep.'

Seeing she wasn't going to be dissuaded he gave in. 'All right. I'll take over in a couple of hours.'

She nodded. 'As you wish.'

With that she strolled away, taking up her position beneath a tree some fifty yards off. She was quite unaware of the gaze that followed her.

The two hours of her watch passed slowly and she found herself stifling yawns. The day's ride and the lack of sleep were beginning to tell now and she was looking forward to her bed even if it was on hard ground. The night air was cool and she shivered a little. Fortunately there were no other signs of life, save for the insects in the grass and the occasional call of an owl. When her limbs grew stiff she got up and walked around a little. It helped but not much. After that she didn't dare sit down again in case she dozed. With the mood Harry was in she didn't want to lay herself open to further criticism. She sighed and leaned back against the tree.

A little later she heard a familiar voice. 'Anything to report?'

Her heart missed a beat. Then she was annoyed with herself. Even now she still was caught out by Harry's ability to move softly. 'No, it's all quiet.'

'You must be worn out by now. Go and turn in.'

'In truth I don't mind if I do.' She made to leave, then hesitated. 'Harry, about what happened before…'

'Forget it.'

'I can't forget it. Nor I think can you.'

His tone became more guarded. 'What is it you wish to say, Elena?'

'That it wasn't your fault.'

'Is that supposed to make me feel better?'

'I wish it may but somehow I doubt it.'

'You'd be right.'

She licked dry lips. 'I can only say that I'm sorry.'

'So am I.'

Her heart sank. The damage had gone deeper than she'd thought and he wasn't ready to talk about it. Better to go now before she annoyed him any further.

'I'll turn in, then.'

'Do that.'

'Goodnight, Harry.' She hurried away, keen to be gone now.

For a moment or two he watched her, grim-faced. Then he leaned against the tree and swore under his breath. He shouldn't have let her go like that and he knew it. She'd tried to make a conciliatory gesture which, after what had passed between them, must have taken a good deal of courage, and he'd behaved churlishly. He'd avoided her all day but it hadn't helped because he could think of nothing else. Elena had got under his skin in all sorts of unexpected ways. It hurt to know that she didn't trust him yet but he knew the reason, so why was he reacting like this? She wasn't ready to consummate their marriage, that was all. He should have kept a sense of proportion. The fact that he hadn't been able to made him angry, but not with her. He wanted her badly, but his need was about a lot more than physical pleasure. Now, in an act of unparalleled stupidity, he'd allowed his pride to drive her away.

Chapter Sixteen

In spite of everything else, weariness won out that night and Elena was asleep within minutes of her head hitting her improvised saddle pillow. She slept deeply and dreamlessly and didn't stir again until after sunrise. When she opened her eyes it was to see Harry bearing a mug of tea. For a moment she stared at him in silent bemusement and then saw him smile.

'Good morning. I won't ask if you slept well since I know that you did.'

'I went out like a light.' She propped herself up on one elbow. 'What time is it?'

'Almost seven.'

'Seven! Heavens, you should have woken me.'

'You looked too peaceful to disturb. Besides, you were very tired last night.'

'Yes, but even so…'

'An hour isn't going to make much difference in the great scheme of things.' He bent down and handed her the tea. 'Here. It'll warm you up.'

As she took the mug her fingers brushed his, a casual touch that brought other thoughts to mind. It was hard to reconcile the man before her with the cold and distant being she had spoken to before.

She eyed him obliquely. 'Did you sleep well?'

'Very well, I thank you.' He paused. 'I'm sorry I was short-tempered last night.'

'It doesn't matter.'

'Yes, it does. My behaviour was churlish in the extreme.'

'You were tired too. It doesn't help.'

He smiled ruefully. 'No, it doesn't. All the same, I apologise.'

'Apology accepted.'

'Thank you.' He squeezed her arm lightly and then straightened. 'Drink your tea. Then we'll be on our way.'

With a rather lighter heart Elena stowed her things and prepared to ride. Concha saw the alteration at once.

'You are feeling better today, I think.'

'Much better.'

'A good rest puts everything in perspective, no?'

Elena nodded. 'It certainly helps.'

She thought back to her conversation with Jack. That too had lent things a different perspective, although she didn't know how best to make use of the information. Now that the *status quo* had been restored she didn't want to unbalance it again. All the same the past could not be ignored when it impinged on the present and threatened to blight the future. While she admired

Harry's courage and his evident loyalty to those he loved, she could not bear to think that he should blame himself for what had happened.

With a sudden flash of insight she understood how she might, unwittingly, have contributed to his state of mind. Did he believe that she held him partially responsible for what had happened at Badajoz? After all, when he had needed her trust she had not given it. That begged the question, why? When she had panicked was it not because she had unconsciously equated an act of love with an act of violence? What did that say about her deeper feelings for Harry? The insight did not make for comfortable viewing.

'Now you look worried again,' said Concha.

'The thought of throwing away happiness does worry me.'

'Why would you? Rather you should embrace the chance.'

'I know, but I cannot.'

Concha didn't pretend to misunderstand. 'It was always going to be difficult, but surely not insurmountable.' She paused, darting a glance ahead to make sure that the men were out of earshot. 'He does not blame you for what happened.'

'No. I think the boot is on the other foot.'

'I'm not sure I follow.'

'When he told me that he was at Badajoz my first reaction was to see him as a British soldier.'

Light dawned in Concha's face. 'And because he was a British soldier he must be equally guilty?'

'Something like that.'

'But he tried to stop the atrocities.'

'I know, but part of my mind still resented him being there at all.' Elena sighed. 'Oh, heavens, I'm not even making sense to myself.'

'That is because it doesn't make sense. His Lordship is not as those others. He is an honourable man, I believe.'

'So do I.'

'Well, then, should you not trust him?'

There was only one answer to that. Elena knew full well that Harry could have used force that night in Seville. It was his right yet he had not done it. *I won't hurt you.* Those words were more than an idle promise; he had meant them. He had offered her a glimpse of something extraordinary and unexpected and she had turned back from that threshold because she hadn't trusted him. The knowledge did nothing to mitigate shame.

'This is such a mess and now I don't know what to do about it.'

'Do you care for him?' asked Concha.

'Yes.'

'Then you must show him that you do.'

'I don't know how.'

'Follow your instinct. It will guide you more surely than words ever could.'

Elena thought hard about that as they rode along. She had no skill in the art of flirtation; the past four years had been spent keeping men at bay and she had become good at it. If she tried such feminine wiles with Harry might he not take it as mere teasing? In the light of recent events he could hardly do other and it likely wouldn't go down well at this juncture. If she were to lead him on and lose her nerve again it would be disastrous. She had already hurt him and didn't ever want to do it again. Some feminine instinct would have been mighty useful, but hers seemed to be non-existent.

Over the next few days their relationship returned to a more level footing but he made no attempt to renew his attentions to her. When they spoke it was as friends and usually on practical matters. Sometimes she would catch him watching her but his expression was always unreadable. Was he regretting their marriage now? What would happen when they got to England? A man like Harry would never lack for female attention. The fear returned that if he did not get affection and warmth from his wife he would find it elsewhere. Plenty of marriages were matters of convenience only where the couple observed the outward forms while they conducted private affairs. The idea was chilling. Dolores and her husband did not live like that; they were happy together and proud of their young family. Elena had never considered having children before but now the idea was oddly appealing. Of course, that presupposed other things... Out of nowhere came the recollection of Harry's kisses, of his hands caressing her naked skin, and a pool of warmth formed in the centre of her pelvis.

'A penny for them.'

A familiar voice jerked her back to reality and she realised that he had brought his horse alongside unnoticed. A rosy flush dyed her cheeks. 'Oh, er, I...I was just thinking about my sister in England.'

He registered her heightened colour with quiet appreciation and wondered what had occasioned it. Aloud he said, 'You must be looking forward to seeing her again.'

'Yes, I am.'

'Well, there is no reason why we should not visit her in Hertfordshire. It's on the way to Castonbury.'

'I have yet to meet my nieces and nephew. Indeed, at one time, I did not think that I ever would.' She smiled reflectively. 'It is hard to live so far from the people one loves.'

'You will have much to tell each other.'

'Yes.' His words were an understatement if ever she had heard one. 'And with any luck you will have much to tell your family.'

'I am more hopeful than I was.'

'Perhaps this coming talk with Sanchez will provide a kind of closure.'

'I think it may. Ordinarily a funeral would do that, as with my younger brother, Edward.'

'A grave leaves no room for doubt, does it?'

'That's well put.'

'I saw the rioters shoot my father but it wasn't until I stood beside his grave that my heart knew he was really gone.'

He returned a wry smile. 'I know what you mean. It's the last point of reference, isn't it? We were able to mourn Edward. My father still does. Jamie has no grave—who knows where his remains may be? All we have of him are memories.'

'And his son.'

'Yes, his son.'

'Surely the family will love the child to honour the memory of his father.'

When he thought back to his former conversation with Ross, Harry felt a twinge of guilt. The best he could say was that the family were keeping an open mind, but *love* was not the foremost word he'd have used to describe their reaction to learning of the child's existence. Fortunately the boy was too young to notice such things, but as hc grew up it was going to matter a great deal.

'Children need affection if they are to thrivc,' she went on, 'and, in the absence of a father, strong male role models.'

'You speak knowledgeably.'

'It's only common sense. How can a boy become a well-balanced man if he has no male guidance?'

'Good point.' Harry reflected that it was also a point he was going to have to address. Jamie would have done no less had their positions been reversed.

'It is hard to lose a parent like that when one is too young to remember. The child will only know his father as a result of what his mother tells him.'

'From what you say I must infer that you like children.'

'Of course. Don't you?'

'Yes, although I confess my experience has been limited—thus far.'

She was suddenly aware of other implications beneath this conversation. One day Harry was going to want an heir. What man did not? After Badajoz it had been her greatest dread that she might be pregnant, but that fear at least had not been realised and it had not been relevant since. The notion that it might become relevant no longer repelled her. The thought was disturbing but somehow not displeasing.

'Then you wouldn't mind broadening your experience?' she asked.

The question took him aback but a swift sideways glance revealed that Elena's expression was quite innocent, or apparently so. He suppressed a smile.

'No,' he replied. 'I wouldn't mind at all.'

Although they had initially been following the river, they were eventually forced to make a detour to avoid a large expanse of salt marsh, a region known locally as Las Marismas. However, the lower-lying countryside was undemanding compared to the mountainous regions they had traversed earlier. Unfortunately the weather, which had been pleasantly warm, gradually changed and became overcast. As the day progressed the cloud on the horizon became as dark as a bruise.

'Looks like we're in for a spell o' damp,' said Jack.

'We'll find somewhere to stay tonight,' replied Harry. 'According to the map it's not far now to Villafranca.'

In this he was correct. However, the only available accommodation was a ramshackle inn that would never have figured on Don Manuel's list of recommendations. For a start it had no individual bedchambers for its guests, only a communal dormitory beneath the rafters. The *patrón* informed them that several of the low cots were already taken and, Harry guessed, all by men. Had he and Jack been alone it wouldn't have bothered him in the least. They'd slept in far worse places. With two women along, and one of them his wife, his response was different.

'I can't subject you to this,' he told Elena.

'Subject me to what?'

'To sleeping in this.'

It was on the tip of her tongue to say that she had spent years sleeping in similar accommodation, but decided it would be impolitic at this point.

'It's not ideal but at least it's dry,' she replied.

'Not ideal? There's an understatement if ever I heard one.'

She bit back a smile. 'If we take four beds together you and Jack can take the outer ones and we the inner two. That way we'll be quite safe.'

He frowned. 'Sleep with a pistol under your pillow.'

'Of course.'

As he turned away to speak to Jack, Elena caught Concha's eye. The maid grinned and lowered her voice.

'In my experience a pistol is not much use against snoring and flatulence.'

Elena gave a snort of laughter and hurriedly turned it into a cough. Harry glanced round. Nothing could have been more innocent than the eyes that met his.

They went down and he made enquiries as to what might be available for dinner. Their host beamed.

'Today we have chickpea and spinach soup.'

'Good. What else?'

'Bread.'

Harry sighed. 'I suppose you have wine?'

'Of course wine, *señor*. What kind of house would it be otherwise?'

The man clearly considered it a rhetorical question because he bustled off before Harry could vouchsafe a reply.

Elena caught his eye. 'The simplest meals are often the best.'

'In that case I'd say we're in for a treat.'

Since the inn had no private parlour the four of them ate in the communal dining room. It was a long room with a timber frame in-filled by adobe bricks. At one time these had been plastered over, but now the plaster layer had crumbled away in places. What remained was yellowed with age. At the far end was a wide hearth where a fire burned. Bunches of garlic, dried herbs and chilli peppers were strung from the smoke-darkened beams in the low ceiling. In the centre of the room was a long trestle table with benches on either side. The wooden floor was covered with a layer of straw. Two small windows looked out on to a fenced yard where chickens scratched. A pig pen stood in one corner and, a few yards distant, a privy.

The other occupants of the dining room glanced up as the newcomers entered, eyed them curiously for a moment and then turned their attention back to their food. The four took their places at the end of the table. A manservant appeared with horn cups and wooden spoons. Presently the soup arrived in a large tureen, and was accompanied by a loaf and a jug of rough red wine. In fact, the soup was good and, with the bread as well, surprisingly filling. They ate hungrily. Outside it began to rain.

Once the food was finished they lingered over the wine and talked quietly. Harry contributed little to the conversation; his thoughts turned inward. Although he was glad that they had at least found shelter for the night, the primitive surroundings made him feel even more determined that, after this trip, he was going to remove Elena to her rightful sphere. When he reflected on the conditions she had endured in the course of their short married life he was ashamed. Elena never complained and said she didn't mind it, but he did. As time went on he found that he minded more and more. He glanced round the room with distaste. Bringing her to such a place was like throwing a diamond into mud. If his family could see this they'd take him to task and no mistake. Furthermore, they'd be right.

He glanced at the woman beside him. In spite of the surroundings, Elena looked quite relaxed, chatting easily with Jack and Concha. Her profile was towards him, its sculpted lines and soft hollows framed by stray curls of dark hair. His imagination stripped away the rough, travel-stained garments and replaced them with the silk jacquard gown. It was a beguiling mental image and resurrected a host of other sensations.

It seemed he wasn't alone in thinking his wife an agreeable sight. He intercepted several covert glances her way. One, bolder than the rest, stared at her in open admiration. Harry's jaw tightened. Shifting position a little he casually pushed aside the front edge of his coat and let his hand come to rest on the butt of his pistol. Then he fixed the admirer with a steely gaze. The other man looked quickly away.

In spite of the surroundings Elena felt relaxed and content. She had shelter, food and the company she would most have sought. Just then she wouldn't have exchanged her lot for anything. She glanced at Harry and saw him smile. He hadn't said much this evening but, now that they were so close to Cádiz, perhaps his mind was on other things.

Eventually, as the hour advanced, the other occupants of the room began to leave. One or two went out the back way, the others heading for the dormitory.

'We may as well follow suit,' said Harry then. 'We've another long day ahead of us tomorrow.'

Jack nodded. 'True enough, my lord.'

Concha caught Elena's eye and then glanced in the general direction of the privy. Elena nodded and the two women rose.

Elena looked at Harry. 'Would you excuse us?'

She and Concha headed for the door. A glance outside revealed that it was still raining. Elena looked at her companion.

'Go on. I'll wait.'

'Thank you.'

Concha sprinted across the yard and entered the privy. Elena watched the rain and felt glad that they weren't going to be sleeping out of doors that night. Even a communal dormitory was better than that. Of course Harry might well disagree. Recalling his reaction she smiled to herself. For a little while back there the tolerant easygoing Englishman had sounded very like a jealous husband. Nevertheless, it was not displeasing.

She was drawn abruptly out of thought by the sound of Concha's voice.

'Get out of my way, clod.'

Roused from her reverie Elena looked across the yard in surprise. Then she frowned to see Concha confronting a stranger. The man had his back to her but his intention was clear enough since, each time Concha tried to step past him, he blocked the way.

'Come now, don't be like that. We could have some fun together.'

The reply was a ringing slap. The man clutched his cheek.

'You'll pay for that, you little slut.'

Seizing the front of Concha's jacket in one fist, he hit her hard with the other. She rocked back from the blow, blood trickling from a cut lip. Pale with rage, Elena let out a furious yell.

'Leave her alone, you cowardly scum!'

The room went suddenly quiet. Harry and Jack looked

round quickly, just in time to see her race outside. Then they were on their feet and striding towards the yard.

Elena grabbed hold of Concha's attacker and tried to pull him away. He glanced round and laughed.

'Two of you now? Even better. We can…' He paused as a hand tapped him lightly on the shoulder. Glancing round again he met Jack's gaze. 'What do you want?'

'Let go of the woman.'

'What's it to you?'

The reply was a head butt. Concha's assailant reeled, blood pouring from his nose. He had just enough time to utter a curse before a clenched fist drove hard into his solar plexus and doubled him over. Moments later a knee snapped his head up. It was followed by a savage uppercut that flung him backwards. Jack paused, flexing his left hand.

Harry grinned at him. 'I'd like to help but I suspect I'd only be in the way.'

'I appreciate t'offer, my lord, but this bastard's mine.'

Jack strode across the intervening space, reached down, grabbed a handful of coat and hauled the man upright again. Then he hit him several more times, driving him back step by step towards the pig pen. As the low rail caught his legs the man was pitched backwards to land supine and groaning in the mud among the hogs. Jack glared at him.

'You're nowt but a pig yourself so you're in t'right company.'

'Well put,' said Harry.

Jack looked anxiously at Concha. 'Are you all right,

lass?' Then seeing her cut lip his expression darkened. 'I should have bloody killed him!'

She managed a shaky laugh. 'I thought you had.'

Elena regarded her in concern. 'I think we should get you inside and tend that cut.'

Harry nodded. 'Good idea.' He glanced towards the knot of bystanders gathered round the doorway. 'We seem to have attracted an audience, don't we?'

As they reached the doorway, he uttered one short and idiomatic sentence and the bystanders parted like the Red Sea. Just then the *patrón* appeared. His astonishment turned to consternation when he learned what had occurred.

'*Madre de Dios!* That ever such a thing should happen in my house!'

Jack scowled at him. 'Stop bleating, you damn fool, and fetch some water and a cloth.'

'And some salve if you have it,' added Elena. 'If not, honey will do.'

As the man scuttled off she drew Concha towards the fire. 'Come, sit down over here. You're all wet.'

'You're wet too.'

'A little damp around the edges,' Elena admitted.

Now that the incident was over the inevitable reaction had set in—anger, disgust and a familiar inner chill. Suddenly the fire seemed very comforting.

Presently the *patrón* returned with the required items. Jack relieved him of them and pulled up a stool beside Concha.

'We'd best get that lip cleaned up, lass.'

He dipped the cloth in the water and set to work. Concha sat still and said nothing, her face impassive, though the sidelong glances she directed at him were more eloquent. Elena left them to it and joined Harry on the other side of the hearth. He eyed her critically.

'Are you all right, sweetheart? You look pale.'

'It's not fear,' she replied, 'it's anger and a gloating pleasure in summary justice.'

'It was deeply satisfying, wasn't it?'

'I can't begin to tell you how deeply.'

'Well, it's over now.' He glanced at the other two. 'And Jack seems to be a competent physician.'

Elena surveyed the little scene in silence for a moment. 'A man of many parts.'

'Indeed he is.'

'I'm glad he's on our side.'

Harry grinned. 'So am I.'

He put an arm around her and drew her closer. His nearness warmed her more than the fire ever could and slowly the tension flowed away and she relaxed against him. Never had he seemed a more solid and reassuring presence than now, and never had it felt more right to be with him.

Jack laid the cloth aside and picked up the pot of honey. He dipped his little finger and then, with infinite care, applied it to the cut lip. Then he surveyed his handiwork critically.

'How does feel?'

'Not so bad,' said Concha. 'At any rate I've felt far worse.' Her gaze softened. 'Thank you, Jack.'

'You're welcome, lass.'

Elena looked at Harry and saw him smile quietly.

Later she lay in bed listening to the sound of rain on the roof. Once or twice she glanced towards Harry's cot but in the darkness it was impossible to know if he was awake or not. Either way it was enough to know he was there. Not that she imagined there would be trouble of any sort now. Between them he and Jack were a force to be reckoned with. She smiled to herself and closed her eyes. In minutes she was asleep.

The morning light revealed that the weather had not improved much. Harry eyed it dubiously through the window as they ate breakfast.

'Do you want to stay here for a while and hope that it stops?' he asked.

'We're so close to our goal now,' replied Elena. 'It seems a pity not to press on. After all, we've been wet before.'

Jack nodded. 'You're not wrong there, my lady.'

'A bit of damp never hurt anyone,' said Concha.

Harry looked at his companions. 'Very well. Onward, then.'

Although he'd felt compelled to offer them the choice he was pleased by their decision. They were tantalisingly close to their goal now. Remaining in this dreary inn held no appeal, and besides, the weather might let up later.

Unfortunately it didn't. It held out all that day and for the two after that. Leaden skies delivered steady rain that soaked through their clothing and turned the road to mud. A series of mean inns provided shelter for the night but, even if the fires smoked and the rooms were not of the cleanest, no one complained. At least they were dry—until the following day when the whole exercise was repeated.

'This will prepare us for England, no?' said Concha as they splashed along a filthy stretch of road. 'It rains often there, I'm told.'

Jack regarded her solemnly. 'It might prepare you for t'south of England well enough, but t'north is a different kettle o' fish.'

'It cannot be wetter than this.'

'Why, in't north of England they'd rate this no higher than mist.'

'Mist! What are you talking about?'

'When it rains there it comes down by t'bucketful for days on end,' he replied. 'It's why t'folk have webbed feet.'

'They do not.'

He raised one eyebrow. 'Have you been to t'north of England?'

'No.'

'Well, then, how do you know?'

'Because you come from there and I'll wager you haven't got webbed feet.'

'That's because I were cured.'

'Cured?'

'Aye, on account of spending so long away from t'place. It were all those years in t'army under t'Spanish sun, I reckon.'

'How can the Spanish sun be a cure for webbed feet? Do Spanish ducks have toes?'

'Of course not. They live in t'water, don't they?'

'*Madre mia!* I suppose you'll tell me next that these northern English folk are excellent swimmers.'

'Well, oddly enough…'

Behind them, Harry sighed. He glanced at Elena and then they both laughed. He reflected again that laughter suited her very much indeed. Even soaking wet and splashed with mud she was still the most desirable woman he'd met in years.

'Does that man's imagination never fail?' she asked.

'Oh, he's just warming up.'

'So is Concha.'

'I admit to being completely outclassed.'

'I cannot see you as a teller of tall tales.'

His expression grew serious. 'I hope not. With you I would always wish to be truthful.'

'And I with you.'

'Not always, I think.' Seeing her troubled expression he smiled. 'You have not said what you truly think about being dragged the length of the country in the pouring rain.'

'I was not dragged. I came of my own accord. Besides, you warned me what to expect at the outset.'

'Hmm. I did, didn't I?' He paused. 'I also warn you that when we get to England things will be different.'

Her eyes widened a little. 'Oh?'

'To begin with you will be permitted to remain indoors on rainy days, and even dry days if you choose.

You will not collect firewood or tend horses or cook food since you will have servants to do those things.'

'Dear me.' She feigned astonishment. 'This sounds like a life of idleness and luxury.'

'It's high time you enjoyed some idleness and luxury.'

'I am not opposed to that.'

'In addition I mean to get you out of those clothes and into something more feminine.'

'You mean you think a pretty gown has more to recommend it than mud-stained breeches? Incredible.'

He grinned. 'I think the gown just has the edge.'

'You will allow that this clothing serves a practical purpose.'

'Indeed it does,' he agreed, 'for now.'

'Well, to be frank, I'm looking forward to putting it aside for more feminine attire.' She grimaced. 'At present I look like something the cat dragged in.'

His eyes gleamed. 'The cat never dragged in anything that looked like you, my dear.'

Something about his expression caused a fluttering sensation in the pit of her stomach. She fought it down. 'Well, that's a relief.'

'I wouldn't say so at all.'

Being unsure what to make of this, she eyed him quizzically. 'You are not so unlike Jack, after all, since I think you enjoy teasing.'

'Only when I can be sure of getting as good as I give.'

'I do my best.'

He grinned, enjoying her. 'You make a formidable opponent.'

'I doubt that somehow.'

What Harry might have said next remained unknown because, as they rounded a bend in the road, they came to a ford. A tributary stream of the Guadalquivir, it would ordinarily have been a simple crossing. However, the recent rain had swollen it considerably and the brown water was much deeper than usual and faster-flowing. They reined in by the edge of the crossing place.

Jack looked at Harry. 'What do you reckon, my lord?'

'There's nowhere else, at least not without making a twenty-mile detour. We'll have to risk it. I'll go first and see how deep it is.'

He walked his mount into the water and slowly began to traverse the stream. Alluvial mud made it impossible to see the bottom. Ordinarily hock-deep, the water at midpoint reached the horse's chest. He felt the animal bracing itself against the flow as it gingerly edged its way forward. Its ears flicked back and forward as though to catch his words of encouragement. They pushed on through and then, on the far bank, Harry reined in and called back to the others.

'The current's strong but it's passable with care. Just take your time.'

Concha came over next, followed by Elena. Her horse sidled a little and snorted, disliking the water, but she used her heels and urged it forward. The river was cold and, as the depth increased, the animal whinnied uneasily. They were just over halfway, and a little downstream of Concha, when it put its foot in a pothole and stumbled badly. It floundered, trying to recover, but, unbalanced by the force of the current, it failed. As soon as she felt the horse going down Elena kicked her feet free of the stirrups. They hit the water. The icy shock took her breath away and a second later she went under. Immediately everything became a confused mass of horse and leather and swirling muddy brown. She struggled gasping to the surface and tried to find her footing but the riverbed was uneven and the current frighteningly strong. It swept her downstream. From somewhere she heard voices calling. Fighting her way back to the surface she sucked in a lungful of air and tried again to find her footing, but the water below the ford was deeper and her waterlogged boots and clothing dragged heavily. As the current took her under again she knew that she was going to drown.

Harry saw the horse go down and heard the cry of alarm as it pitched Elena over its shoulder. For a second or two she went under, then, to his relief, surfaced again. The horse found its feet and plunged towards the shore. Harry expected to see Elena towed in after it, clinging on to its tail, but when it didn't happen and the current carried her away downstream he paled. Leaping off his horse, he flung his coat over the saddle and then plunged into the water. He was a strong swimmer but the tug of the current was stronger. Moreover, he couldn't immediately see Elena. The sensation of dread that followed was colder than the water. He cast around in desperation, seeking some trace of her. Then, at last, he glimpsed her head above the surface. Relief displaced dread and he struck out in her direction. He was only feet away when she went under again. Harry sucked in a lungful of air and dived.

Elena struggled against the water drag, kicking for the surface, eyes stinging, lungs parched and burning. She could see lighter water above her but she was tiring rapidly and every movement was an effort. The weight of her sodden clothing pulled her downwards. Then the light began to recede and the water darkened around her. Bubbles of air streamed from her mouth. She was vaguely aware of something solid against her back and then a strong arm locked around her chest and began to haul her upwards. As her head broke the surface she gasped, coughing and choking and spluttering. Then she heard Harry's voice in her ear.

'Don't be afraid. I'll get you out of this.'

Chapter Seventeen

Harry made no attempt to fight the current. Instead he let it carry them for another two hundred yards until a curve in the river brought them naturally into the shallows where the water was slower and only thigh-deep. Finding his feet at last he put an arm around Elena's waist and dragged her upright. He felt her stagger and glanced down at her pale face. Her skin was icy to the touch but she was alive. He frowned, his emotions torn between anxiety and relief. Lifting her bodily out of the water he waded ashore and sat her down carefully on the shingle bank. Then he knelt beside her.

'Elena? Elena, look at me.'

She became aware of a man's coat, wet and rough against her cheek, and grey eyes looking anxiously into hers. Rather uncertainly she stared back.

'Are you all right, sweetheart?'

She nodded, eventually finding her voice again. 'I…I think so.'

'Thank heaven for that. You gave me quite a fright back there.'

'My horse fell in a hole. For a while I really thought I was done for.'

'Surely you didn't think I'd give you up so easily?'

Her gaze held his. 'I'm glad you didn't. Thank you.'

'No thanks are required.' He surveyed her critically. 'What is required is to get you indoors in front of a fire. You're chilled to the bone and paler than a lily.'

He hauled her onto her feet. Just then Jack and Concha appeared with the horses. When they saw their companions alive and apparently unscathed their relief was evident.

'*Madre mia!* I feared we had lost you,' said Concha.

'I thought so myself for a while,' replied Elena, shuddering.

'You look awful. Ghastly pale.'

Jack frowned. 'We'd best get you in t'warm, my lady.'

'My thought exactly,' said Harry.

'Next town's not far off. According t'map, it's not above a mile up t'road.'

Harry nodded, privately thanking heaven that they weren't stuck in the middle of nowhere. 'Right, we'll go there at once.'

With the aid of his arm Elena staggered to her horse, feeling very cold and uncharacteristically shaky. The thought of another ride was distinctly unappealing, but there was no choice about that now. She eyed her mount with misgivings; somehow it seemed a lot bigger than it had before, its back much further away. In the event she was spared the trouble of mounting. Assessing the situation with complete accuracy, Harry picked her up and she experienced a brief sensation of weightlessness as he tossed her lightly into the saddle. Then, keeping a firm hold on her reins, he remounted his own horse and they set off.

Fortunately, Jack was right: it wasn't very far at all to town. He and Concha lost no time in locating an inn and bespeaking rooms. The place was unpretentious but it was clean. Harry lifted Elena off her horse and carried her indoors, firing off a series of instructions to the startled *patrón* as he went. Within a relatively short time Elena found herself in a spacious private chamber in front of a cheerful fire. Harry set her down and surveyed her critically.

'We need to get you out of those wet things.'

'You're wet too.'

'I'll worry about that presently. Right now I'm more concerned about you.' He stepped closer and unfastened her jacket, dragging it off her shoulders. Then he sat her in a chair and bent down to pull off her boots.

'Can you manage the rest?'

She nodded dumbly.

'Good.' He handed her a couple of linen towels. 'You'll need these.'

Leaving her to get on with it he began to peel off his own wet clothing. Elena struggled out of her sodden breeches and then glanced round. Harry had his back to her so she pulled off her shirt and, with fumbling fingers, wrapped the first linen sheet around herself.

Then she turned towards the fire again and began to dry her hair with the other while he finished undressing. He stripped and fastened a towel around his waist. The sight of that hard-muscled body sent a tremor through her that had nothing whatever to do with cold.

Unaware of the inner turmoil he was causing, he set to, draping their wet clothing over chairs to dry in front of the hearth. When he had done that he straightened and turned towards her, regarding her critically. Under that penetrating stare Elena felt suddenly self-conscious.

'I look like a drowned rat, don't I?'

'Not the expression I was going to use,' he replied. 'But you still look mighty pale, my sweet.'

'Do I?'

'You'll feel better with some hot food inside you. Shall you object to dining in here?'

She returned a wry smile. 'I think it would be best under the circumstances.'

He grinned. 'So do I. The sight of you like that would cause a local scandal.'

She thought that the same could be said of him, but ventured no reply.

He went to the door and summoned Jack, who had been loitering in the corridor for the purpose, and sent him off for some food and a jug of mulled wine. A short time later the servant returned with the wine and the intelligence that the food would follow. Harry relieved him of the jug and goblets and, after delivering an injunction to take himself off and find something to eat, bade him farewell and shut the door. Then he poured two generous measures of wine and handed one to Elena.

'Drink this. It'll warm you.'

The wine was sweet and fragrant with cloves and cinnamon. She took a sip and swallowed, feeling the hot liquor carving a path all the way to her stomach. It was also dangerously heady, rather like the man opposite. Slowly the combination of inner and outer warmth began to take effect with a painful tingling in her hands and feet.

Seeing some of the colour return to her face Harry felt more reassured. It had been no lie when he said she'd given him some anxious moments earlier. His heart had been in his mouth. For a little while he'd really feared he might not find her. The thought of the alternative turned him a lot colder than the river ever had. In that moment he truly understood how much she meant to him. He also knew he wasn't going to fail her as he'd failed Belén.

A discreet knock distracted him. When he opened the door this time it was to see Concha bearing a large tray. On witnessing Harry in such a state of undress her eyes widened. She shot a swift glance past him to Elena and, on seeing her mistress in like case, sent a conspiratorial smile that way. Then she handed over the tray and left them.

Harry pulled the table closer to the fire and laid two places. Then he set out the dishes and drew up two chairs. The tray bore a tureen full of rich and savoury stew. It was accompanied by a loaf of fresh bread. It was a simple meal but it tasted delicious and they ate hungrily. Gradually the chill receded and was replaced by contented warmth. Afterwards they lingered over the rest of the spiced wine. Harry leaned back in his chair, surveying her over the rim of his cup.

'Better?'

'Very much better,' she replied.

'You look it.' It was an understatement, he thought. Her colour had returned and, now that her hair had dried, an unruly mass of dark curls tumbled over her bare shoulders. The linen towel clung to the contours of her figure and, since it finished just above her knees, left a pleasing amount of shapely leg on view.

Aware of his scrutiny to the last atom of her being, she realised that she should have felt embarrassed or ashamed, but she didn't. Those feelings were long gone. When Harry looked at her it engendered a very different sensation.

'Thanks to you,' she replied. 'It's thanks to you that I'm here at all.'

'I beg you will not mention it.'

'Not mention it?' She regarded him incredulously. 'You saved my life, Harry, and risked your own to do it.'

His gaze locked with hers. 'You are too precious to lose. I did not know how precious until that moment.'

With an effort she managed to keep her voice level. 'You don't know how much it means to hear you say that.'

His heart performed an unusual and risky manoeuvre. He hesitated, fearing to ask the next question but knowing he was going to anyway. 'Then am I to understand that the sentiment is returned?'

'Yes, it is returned. I wanted to tell you before but, in view of what had happened, I didn't know how.' She rose from her chair and moved round to his side of the table. Taking his face in her hands she bent and kissed him. 'It took an icy bath in the river to bring me to my senses.'

Harry put an arm about her waist and drew her on to his lap. 'I think I am the one who needed bringing to my senses.'

Her arms slid around his neck and she kissed him again, gently at first, then more deeply. He tasted of wine and cloves and cinnamon, a combination that was exciting and erotic. His tongue flirted with hers, inviting and getting a like response. She pressed closer, breathing his scent, revelling in the touch of his skin beneath her hands and the play of muscles across his shoulders. As she moved, the towel slipped a little. Strong warm hands caressed her back and shoulders. The towel slipped further, uncovering her breasts and, as flesh met flesh, the kiss became passionate.

Eventually Harry drew back a little, heart pounding, and his gaze locked with hers. 'If this doesn't stop now, my sweet, it isn't going to stop at all.'

'I don't want it to stop.'

For a moment he wasn't sure if he'd heard aright but the expression in those dark eyes held an unmistakable invitation. 'Are you quite sure about this, Elena?'

'Yes, I'm sure.'

He scooped her up and carried her across to the bed. Kneeling on the mattress he drew her to her knees in front of him, letting his hands ride her waist, pulling her closer. His mouth brushed hers, light, teasing, then gradually more insistent. He wanted her so badly it hurt, but he had no intention of hurrying this. Nor did he intend to make any demands. It was solely about giving her all possible pleasure. Thus his exploration of her body was leisurely and thorough, every caress designed to arouse and increase desire. His lips moved from her mouth to her cheek and thence to the lobe of her ear. He nibbled lightly, sending a delicious shiver the length of her, but what she felt now was increasing excitement, not fear.

He resumed, moving lower, kissing her neck and throat and then her breasts. Recalling her response the last time he'd done this he took a soft peak in his mouth, teasing gently. He heard her gasp, saw the rosy flush that bloomed along her skin. He unfastened the towel and discarded it along with his own. Then he resumed, sliding a hand down her back to her hips and buttocks. The other caressed her belly, moving thence to the secret place between her thighs. Very gently he found what he was seeking and stroked.

Heat flooded her pelvis and deep within it a coil of tension formed and grew. As he continued stroking the sensation intensified producing slick wetness. Blood became fire. She shuddered, arching towards him, carried on a shock wave of exquisite pleasure. It was followed by another and another.

'Heavens! Harry, please…'

Slowly he lowered himself on to his back. 'Sit astride me, Elena.'

Her eyes widened in brief astonishment but she moved to obey nonetheless. As she straddled him he slid into her. She caught her breath, her entire body resonating with him, wanting this, revelling in the feel of him inside her. Instinctively she moved with him, in a slow delicious rhythm. Gradually, the rhythm increased and he moved deeper, but there was no pain and no fear, only increasing delight.

Harry smiled and received an answering smile in return. He knew then he'd been right. This time she was with him, part of him. Her beautiful eyes were dark with passion, their expression not of terror now but ecstasy. His hold on her hips grew stronger and pulled her down, thrusting harder. He heard her gasp, felt her body arch and quiver. Then he let go of his restraint and joined her in a final shuddering climax. Breathless now he slumped back on the bed, his heart thumping against his ribs. He had expected to enjoy the experience but the intensity of it took him by surprise. She had possessed him body and soul.

'That was incredible.'

She smiled and leaned down to kiss him. 'Yes, it was. More than I ever imagined it could be. Thank you.' She paused. 'How did you know to do this?'

'When you panicked before it was because I was

pinning you down. It was a stupid mistake and one I didn't want to repeat. I guessed that if you didn't feel trapped you'd enjoy it a lot more.'

'You were right, on both counts.'

'I'm glad. I never want you to feel frightened of me again.'

'I didn't trust you enough and I'm sorry for it.'

'How should you have trusted me? You had only nightmare experience to judge by, and I was thoughtless enough to remind you of it.'

'I shall not be afraid now.'

'Indeed I hope not.' He paused, regarding her quizzically. 'Do you mean to stay there, my sweet? I'm not complaining, of course, but I'd rather like to hold you.'

She grinned and came to lie down beside him. He drew the coverlet over them and pulled her close, sharing his warmth. Elena rested her head on his shoulder. It was reassuring and dependable like the steady rhythm of his heartbeat under her hand. With a small sigh of contentment she closed her eyes and smiled. She was truly his wife now and he had made her a woman again. While he hadn't actually said that he loved her, his actions today showed that he did care. It was enough for now.

Chapter Eighteen

Later they rose and dressed. Elena donned one of her muslin gowns. It was a little creased from the saddle-bag but, having been on one of the pack horses, it was at least dry. Then she combed her hair and arranged it in a simple knot. Scanning her reflection in the mirror she thought the result was a vast improvement on the bedraggled creature she had been only a few hours ago.

Harry appeared over her shoulder. He slid his arms around her waist and dropped a kiss in the hollow of her neck. The touch set her skin tingling. She smiled and turned round, twining her arms around his neck. Then she kissed him back.

He looked into her face. 'Have you any idea what a bewitching creature you are?'

'If you want to tell me I'm prepared to listen.'

'I'd rather show you than tell you.' A more lingering kiss followed this. Then he drew back again. 'I wanted to do that the very first time I set eyes on you, but I didn't dare. Of course, I was thinking of you as a would-be nun at the time.'

'I hope you are over that misapprehension.'

'The extent of the error is now clear to me.'

'I'm glad of that.'

'I was happy to be corrected.' He glanced over her shoulder towards the window. 'It seems to have stopped raining at last. Would you care for a walk? We should be in time to join the evening *paseo*.'

'The *paseo* would be lovely.'

Just then he could have suggested that they clean all the muddy tack or muck out the stables. It wouldn't have mattered as long as they were together. After so many years of independence the extent of her neediness now took her unawares, like the deep-seated emotion she felt for this man. She didn't know when she had begun to love Harry, only that she did. It was no young girl's infatuation this time, but a lifelong passion. To lose him would be to lose a part of herself.

They strolled in companionable silence for a while, enjoying the relative novelty of a dry evening. The air was clear, scrubbed clean of haze and smelling pleasantly of wet earth and vegetation and wood smoke. The light was fading now and, when they reached the local plaza, lanterns had already been lit. As Harry had predicted the cessation of the rain had brought others out of doors for the customary evening stroll. Above them the sinking sun laced the clouds with streaks of red and gold. Harry eyed it with increasing optimism.

'I think this might well clear by morning.' He paused.

'Will you be strong enough to resume the journey by then?'

Elena smiled. 'I shall be quite able to do so.'

'Are you sure? It won't matter if you want to leave it a little longer.'

'What matters is to reach Cádiz and find Sanchez.'

'All the same,' he said, 'you've had a nasty experience.'

'Thanks to you it wasn't much worse.'

'I once failed two people who trusted me. I'll not let that happen again.'

Elena looked up quickly. 'What happened to Belén was not your fault, Harry.' She took a deep breath. 'Nor was Captain Radcliffe's death.'

It stopped him in his tracks and, drawing her aside, he fixed her with a piercing stare. 'What do you know of Radcliffe?'

Her heart began to thump. Had she ruined everything with yet another inappropriate remark? It was too late to retract it now. The only way was forwards. With a calm she was far from feeling, she met his eye.

'Jack told me what happened.'

'Did he indeed?'

'You must not be angry with him—it was I who solicited for answers.' She paused. 'After you told me about Badajoz I guessed there were still things that had been left unsaid.'

'With good reason.'

'I wanted to understand and Jack was the key.'

'Jack only knows part of the truth.'

Her gaze met and held his. 'He told me that you risked your own life to try and save your friend. There's nothing shameful in that.'

'It was not enough.'

'The odds were overwhelming and those men were crazy with drink and bloodlust.' She shuddered. 'Nothing would have stopped them. I was there, Harry, and I know this for truth. It was the stuff of nightmares.'

He paused. 'Do you still dream about it?'

'Sometimes.'

'I did not understand the meaning of nightmare until Badajoz.'

'It was a miracle that those men did not kill you too.'

'But for Jack they would have done. For a long time I wished they had.' He let out a ragged breath. 'John Radcliffe was a fine officer and one of the most decent men I ever met. I was privileged to know him and to be numbered among his friends.'

'If he was all you say, he would not wish you to carry a burden of blame for what happened.'

'Even so…'

'What if things had been the other way round? Would you have blamed him?'

'Of course not.'

'Well, then, why do you continue to blame yourself?'

'Radcliffe's death is the least of my guilt,' he replied.

'I don't understand.'

'I know you don't.'

His expression sent a chill through her, but having

come so far she was not prepared to duck the issue any more. Too much depended on it. 'I want to, Harry.'

'I warn you now, it isn't pretty.'

Her gaze burned into his. 'The past isn't pretty? No one knows that better than I, but if you want us to have the future you spoke of, we have to face the truth no matter how ugly it is.'

For a long moment he was silent. Then he nodded slowly. 'All right.'

Elena waited, her eyes never wavering from his.

'The shock of Radcliffe's murder was profound, yet by the end of that night what I felt was not grief. It was bitter resentment. He was the reason I could not save Belén. If I had gone straight to the house I might have got her out, but as those brutes attacked him, he called out my name, you see.' He swallowed hard. 'So I stopped to help him.'

'You could not have done anything else. You could not leave your friend to die.'

'And yet afterwards I wished I had.' He paused. 'I would have sacrificed my best friend to save Belén.'

Elena paled, trying and failing to find the right words, as her mind wrestled with the implications of what she had just heard. Harry, seeing her expression, thought he understood it.

'Now you know what kind of man you have married.'

'You did the honourable thing and still lost two people whom you loved. It is hardly surprising that you should feel conflicting emotions about it.'

'Conflicting emotions? Say rather, perfidy.'

'You judge yourself too harshly.'

'And how do you judge me, Elena?'

'As a man trying to come to terms with a nightmare.'

The grey gaze locked with hers. 'Do you still want a future with him?'

For a moment she was dumbfounded. Then, with an effort, she recovered her wits. 'Yes, I still want that.'

'It's more than I deserve.'

'You deserve to be happy. I should like to make you so.'

'You do make me happy.'

He did not speak of love, but she was glad that he did not try and pretend. In any case, what would have been the point when he had just revealed where his deeper feelings lay? Harry cared for her, but it was Belén who held his heart. For her he would have sacrificed his friend, his fortune and his life. Elena had once dreamed of finding a love like that, had hoped it would be with Harry, but knew now it wasn't going to happen. She had heard it said that in any relationship one heart was always warmer than the other. Clearly she would have to be that one. She summoned a tremulous smile.

'I'm glad.'

They resumed their walk round the square and then, by tacit consent, began to retrace their steps to the inn. Neither one spoke but now the silence had a different texture. Pretence was at an end between them, as she had wanted it to be, but it had not brought a lightening of the spirit. Instead it had killed off her most cherished ambition. Now she could only hope that she had enough love for two.

As Harry had predicted, the following day dawned fair. Moreover, their wet garments had dried out and, since they were in town, they were able to restock their provisions before continuing with their journey. The roads were still sticky but the sun would dry them in a few hours.

'At least we'll be free of dust for a while,' said Concha.

Elena nodded. 'Yes, there is that.'

The end was almost in sight now and she was glad for Harry, knowing that what he sought was almost within his grasp. She allowed her imagination to move ahead, to England, when they could live properly as man and wife. How much she wished for that. She would do everything in her power to make it work. Even if she was not the love of his life it did not mean that they could not be happy together. Plenty of married couples were in the same situation but they managed well enough and perhaps, in time, he might develop deeper feelings for her.

After so many years of wandering and uncertainty the thought of having a proper home held a strong appeal. She wanted to visit his home too, wanted to meet his family, to be part of something once more. She even began to entertain the hope of children one day. It would be good to give Harry a son—several sons, perhaps. That inspired other, deeply pleasurable thoughts.

She smiled ruefully. For the next few days they would have to camp in the open again which meant that they would no longer have the privacy they had enjoyed before. For that reason alone Cádiz could not come soon enough.

'You look thoughtful,' said Concha.

'I was thinking about England.'

'Ah, yes. It will be interesting to see, no?'

'I believe it will.'

'Do you think it really rains as much as Jack said?'

'I sincerely hope not,' said Elena.

'What about living in a foreign country? Does it not worry you?'

'Not unduly. I suppose it will be strange at first, but in time I imagine that will change.'

'Customs may be very different there.'

'Some of them, no doubt.'

'Well, at least we won't have a problem with the language,' said Concha. 'English is a barbarous tongue but I'm glad now that I learned it.'

'Yes, life would be very difficult else.' Elena paused. 'Do you want to go to England, Concha?'

Her companion regarded her quizzically. 'Why do you ask this?'

'It's the first time I have asked. Up to now I've only made assumptions.'

'I will go where you go, as always.'

'No one could have had a more loyal companion and friend. We have been through a great deal together, you and I, but I will not ask you to live in a strange land if it is contrary to your wishes.'

'Then I will tell you directly that it is my wish to go there.' Concha glanced in Jack's direction. 'Even if some of the inhabitants are a bit odd.'

Elena grinned and lowered her voice. 'That is not so much concerned with Englishness as with being a male.'

Concha gave a snort of laughter. '*Así?* Well, you may be right. I'll be able to judge much better when we get there.'

For all her light-hearted words to Concha, male behaviour was very much on Elena's mind. After that last discussion about Badajoz and the revelations concerning Radcliffe, the matter had not been mentioned again. To all outward appearance, Harry was quite himself. He was courteous and considerate, but she sensed the underlying tension in him. Moreover, although he discussed neutral subjects readily enough, he never touched on the personal. Elena didn't make any attempt to do so either, guessing he still had much to come to terms with. That would only be achieved in his own time. All the same, it saddened her to be shut out of his confidence.

As the sun returned and dried the road they made good progress. The following afternoon Jack bagged a hare. Later, when they made camp, Concha went foraging for herbs. Those went into the pot as well, along with onions and potatoes from their supplies, and that night they dined off delicious hot stew.

'You cook well, lass,' said Jack appreciatively. 'I say that for you.'

Concha's lips twitched. 'Praise indeed.'

'Aye, well, credit where credit's due.'

'I'll try not to let it go my head.'

'I'm sure it won't. I never met anyone less conceited.'

To Elena's surprise, Concha's cheeks turned an attractive shade of pink and, for the first time since the start of the journey, she made no reply. Elena looked at Harry and intercepted a quiet smile.

'Where did you learn to cook, lass?' Jack continued.

'From my mother mostly,' Concha replied.

'She must have been good, then.'

'She was skilled at making nourishing meals out of very little.'

Jack nodded. 'It's a real art is that.'

'The poor learn it early.'

'That they do, lass. They learn about hunger an' all.'

'After we entered the service of Doña Elena's late, honoured father, hunger never troubled us again,' said Concha.

'He were a good man by all accounts.'

'The best of men,' she replied. 'But for him we would both have perished. When want drove my mother to steal fruit from his orchard, Don Pedro's steward apprehended her. If it had been up to him she would have hanged and I would have starved. However, Don Pedro listened to her story. Instead of hanging her he gave her employment in his house, and he permitted her to bring me too. We never gave him cause to repent it.'

Jack's expression was hard to read but his eyes said a great deal more. 'I'll wager you didn't. Such men are rare indeed.'

'Yes, they are. I was privileged to have known him.'

'Aye, you were. Would that I'd met such a man when I were a lad.'

Elena reflected that her father would probably have liked Jack Hawkes. While Don Pedro wouldn't stand any nonsense, he had ever been a man to recognise determination and courage. Unfortunately the point was academic now. Jack would never meet her father and neither would Harry. She would never see her parent again. She smiled sadly and then got to her feet.

'I'll take the first watch.'

Harry looked up quickly. 'Would you not rather rest awhile? It's not so long since your accident, after all. I'd be happy to take the first.'

'It is no matter, truly, though I thank you for the offer.'

She strolled away and, finding a suitable spot, settled down to wait. Although they had encountered no more brigands it didn't pay to be careless, especially as they were so close to their goal now. She glanced up. A clear starlit sky gave promise of more fine weather to come. That was a relief anyway. In the cooler winter season rain tended to arrive in short intense bursts which lasted a few days and then were followed by spells of unbroken sunshine.

Her thoughts went thence to England, by all accounts a much wetter land. She smiled to herself. Dolores had accustomed herself to it, so there was no reason why she should not too. She tried to visualise Castonbury Park. From what Harry had said it must be a grand house and, no doubt, a fine estate. Would his family welcome her? Would they be prepared to accept a foreigner in their midst?

Soft footfalls penetrated her consciousness. In seconds she was on her feet with a pistol in her hand.

'It's all right.' Harry hove into her line of vision. 'It's only me.'

Elena lowered the pistol and relaxed a little. 'You move so quietly.'

'Now that *is* hurtful. I was trying to make a noise.'

The plaintive tone raised a smile. 'Next time try harder lest you get a ball through your heart.'

'I'll bear it in mind.'

Elena regarded him quizzically but the darkness hid his expression. 'Did you wish to tell me something?'

'To ask if you're all right. I was afraid the conversation about your father might have upset you.'

'No, it didn't. I miss him but it doesn't pain me to speak of him.'

'I wish I might have known him.'

'You would have got on well, I think. The two of you would have found much common ground.'

'He's a man whose behaviour I should wish to emulate,' he replied.

In truth it was only part of the reason he was there. While he had wondered about her private reaction to the earlier conversation it also served as an excuse to be alone with her. He hadn't realised until then how much he wanted that. Fond as he was of their two companions Elena had become as necessary to him as breathing.

'We haven't spoken much since we left town,' he said. 'I didn't want you to think it was deliberate policy.'

'You've had other things on your mind.'

'Yes.'

Their earlier conversation about Captain Radcliffe had opened up a dark place to the light of day and it didn't make for pleasant viewing. At the same time he couldn't be sorry that he'd told her. Pretence was at an end and she knew now who he was. He just hoped that, in time, they could draw a line and move on.

'I hope to make up for it later,' he continued.

Her pulse quickened a little at the implications. 'I'll remember you said that.'

Harry grinned. 'I shall not need reminding.'

Four days later they got their first glimpse of the sea, a deep blue smudge against the paler horizon. As Harry pointed it out Elena stared in wide-eyed wonder.

'This is the first time I ever saw the sea,' she said.

'Or I,' said Concha.

He surveyed them in momentary shock, then, on reflection, realised it wasn't surprising. Spain was a big country and, probably, very many of its citizens never saw the sea.

'You'll soon be able to have a much closer look.'

Elena smiled. 'I can hardly wait.'

Her expression just then was indicative of almost childlike excitement and he was unexpectedly touched.

'We'll make time to look.'

'Will we see whales?'

'I don't know about whales, but there may be dolphins.'

'There was a picture of a dolphin in one of my father's books. I should very much like to see the real thing.'

'They tend to travel in groups,' he replied. 'It's quite something to behold.'

'Aye,' said Jack. 'It is that. They're playful creatures and can follow a ship for days wi'out tiring. They've even been known to help drowning sailors to safety.'

Concha regarded him askance. 'Is this another of your tall tales?'

'It's true, honest. First mate on t'troop ship told me and he swore on t'bible it were so. Cross me heart an' hope to die.'

'Well, it may be as you say.' She paused. 'What do these dolphins do the rest of the time?'

'They hunt fish, I suppose. No one knows for sure.'

'What is it like to travel on a ship?' asked Elena.

'Like being drunk, my lady, only wi'out getting merry—until you get your sea legs that is.'

'Sea legs?'

'When you grow accustomed t'movement o' t'ship.'

'Oh.' She looked at Harry. 'Does the voyage to England take long?'

'Three weeks, perhaps, a little less with fair weather and a following wind.'

'It will be an adventure.'

He eyed her with amusement. 'Have you not tired of adventures yet?'

'On the contrary, I think life would be dull without them.'

'I suppose it would. All the same, a little peace and quiet in between times would not go amiss.'

They rode on and soon the roofs of the town came into view. Situated on a peninsula, Cádiz was an important centre for shipping and trade. Its harbour was protected by a great fortress which, despite all their efforts, had never been taken by the French. A little further along the coast was Cape Trafalgar, off which the British had won their great naval victory eleven years earlier.

'It doesn't seem quite real to be here, does it?' she said.

'No. All the same, I'm glad we are.'

'Very soon now you will have the proof you need.'

He smiled. 'Let's hope so.'

Privately he was hopeful. They had come so far and endured so much. It couldn't all be for nothing.

'We'll find somewhere comfortable to lodge,' he went on. 'Then I'll make enquiries about Sanchez.'

Elena returned the smile, guessing at some of his thoughts just then. For the rest of them it was the end of a long and arduous journey; for him it was the culmination of an ambition. After that she supposed they would take ship for England. The thought filled her with a mixture of anticipation and trepidation. The next few weeks were going to be filled with new experiences. After that, something infinitely more exciting beckoned. That thought turned her mind in another direction.

Since they had been on the road there had been no opportunity to share his bed. Nor had he attempted to create any others. He had told her his apparent neglect was not a matter of deliberate policy but, having waited days now for him to make a move, her patience was at an end. Clearly she was going to have to take the initiative. A few weeks ago the idea would have been unthinkable. It was still rather alarming, but now the thought excited her as well. She smiled to herself. If His English Lordship imagined that she had forgotten his promise he was much mistaken. It was he who needed reminding, after all.

They made their way through the bustling streets and at length found La Gata Negra, the hostelry that Don Manuel had recommended. In this at least his judgement had been unimpaired. Like all his other recommendations, the Black Cat was clean and orderly and employed well-trained staff. Harry bespoke accommodation and gave orders about the horses. Then they went in. A manservant showed them to their rooms.

Elena stepped over the threshold and looked around. The chamber was large and surprisingly well furnished with a bed, washstand, dresser, two chairs and a couch.

'Does it meet your requirements?' asked Harry.

'Indeed it does.' She glanced at the couch again. 'In fact, it exceeds expectation.'

He closed the door behind them. 'I hope it's the last time we'll have to do this for a while. Living out of saddlebags is all very well, but I confess I've had my fill of it.'

Elena shrugged off her jacket. 'I know what you mean.'

He dumped the saddlebags and removed his coat, tossing it onto the bed. 'Yes, but I promise you things are going to change.'

'That's good.' Elena sat down on a chair and tugged off her boots. Then, without haste, she unfastened her breeches and took those off too.

Harry watched with increasing interest. 'When I spoke of changing I didn't expect to be taken quite so literally.'

Elena untied the ribbon at the back of her neck and shook her hair loose. 'Is that a criticism?'

The accompanying sidelong look was distinctly seductive and his breathing quickened. 'By no means.'

Elena untied the laces at the neck of her shirt and let the fabric part. 'Well, I have a complaint to make.'

'Indeed? What complaint?'

'It may take some time to tell you.'

'I'm not in a hurry.'

She advanced until she stood before him. 'I'm glad to hear that, my lord, because I do require your complete attention.'

His hands came to rest on her waist. 'You have it.'

'Are you quite sure?' Her lips brushed his, lightly teasing. 'I should not like to think you were distracted.'

'Distraction would be impossible.' He nuzzled her neck. 'So tell me what displeases you.'

Her arms went around him. 'Do you know how long it is since last we made love? Six whole days!'

'Six days...seven hours...and thirty-five minutes,' he replied, punctuating each phrase with a kiss.

Elena caressed his back. 'Worse and worse.'

'I can see I'm going to have to make amends.'

'You know I have some ideas about that.'

'Really? What ideas?'

She edged closer still, moulding her body to his. Then, applying gentle pressure, she walked him slowly backwards. 'If you would like to sit down on that couch I'll explain. I think you might find it interesting.'

When he had complied Elena sat astride his lap. He raised one eyebrow.

'This does look interesting.'

'Indeed I hope so.'

Leaning forward a little she kissed him while her hands sought the fastenings of his breeches. His heart-beat quickened. He watched as, with slow delibera-tion, she unfastened the buttons and tugged aside the shirt beneath. Then her fingers closed round him and stroked.

'Still interested?' she asked.

Harry drew in a sharp breath. 'Oh, yes.'

The stroking continued and heat flared in his groin. In moments he was erect. Her fingers continued to tease, creating sensations so exquisite he thought he might die. She shifted position a little to accommodate him. With a groan he slid inside her. His hands cupped her buttocks, pulling her closer. Then her mouth was against his ear, nibbling the lobe softly and sending a delightful shiver the length of his body.

'Do you know I'm beginning to believe you?' she murmured.

He bent and kissed the tops of her breasts. 'I hope to convince you, but it may take some time.'

Elena grasped the hem of her shirt and casually pulled the garment off. Harry's heart performed an unwonted and exceedingly dangerous manoeuvre. Until then he'd thought he couldn't possibly be more aroused. She began to rock slowly. He gasped.

She regarded him speculatively. 'So we're going to be here for a while, then?'

He caressed her naked skin. 'Indeed we are.' His lips resumed what they had begun. 'A very…long…while.'

Chapter Nineteen

Later Harry sent out for food which they ate in their room. Afterwards he carried her back to bed and resumed what they had bcgun. Her passion astonished and delighted him, but more rewarding than all of that was the knowledgc that she was offering him her trust. The shadows of the past had been banished and he was careful to do nothing that might recall them, so that his exploration of her body was tender, each caress an act of homage. Elena was innately sensual and her passion was awakened now. Gradually, and with infinite patience, he introduced other possibilities to their lovemaking and discovered in her a willing pupil. The night was far advanced before they slept.

Elena woke first, her entire body suffused with warmth and a sense of well-being. Turning her head she looked at the man beside her, drinking in every detail of his face, her heart full. He had taken her to places beyond imagination, initiating her further into the art of love. Far from being repelled or frightened she had enjoyed every moment. It seemed a paradox that submission to a man could make her feel whole again, but it undoubtedly had. She smiled and dropped a kiss on his breast.

Harry opened his eyes and smiled. 'Is that how you mean to wake me each morning?'

'If you wish.' She returned a sultry glance. 'Or if you prefer I could do this.' She shifted position a little and kissed him on the lips.

'Better and better.'

She repeated the gesture. 'I'm glad you approve.'

'I approve very much.'

Her gaze held his. 'I'd like to have more than your approval.' She hesitated. 'I love you, Harry.'

He stared at her dumbfounded, unable to believe he had heard aright. Their compatibility delighted him on many levels; that her heart was involved as well seemed more than he deserved. As the implications began to sink in, he experienced a variety of unwonted sensations which only added to surprise and compounded mental confusion. He was far from indifferent to Elena. It had happened so gradually that he'd hardly been aware of it. Somewhere along the way his feelings for Belén had been…not supplanted exactly, but they had subtly altered. Her memory would always be with him, but the attendant grief and loss had abated and been replaced by hope. A part of him still felt guilty that it should be so and it warred with the rest that wanted to move on, to find fulfilment and to love again. Having spent years concealing his emotions and almost never giving them expression, he was at a loss now to explain what he felt.

'Elena, I...' He broke off, searching for words. 'You must know that I also care for you very deeply.'

His hesitation and embarrassment didn't go unnoticed and her heart sank. She had taken a risk in declaring herself hoping that, by being open with him, he might then tell her what he truly felt. And indeed he had. Only it was not what she had been longing to hear. *Care for* was not the same as love. She had earlier surmised that Harry was the kind of man who would not give his heart easily; her intuition had proved correct.

She summoned a tremulous smile. 'I'm glad.'

'You should never doubt it, sweetheart.' He kissed her cheek. 'You are very important to me.'

Her throat tightened. At least he hadn't pretended, and he had let her down gently, although, at that moment, she almost wished he had lied to her.

'It's getting late. We should get up.'

He slid an arm about her waist. 'There's no immediate hurry, is there?'

Elena turned away. 'You have an appointment to keep, remember?'

He'd temporarily forgotten about that and now felt strangely torn. He knew that she had withdrawn from him, that there were things unspoken between them, but he was uncertain how to broach so sensitive a subject. With a feeling akin to disappointment he watched as she climbed out of bed and donned her shift. He sighed. Clearly the moment had passed. They would have to talk later.

It was perhaps an hour later when he set out from the inn on the last stage of his quest. He had been given directions by the *patrón* of La Gata Negra. However, the enquiry had elicited a look of surprise and the intelligence that the address was not in the most salubrious part of town.

'If you go there it would be as well to go armed, *señor.* Although trouble is unlikely during the hours of daylight one cannot be too careful.'

Harry thanked him for the advice. The *patrón* bowed and, after ascertaining there was nothing more his distinguished guest required, he left.

'If t'neighbourhood is as he describes, it'd be as well to go accompanied an' all,' said Jack, who had been present during the conversation. 'Happen you might need someone at your back.'

'I'd be glad of the company,' replied Harry.

Thus it was that the two of them made their way from the bustling main thoroughfare into smaller side streets. Here the buildings were closer together and humble in appearance. The cobbles were littered with rubbish and, in places, slick with dirty water; the air was thick with the smells of decay and stale food. Cur dogs picked through the detritus, oblivious to the passers-by. The latter regarded the newcomers with covert and curious glances but no one made any attempt to impede their progress.

Once or twice they paused to ask directions and, at length, came to the street in question and found the house. It was unremarkable and, like all the others, its lower windows were shuttered and barred. A stout wooden gate gave on to the roadway. When Harry knocked, the sound echoed behind it. At length an elderly woman appeared. She was clad all in black. The dress had seen better days but the wearer contrived to look neat all the same. When she asked the visitors their business her tone was polite.

Harry gave his name and asked for Sanchez. The old woman nodded.

'You had better come in.'

They followed her into a small courtyard and thence into the house where they were shown into a small parlour. Although sparsely furnished it was spotlessly clean and smelled of beeswax polish. The old lady excused herself and left them alone. Harry listened to the sound of her retreating footsteps and then low, urgent voices, hers and a male's.

A few minutes later the door opened again to admit a man of middle years. He was of average height and stocky frame, his lined face homely rather than handsome, and framed by greying brown hair. Dark eyes surveyed the visitors with wary interest. His gaze passed over Jack and came to rest on Harry, taking in every detail of his appearance. As he did so his eyes widened a little.

'You will forgive the lack of ceremony, my lord. I was not expecting so exalted a guest.'

'I am not here to stand on ceremony,' said Harry. 'I am come to seek Señor Sanchez.'

The older man frowned. 'I am he, but I fear you have the advantage of me.'

'Señor Xavier Sanchez?'

Understanding dawned in the man's face. 'Xavier is my nephew, but I regret to say that he is from home at present.'

Harry's heart sank. 'May I ask when he will return?'

'I do not know. I have not seen him for some time.'

'This is most unfortunate for my business is pressing and I have travelled a long way to find him.'

'May I ask the nature of your business?'

As Harry gave him the gist, the older man listened carefully, his expression indicative of concern.

'This is indeed a matter of importance.'

'It could not be more so to my family.' Harry paused. 'I wonder, might it be possible to get a message to your nephew?'

'As I said, I don't know his exact whereabouts.'

'But you do know those who might.'

For a moment his gaze locked with that of Sanchez. The latter nodded slowly.

'Perhaps.'

'I'd be much obliged if you would make enquiries.'

'I'll see what I can do.'

'I know that my late brother was involved in matters of a sensitive nature, and that this might make your nephew cautious. He has no need to be. My enquiries relate only to the circumstances of my brother's death.'

Again, Sanchez nodded. 'If you will leave your direction I will send word when I know more.'

'I thank you.'

Harry suspected that the man already knew more than he was prepared to say at this stage, but could understand the reasons for reticence. In the Intelligence Service discretion was of paramount importance: careless talk could and did cost lives. At the same time it was frustrating to be so near his goal and yet still be denied the proof he sought. For now though, he accepted that there was nothing else to be done. It would be folly to alienate the uncle and jeopardise all chance of finding the nephew. Harry had always known something like this might happen but, all the same, the sense of anti-climax was strong. He saw the same emotion in Jack's face. For the first time the thought occurred that Xavier Sanchez might not wish to be found. Harry paused, framing his next words carefully.

'If…when…you get word to your nephew, tell him also that I am not come to apportion blame.'

The dark eyes never wavered but their gaze softened a little. 'I'll do that, my lord.'

'Then I hope to hear from you soon.'

Harry offered his right hand and, after a brief hesitation, the other man took it, his grip sure and strong. Then he smiled faintly.

'Vaya con Dios.'

Harry and Jack left the house a short time later and

retraced their steps to the inn. For a little while neither one spoke. Then, eventually, Jack threw his master a sideways glance.

'He'll get word to his nephew, I'm thinking.'

'Yes. I imagine he won't find it too hard.'

'He knew a lot more than he was letting on. I'd like to have searched t'rest of t'house.'

'That thought was in my mind too, but it would have been most unwise to try.'

'Aye, true enough.' Jack sighed. 'What now, my lord?'

'We wait. There's nothing else we can do.'

'If Xavier Sanchez has any sense of honour he'll meet you.'

'So I hope,' replied Harry.

On their return to the inn, he went in search of Elena and found her with Concha in the garden at the rear of the premises. Seeing him approach the maid rose and left them. Harry took the seat she had vacated. Elena regarded him with mingled anxiety and embarrassment. However, he seemed unaware of it. It was as though that earlier scene had never happened. Forcing hurt aside she decided to take her cue from him.

'Was your visit successful?'

'Yes and no.'

She listened with quiet attention while he explained what had happened.

'It sounds as if the uncle was exercising caution,' she said.

'My thought exactly.'

'It's understandable, in the circumstances.'

He smiled ruefully. 'Frustrating too, but there's not much to be done about that. While we wait, perhaps you'd care to explore the town.'

'I'd like that.'

'Well, then, I'm entirely at your disposal.'

The bustling harbour with its forest of ship masts was an enthralling sight, like the mysterious sacks and bales and barrels on the quayside. The smell of fish and spice mingled with rope and tar and seaweed, and the sunlit air resounded with male voices speaking in Spanish, Portuguese, Italian, French and Arabic. It suggested a world apart from the one Elena had previously inhabited, a world that was strange and exotic and exciting. She was entranced.

Curious and admiring glances came her way but, being rapt in the wonder of it all, she failed to notice. Harry, on the other hand, did. It came as no surprise that other men should want to look at his wife and he was happy to let them look. He'd have been less than human if he hadn't enjoyed their envy. In contrast, Elena seemed quite oblivious to the attention and wanted to know about the ships and their cargoes instead. Harry, privately amused, did his best to answer.

Later they left the harbour and strolled thence to the Barrio de la Viña, an area of the old town with close proximity to the shoreline and the Playa de la Caleta, an impressive expanse of sand stretching between the fortresses of San Sebastian and Santa Catalina. Elena surveyed the view with shining eyes.

'Homer's wine-dark sea,' she murmured. 'It's more beautiful than I'd ever imagined.'

Her unfeigned enthusiasm recalled the first time he had ever set eyes on the sea. 'It's quite something, isn't it?'

'I can easily understand why men are drawn to explore it.'

'It has a siren voice but it is not without its perils.'

'So I have heard.'

'In England there is a growing fashion for sea bathing,' he said.

'Men are so fortunate.'

'Women enjoy it too, I believe.'

Her eyes widened. 'Women? Really?'

Harry grinned. 'Yes, really.'

'I should like to try that.'

'If you wish I will take you to Brighton and you can essay the waters there.'

'You wouldn't mind?'

'No, why should I?'

There were several things that she might have said in reply. Instead she tried to imagine what her former betrothed would have said if she had ever suggested such a thing. Visualising his probable expression, she could only smile to herself. Jose and Harry were as different as paste from diamond.

'Be warned though,' he continued. 'The water is likely to be much colder than here.'

'I'll brave it just for the experience.'

'Would you like to try now?' Without warning he swept her up and strode towards the water's edge.

Elena shrieked, protesting vigorously. 'Harry, no! Put me down!'

'You said you wanted to swim.'

'Yes, but not now!'

'No time like the present.'

'You wouldn't.'

'Wouldn't I?'

As the next wave rolled in and he made to throw her into the water, she uttered a despairing wail, clinging to him for dear life. The wave broke sending lacy foam racing up the strand. Instead of dropping her, Harry retained his hold and, at the last moment, turned and fled from the advancing water, eventually setting her down safely above the waterline. Heart pounding she glared at him in disbelief.

'*Bruto!* I really thought you were going to throw me in.'

Far from expressing contrition the reply was a guffaw of laughter. It was infectious and she caught it.

'You're a wicked man, Harry Montague. You know that?'

'No, my sweet, a wicked man would have thrown you in. As it is, I'll settle for a lesser penalty.'

She eyed him with mock hauteur. 'And what is that?'

'A kiss.'

'Do you think I'm going to kiss you after that?'

The grey eyes gleamed. 'Do you really think you will not?'

'Kiss me if you can, my lord.'

He reached for her waist but Elena dodged out of the way, laughing. Harry lifted an eyebrow.

'Come here, Elena.'

'No.'

'No?'

His expression was suggestive of polite interest. Then he lunged towards her. She dodged again, feinting and weaving to elude him. Undaunted he pursued her, coming dangerously close to success several times. Realising her peril, Elena turned and fled. He caught her in half a dozen strides. An arm of steel slid around her waist and drew her round to face him, both of them breathless and laughing. For several heartbeats they remained thus before laughter faded and became something altogether more intense. She swayed towards him, surrendering to his kiss. His hold tightened, crushing her against him, and the kiss became passionate. She returned it hungrily, wishing only that it had been motivated by love.

Chapter Twenty

Harry did not expect to hear from Señor Sanchez for several days at the earliest, so he was pleasantly surprised when, after only two, he received a note requesting him to return to the house. He tried not to let excitement run away with him, but it was difficult. Elena saw the strain in him and understood it.

'I do hope this meeting will bring all you wish for, Harry.'

He raised her hand to his lips. 'Thank you. I hope so too.'

'You cannot have come so far for nothing.'

'Let us trust that the Almighty hasn't so cruel a sense of humour.'

It had been a long time since she had trusted the Almighty over anything, but she didn't mention it. Harry needed support now, not cynicism. She smiled.

'Let us trust to a favourable outcome.'

'I'm sorry to leave you again, but it won't be for very long.'

'You need have no anxiety over that. I shall occupy myself until you return.'

'Truly you are a gem among women.'

She conquered hurt. A gem was all very well, but it was not the same as being the love of his life. 'As long as you know that.'

Harry's gaze gleamed. 'I have known it for some time, my sweet.' Reluctantly he released his hold on her hand. 'I'll be back soon.'

'Buena suerte.'

'Thank you. I need all the luck I can get.'

After he had gone, Elena paced the floor awhile in pensive silence. Then, needing some fresh air, she betook herself to the garden once more. It was pleasant to sit in the sunshine and feel the warm breeze life her hair off the back of her neck. Soon she would have to accustom herself to a new country and a new climate, but the thought didn't dismay her. As long as she was with Harry it didn't matter. She had never imagined that she could feel so much for one man, but he had become indispensable to the point where it was impossible to visualise life without him. When they were together he had her full attention; when they were apart she thought about him all the time. He had but to enter a room for her heart to leap. His slightest look or touch was sufficient to set every nerve tingling. She wished it could be the same for him, but his heart was spoken for and her rival was unassailable. One could not compete with the dead.

* * *

Just then, the subject of her thoughts was engrossed in rather different ones of his own. For all that he tried to control it he couldn't quite suppress the feeling of anticipation building in his breast. Sanchez wouldn't have sent for him unless he had something significant to relate, and that meant he had been in contact with his nephew. Harry could only hope that Jamie's erstwhile companion did indeed have a sense of honour. He could not imagine his late brother remaining long in company with a man who had not. The memory of Jamie was poignant and no doubt always would be, but, God willing, his family would eventually know the truth.

Being certain of the way now, he and Jack made good progress and arrived at the Sanchez house within half an hour of leaving the inn. They were admitted and shown into the same room as before. They had not long to wait before their host appeared and with him another, younger man, whom Harry put in his early thirties. He was slightly taller than the uncle but, like him, of a stocky build. A distinct facial resemblance was there too, especially about the mouth and nose. Harry's heart began to beat a little faster.

The older man smiled and inclined his head towards his guests. 'Thank you for coming so promptly, my lord.' He gestured towards his companion. 'May I present my nephew, Xavier?'

Gladness and grief mingled in Harry's breast and, for a moment, made it difficult to speak. He conquered it.

'It has long been my most ardent wish to speak with

you, *señor.* Believe me when I say you have my gratitude for agreeing to this meeting.'

'My uncle outlined the reason for your visit,' replied Xavier. 'I could do no less.'

The older man interjected. 'I hope that you will forgive my earlier reticence, my lord, but I could not commit my nephew to a meeting like this without first consulting him.'

'Understandable,' said Harry, 'given the circumstances.'

'The matter is delicate and no doubt you will wish to be private. I will therefore leave you to talk.'

With that he excused himself. Jack, receiving a look from his master, followed in his wake, closing the door behind them. For a moment or two, neither Harry nor Xavier spoke. Then, the latter gestured to a chair.

'Please, won't you sit down, my lord?'

Harry accepted the offered seat and watched as his companion took the one opposite. Xavier surveyed him steadily.

'Ask me what you will and I will answer as truthfully as I can.'

'I know that you and my late brother were colleagues, and that the work you undertook was concerned with intelligence.'

'That is so.'

'What I need to know are the details concerning his death. Until those are established the rightful heir cannot succeed to his inheritance. It is a matter of supreme importance for my family.' Harry paused. 'But, quite apart from the legal reasons pertaining to this, there are more personal ones.'

'I understand.'

Harry nodded. 'If you will, then, tell me what occurred that day.'

'It was during the British push for Toulouse. We—your brother and I—had been on a mission to gather intelligence about French troop numbers and movements. The situation was chaotic as it always is in times of war, and reliable information hard to come by. We were sent ahead to reconnoitre and then report back.'

'To whom?'

'To Sir George Scovell.'

Harry lifted an eyebrow. He knew the name well. Originally part of the Fourth Queen's Own Dragoons, Scovell had proved to be an expert at deciphering codes, in particular the Grand Chiffre which had provided the allies with information crucial to Wellington's victory at Vittoria. Scovell had also been in charge of the motley crew known as the Army Guides, men of differing nationalities, chosen for their linguistic abilities and other individual skills, who had gathered information vital to the war effort.

'I see,' he said. It was quite true. The bigger picture was now beginning to emerge with startling clarity. Yet it should have come as no surprise to discover that Jamie had worked for Scovell. The man had only ever employed the best.

'The river was running higher and faster than was usual,' Xavier went on. 'However, the nearest bridge was ten miles away, and we had reason to believe it was being held by the French in any case, so we decided to risk the crossing.' He sighed. 'Jamie went first. It was ever his way.'

'Yes, it was.'

'He was about halfway across when his horse stumbled and lost its footing. It went down and took Jamie with it. I saw him come to the surface but he couldn't find his feet because of the current or the uneven river bottom—or both.'

Harry felt a chill prickle along his neck as he experienced a moment of *déjà vu*—he saw Elena's horse stumble and fall, saw her pitched into the water, felt its cold shock on his own flesh as he went in after her… With an effort he controlled his voice.

'Go on.'

'Jamie surfaced and struck out for the shore.'

'My brother was a strong swimmer. The distance would have been easy for him.'

'Yes, but he was wearing a heavy greatcoat and boots as well as his other clothing. And he was armed. The weight must have dragged him down and then the cold and the current did the rest.' Xavier paused. 'I rode in after him but it was as though the river had swallowed him up. I rode downstream for some way, hoping he might be washed ashore, but there was no trace of him.'

Harry drew a deep breath, seeing it all in his mind's eye. In the same way, but for the grace of God, he might have lost Elena. The parallels were uncanny and he felt suddenly cold.

'I'm sure you did all that you could,' he said. 'What happened afterwards?'

'I continued with our mission. Jamie insisted that if anything were to happen to one of us, the other would ensure that the task was completed. I knew I must keep faith with him. Therefore, as agreed, I reported in with the military information and informed the authorities of his loss.'

'Another of my older brothers was serving in Spain at the time. He tried to find you after he was given the news, but could not.'

'Sir George had more work for me to do and, as usual, I was not permitted to divulge its nature to anyone, nor where I was going.'

Harry could well believe it. Personal grief had no bearing on the machinery of war, and Scovell would never have employed a man who could not be discreet.

'I feel privileged to have met and worked with your brother, a man both trustworthy and likeable.'

'Thank you.' Harry smiled faintly. 'He had that effect on many people.'

'You must have cared for him very deeply, I think.'

'Yes.' Just then Harry found it impossible to articulate his feelings. Although he had known the broad outline of the story for a long time, hearing it related at first hand brought it home more sharply than ever before, underlining the reality of his brother's death. With an effort he gathered his thoughts. 'Will you set down the facts in writing, and then swear to their veracity in front of witnesses?'

'If you wish.'

'It is imperative. My family needs to know the truth.' He paused. 'One more thing…what can you tell me about my brother's marriage?'

Xavier regarded him in surprise. 'I know nothing of the matter, my lord. My conversations with your brother were concerned with our work.'

'But you knew he was married?'

'I assumed he might have a wife back in England. It was not unusual among the officer class.'

'Not England. Not then anyway. My brother was married in Burgos, during the war.'

'In Burgos?'

'Yes, to a Miss Alicia Walters.'

'I regret that I never had the pleasure of meeting the lady.'

'It was something of a whirlwind romance, I understand.'

'It must have been, my lord. We were there for less than three weeks.' Xavier gave a self-deprecating smile. 'I imagine he must have met her some time before that.'

Harry stared at him. 'You were with Jamie in Burgos?'

'Yes, I was with him. Well, not all the time, of course. As he was an officer we mixed in rather different social circles.'

'But surely, if he had married you would have known about it?'

'Not if he chose to keep it a secret. Besides, it was never my place to enquire about such things.'

'No, I suppose not.'

'All attention was on the advance into France. If a couple chose to slip away and marry they might have done so without attracting undue attention.'

'I believe the wedding was performed by an army chaplain. It would not have gone unremarked.'

'Stranger things have happened in times of war,' replied Xavier. 'You could ask the man.'

'So I could—if he were alive.'

'The witnesses, then.'

'Dead too, I understand.'

'Your brother was always discreet, my lord, and silence can be bought when necessary.'

'True—on both counts.'

Xavier nodded. 'I will reproduce this story in writing and bring the document to you tomorrow. Then, if you wish, I will swear to its veracity before witnesses of your choice.'

'I'm obliged to you.'

'I think the obligation is mine, my lord.'

The two men rose and shook hands, arranging to meet at eleven the following morning. Then Harry took his leave. Jack was waiting in the courtyard and now threw his master a quizzical look. When it appeared to go unnoticed he claimed the privilege of a trusted aide.

'Might I ask if your visit was a success, my lord?'

'Yes, Jack, it was. I have the information I came for. The formalities will be concluded tomorrow.'

'That's splendid. Congratulations, my lord.'

'Thank you.'

'Journey weren't a wasted effort, after all.'

'Indeed not.'

For all that the tone was level Harry's mind was whirling as he tried to assimilate what he had learned from Sanchez. Jamie had always played a deep game and always for his own reasons, but this was beyond everything. Had he kept his marriage secret because he knew his family would disapprove of his bride's lowly connections? Was he intending to wait until it was a *fait accompli* before breaking the news? It seemed most likely and, of course, his brother hadn't intended to get killed. Jamie went his own way and once his mind was made up he remained resolute. If Alicia had won his heart he would have married her even if Napoleon's entire army had tried to prevent it.

Harry could not blame his brother for following the dictates of his heart. Had he not done the same with Belén? A doctor's daughter, no matter how attractive and well-educated, would never be considered a suitable wife for the son of a duke—even a younger son. Not that he'd cared a jot for that. He smiled ruefully to himself. It seemed he'd had even more in common with Jamie than either of them had known. And now there was Elena. Her breeding was impeccable, her lineage every bit as good as his, but she was still a foreigner. His family were just going to have to get used to the idea for she had found a place in his heart that no one else could fill. He didn't know exactly how or when that had happened, only the truth of it.

Now that his quest was finally over he could put his mind entirely on their future. There were so many things to be discussed. Elena had never been asked what she wanted. Forced into marriage, she had followed him uncomplainingly, made light of discomforts and dangers, and been supportive in every way possible. It was high time that he began to put her first, to treat her as the lady she was.

On his return to the inn he found her in their chamber. She had been reading a newspaper but, hearing him enter, rose eagerly to greet him. He possessed himself of her hands and kissed them. Then he sat down, drawing her with him onto the window seat, and related the substance of his conversation with Xavier Sanchez.

Elena smiled tremulously. 'Oh, Harry, at last. I'm so pleased for you.'

There could be no doubting the sincerity in her tone or the expression in her eyes. Both warmed him inexpressibly.

'I am pleased for both of us,' he replied, 'since now we can put this business behind us and get on with our lives.'

'I want that very much.'

'So do I.' He paused. 'I'd like you to be present when Sanchez brings the papers tomorrow.'

It took her by surprise but it was not displeasing. 'Of course, if you wish it.'

'I do wish it. After all that you have endured I think it only right you should be there to witness the success of the mission.'

Her heart gave a queer little leap. 'Thank you. I'd like that very much.'

In truth it was a courtesy that she had not expected. In her experience women were not generally consulted on such matters, much less admitted to a man's confidence. Once again she acknowledged that Harry was not as other men. Since she had met him she had been compelled to reappraise the norm in regard to a woman's role, and it only increased her esteem for him.

'As to the rest,' he went on, 'shall you like living in England, Elena? We must go there for a while at least. Quite apart from the legal matters to be dealt with my relatives are entitled to know of our marriage and will be agog to meet you. But, after that, there is no absolute necessity to remain if you dislike the idea.'

Her eyes widened a little. 'Why should I dislike it?'

'I don't know. I hope you will not but…'

'But what?'

'It seems to me that no one has ever asked you what you would like.'

'Then I will tell you.' Her gaze met and held his. 'I would like us to have a proper home, and a family. Whether that home is in England or the outer reaches of Mongolia doesn't matter to me, as long as we can build a future together.'

The grey eyes warmed. 'We will build a future together, Elena, and we most certainly will have a proper home, although you may be relieved to learn that Mongolia doesn't figure in the equation.'

'In truth that is something of a relief.'

He grinned. 'As to the rest…I hope for that too, and promise to do my best to help bring it about.'

'I mean to hold you to your promise, my lord.'

Harry crossed the room and locked the door. Then he rejoined her. His expression sent a delicious shiver down her spine.

'A promise should always be kept and as soon as possible.'

Elena rose and slid her arms around him, wishing she didn't want him so badly. 'My thoughts exactly.'

Chapter Twenty-One

Xavier Sanchez arrived punctually at eleven the following morning and was shown into the private chamber where Harry and Elena awaited him. If their visitor was surprised to see her there he recovered quickly and made his bow politely. When Harry had performed the necessary introductions and invited their guest to sit, he got straight down to business.

'Have you brought the document we discussed?'

'Of course.' Xavier reached into his coat and drew out a sheaf of folded papers. 'Everything that I related is set down here.'

Harry took the proffered papers and opened them, scanning the contents. Having done so, he nodded. 'This seems to be in order. All that remains now is to have them attested and signed under oath.'

'In good time, my lord.'

'What do you mean?'

'That there is rather more to this tale than I have told you.'

Harry frowned. 'Yesterday you affirmed that it was truth. Are you now saying that it is not?'

'By no means. It is true, as far as it goes.'

Elena darted a startled glance at Harry but he didn't see it: his attention was fixed on the man opposite, his expression steely. In that moment he reminded her of nothing so much as a hunting hawk, fierce and potentially dangerous.

'I think you had better explain that remark,' he said.

Xavier met his gaze steadily. 'There are aspects to the affair that I have no authority to divulge but, in view of the circumstances, it seemed to me that you ought to be told everything. Therefore, after you left yesterday, I went to consult my superiors.'

'Go on.'

'When I explained the situation they agreed with me.' Xavier paused. 'One of them offered to accompany me today. I think you should meet him.'

Harry's jaw tightened. 'This had better not be a trick, Sanchez.'

'No trick, my lord, only a regrettable need for caution.'

'Very well.'

'I'll bring him to you now.'

'Do that.'

As Xavier rose to leave the room, Elena looked anxiously at Harry. His anger, though controlled, was almost palpable. Underneath it all she saw the strain that he normally concealed so well, and her heart went out to him. With a sense of foreboding she wondered what more they were about to discover. Surely the prize could not be snatched away now? That would be too cruel to contemplate. She drew a deep breath and locked her hands together in her lap, forcing herself to adopt an expression of calm she was far from feeling.

In the corridor outside she heard footsteps, and then male voices, speaking low. A few moments later Xavier returned with another man, a stranger who walked with aid of a cane. He looked to be about thirty, or a little more. Taller than his companion, he was possessed of a lean, athletic build. His clothing, though serviceable, was of good quality and clearly spoke of the gentleman. The face was arresting. Undoubtedly handsome, it was at present pale and a little drawn, as though its owner had been ill and was but lately recovered, and a vivid scar marred the left cheek. Yet, with its chiselled lines and piercing grey eyes, it was eerily familiar.

For the space of several heartbeats each man took the measure of the other in silence. Then the stranger spoke.

'Hello, Harry.'

The words dropped into a well of stillness for Harry might have been turned to stone. He too was very pale, his gaze fixed on the other man's face. Then, with a visible effort, he gathered his wits and found his voice.

'Jamie?'

'Yes.'

Elena's heart seemed to miss several beats. Then, as her brain caught up with her eyes, she understood why the stranger had looked so familiar. Beside her Harry continued to stare. Gradually shock and incredulity gave way to realisation.

'Dear God! Jamie!'

He crossed the intervening space and clasped his brother by the shoulders. The warm and solid flesh beneath his hands was undoubtedly real, like the grey gaze that met his own. When he looked into his brother's eyes, the last shred of doubt vanished.

'It is you.'

That knowledge brought a surge of emotion so powerful it assumed the intensity of physical pain. Then wordlessly the two men embraced in a hearty hug. When eventually they drew back Harry looked from his brother to Sanchez.

'Why didn't you tell me before?'

'Xavier is not to blame,' said Jamie. 'He was just following orders.'

'Even so…'

'Once he learned why you were here he came to find me.'

'I should think he did.' Harry's throat felt suddenly tight. 'Why, Jamie? How could you do it?'

'It's a long story.'

Elena rose from her chair. 'You two will have much to say to each other. I'll leave you to talk.'

Harry gave her a grateful smile. She returned it and then headed for the door. Sanchez followed her.

'I'll be in the next room if you need me,' he said.

When the door closed behind them Harry turned to

his brother. 'I was never happier to see anyone in my life, but, by heaven, you've got some explaining to do.'

'I know it.' His brother gestured to the chairs. 'Shall we sit down?'

In truth Harry was glad to obey. Now that the initial shock was wearing off he found himself trembling with reaction.

'Have you any idea of the heartache you've caused our family?' he demanded. 'Dear God, man! When he learned of your loss Father was beside himself. Then, when he discovered that Edward had been killed, the poor man almost lost his mind.'

Jamie's pallor intensified. 'I am truly sorry, on both counts. I didn't hear about Edward for some time after the event. Even now it's hard to believe he's gone.'

'I know. Almost every family of our acquaintance lost someone at Waterloo.'

'You were there, I collect.'

'Yes, and I hope to heaven that it's the last battle I ever see.'

'Battles take many different forms,' replied Jamie. 'Some are conducted far from the public gaze.'

'The business that engaged you, for instance?'

'Just so.'

'Well, you have a worthy ally in Sanchez,' said Harry. 'He gave a most creditable performance—each detail of your alleged death was utterly plausible.'

'It was intended to be.' Jamie glanced at the handwritten papers on the table nearby. 'However, if you look at his account again you'll find that the word *death* is never actually used. Nor was it when Xavier informed the authorities of my supposed accident. That is the interpretation of events that others put on them.'

Harry stared at him. However, when he thought back to the previous day's conversation it struck him that Sanchez hadn't used the word then either. He had spoken only of loss and disappearance. Harry's imagination had done the rest, as was the intention. Some of the other remarks were also ambiguous: *I feel privileged to have met and worked with your brother, a man both trustworthy and likeable.* At the time he'd heard only the past tense; his brain had missed the opening verb and the entire lack of one in the latter part of the statement. Admiration mingled with anger, the latter chiefly directed at himself for being gullible.

'A simple trick, but a clever one,' he said. 'Deucedly clever.'

'The simplest ideas are invariably the best.'

'I just hope it was worth it.'

Jamie continued to survey him steadily. 'You shall judge for yourself.'

'It'll make a change to hear the truth.'

'The mission to reconnoitre French troop movements was genuine, as far as it went. However, it was always intended that Xavier and I should part company at the Bidasoa River. He would go ahead and collect the necessary intelligence before returning to report the unfortunate accident, and I would be free to undertake a very different task.' Jamie paused. 'In order to succeed I had to disappear and adopt an entirely new identity.'

'You have been gone for two years. What the devil could have taken so long?'

'Initially my absence was supposed to be for a shorter time, but the matter became more and more protracted. I was following orders.'

'Are you going to tell me?'

'In outline, yes. There are some things I may not reveal.'

'Understood.'

'As you are doubtless aware, towards the end of the war the Spanish monarchists wanted to be rid of Joseph Bonaparte and see King Ferdinand restored to power.'

'Who could blame them? Bonaparte was an upstart and a usurper.'

'Quite so. However, the liberal elements wanted assurances that Ferdinand would govern in accordance with the Constitution.'

'He only ever seemed lukewarm on that score.'

'An understatement if ever there was one,' said Jamie. 'The man is a tyrant, pure and simple. Thus it was not surprising either that there should be an attempt to remove him in his turn. Intelligence got wind of it.'

'And they sent you to find out more.'

'It suited British interests to leave Ferdinand where he was,' replied Jamie. 'My task was to scotch the plan by infiltrating the group.'

'Dangerous work.'

'It almost did get me killed.'

'So I see.'

'By then though, I'd learned enough to halt their ambitions.'

'So you were successful.'

Jamie gave a mirthless smile. 'The plotters are either dead or in prison, but the most ironic aspect of the whole business is that now I wish their plan had succeeded.'

Harry frowned. 'Is Ferdinand so bad?'

'He's ruthless, vengeful and cruel, a man for whom I have come to feel nothing but contempt.'

'I see.'

'I swear to you if I'd known what he was I'd have refused the assignment.'

For a moment Harry was silent, trying to assimilate it all. 'You did what you thought was right at the time. It's all any of us can do.'

'I've given two years of my life to a cause I now detest.'

'It's easy to be wise after the event.'

Jamie sighed. 'That part of it is over at any event.'

'You mean there's more?'

'Some loose ends to tie up, let's say.'

'You're needed back in England, Jamie. Quite apart from all the emotional drama the family is in a parlous financial situation. Father made some disastrous investments a while ago and the repercussions have been considerable.'

'I had no idea.'

'How should you?'

'Is it really so bad, Harry?'

'We're like to lose everything if you don't return soon.'

'Good God!'

'Then of course there's the matter of your wife and child.'

Jamie's eyes grew wide and he looked thunder-stricken. 'What are you talking about?'

'I'm talking about Alicia and Crispin, who else?'

'Alicia?' He seemed even more surprised, if that was possible. 'Alicia who?'

'Did your injuries also include loss of memory?'

'My memory serves me perfectly well. I was never married to anyone called Alicia and, to the best of my knowledge, have never sired a son either.'

Harry was suddenly very still, his mind reeling with the implications. Jamie frowned.

'Why the devil should you think otherwise?'

'Because, some months ago, that same lady arrived at Castonbury claiming to be your wife,' replied Harry. 'She's the reason I came to Spain. Until your death could be proved the inheritance could not pass to the rightful heir.'

'This woman's son, I collect.'

'Correct.'

Jamie regarded him in disbelief. 'You believed her?'

'We believed you dead, and her story was plausible.'

'What story?'

'That the two of you married in Burgos just before the push for Toulouse. You had to leave shortly after the wedding, and she didn't know then that she was with child.'

'It's arrant nonsense! What proof could she offer?'

'A wedding certificate.'

'A forgery.'

'She had your signet ring, Jamie.'

His brother's jaw tightened. 'I lost the ring. It was stolen not long before the push for Toulouse.'

'I see.'

'She must have obtained it somehow.' Jamie ran a hand through his hair. 'It's incredible.'

'It's a carefully orchestrated fraud and, I suspect, by more than one person.'

'They must have had enough detail about me to think they could get away with it. That argues it involves people whom I knew.'

'My thought too.' Harry paused. 'The woman may be using an assumed name. Did you meet an Alicia while you were serving here in Spain?'

Jamie shook his head. 'No. None of the officers' wives anyway.' Then he paused, frowning. 'Wait. There was an Alicia, a lady's companion or some such thing, attached to the household of a chap named Chambers. We attended a few of the same dinner parties.'

'Can you describe her?'

'Lord, let me think. Smallish build, blonde hair, quite pretty if that's your taste. She was well-spoken and seemed to be educated, had a refined sort of manner.'

Harry smiled grimly. 'That's her, it has to be.'

'If it's the woman I'm thinking of I'll go bail she didn't dream up this plot herself.'

'I doubt that too. All the same, she plays the part well enough.'

'Surely the family must have looked into her story.'

'Of course. Giles and Ross have made a concerted effort to find out more. It was their thought to seek out the chaplain who performed the marriage and the witnesses to the ceremony, but enquiry revealed them to be dead.'

'How very convenient.'

'Indeed. When those lines of enquiry drew a blank, they asked me to come to Spain and see what I could discover here.'

'What beats me is how this woman got hold of my ring.'

'You said it was stolen.'

'Yes. I'd been socialising with some of my fellow officers and, to be frank, we were all rather foxed. I vaguely recall getting back to my lodgings, but nothing else until I woke up next morning. It was then I discovered the ring had gone.'

'But surely none of your fellow officers would have taken it.'

'I was reluctant to think so.'

'Could someone else have come in while you slept?'

'Maybe. I can't think who though. The house had been requisitioned for military personnel.'

Harry looked thoughtful. 'Then it would seem to be the work of someone connected with the army.'

'I fought side by side with those men, shared all manner of hardship with them. It creates a bond like no other. I cannot think that one of them would have done such a thing.'

'It *is* hard to believe,' admitted Harry. 'But I've a strong suspicion that if we discover who took the ring we'll eventually find out who perpetrated this plot as well.'

'You've been put to a great deal of trouble on my account, Harry. I can only apologise for it.'

'You're alive. That's what matters.'

'I feel so completely out of touch with everything and there's so much I want to know.'

'Dine with us tonight and I can tell you.'

Jamie smiled faintly. 'Us?'

'I'm married now.'

'Good Lord! Congratulations!'

Harry returned the smile. 'Thank you.'

'May I ask the lady's name?'

'Elena. You met her briefly.'

'Not that lovely creature I saw earlier?'

'The same. If my wits hadn't gone begging I'd have introduced you properly.'

'Well, you'd had quite a shock.' Jamie eyed him curiously. 'When did all this come about?'

'A few months ago.'

'And you dragged your new bride the length of Spain on my account? I'm mortified.'

'It's not as you might imagine.' Harry grinned. 'I didn't meet Elena until I arrived in this country.'

'A whirlwind romance?'

'In a manner of speaking. It's another long story too.'

'I can't wait to hear this.'

He sat in silent astonishment as Harry related the essential facts regarding his meeting with and marriage to Elena. He omitted the personal detail, those things he would not share with anyone save her. All the same it was a lively and entertaining account and by the end of it Jamie's eyes gleamed.

'You're a dark horse, Harry, and no mistake.'

'You're a fine one to talk.'

'I suppose I asked for that.' Jamie grinned. 'All the same I'm sincerely pleased for you. She sounds like a marvellous girl.'

'She is, in every way.'

'The uncle is a double-dyed villain though. I'd like to run him through.'

'I'm before you there,' said Harry. 'Or I would be if it were acceptable to slay one's relations.'

'He ought to be the exception that proves the rule.'

'Undoubtedly. As it is, he escapes unscathed. Fortunately we shan't meet again in all likelihood.'

'Good riddance.'

'Enough about him. We have more important things to talk about.'

'Agreed.' Jamie paused. 'I can't tell you how good it is to see you, Harry. I feel better than I have for a long time.'

'Do your injuries still pain you?'

'Most of it is superficial. The leg's a nuisance, but it'll heal eventually.'

Looking at his brother's relative pallor, Harry guessed there was a lot more that Jamie wasn't saying but he didn't probe. If Jamie wanted him to know he'd tell him. Just then it was enough to know his brother was alive. Now that the first shock was over, it had been replaced by delight and a rising sense of excitement. He tried to imagine the reaction at Castonbury when they heard the news. Their father would be beside himself with joy and the black cloud that had hung over the future would be lifted at last. Of course, there was the matter of fraud to be exposed too, but that would keep for now.

'I'd like you to meet Elena. May I fetch her?'

'The sooner the better,' replied Jamie. 'I cannot wait to make her acquaintance.'

Harry stepped out into the corridor where he found Jack and Concha, waiting at a discreet distance. They greeted him with wide smiles.

'Doña Elena has told us the glad news, my lord,' said Concha. 'I am truly most happy for you and for your family.'

Jack nodded. 'Concha speaks for us both, my lord.'

'Thank you,' replied Harry. 'Though I suspect I have the monopoly on that emotion at present.'

'If this don't beat all, eh?'

'Indeed.' Harry glanced at adjoining door. 'Is Sanchez still here?'

'He is that, my lord.'

'I need to speak to him. In the meantime, Concha, perhaps you'd inform Lady Elena that we shall have a guest to dinner this evening.'

As the two departed, Harry went into the adjoining room where Sanchez waited. For a moment the two men faced each other in silence.

'Under other circumstances I might be angry with you,' said Harry. 'As it is, I find that impossible since my brother has been restored to me safe and well.'

'I regret that the deception was necessary, my lord.'

'I think my brother could scarcely have chosen a more worthy colleague.'

'You are gracious.'

'Not in the least. You have played your part to perfection.' Harry paused. 'There's just one thing more I'd like to know. How came you and he to be in Cádiz together?'

'It was prearranged.'

'Am I right in thinking that the two of you have been in contact for some time?'

'We never lost contact,' said Sanchez.

Another piece of the puzzle slotted into place in Harry's mind. 'You were on the same mission, which is why you disappeared too, after you had reported the accident.'

'Just so, my lord.'

'Very neat.'

Sanchez made no reply, merely surveyed him with a level gaze.

'If I need to speak with you again will I find you the same way?' asked Harry.

'Of course.'

'Then I'll say farewell for the time being.'

Sanchez inclined his head in acquiescence. Then he headed for the door, pausing briefly on the threshold. *'Hasta entonces.'* With that he was gone.

Harry was distracted by the sound of a light step and looked up to see Elena. She greeted him with a smile and a warm hug, her excitement barely contained.

'I'm so pleased for you, Harry. More than I can say.'

He lifted her off the ground and swung her round before bestowing on her a resounding kiss. 'It's bloody marvellous, isn't it?'

'Never in a million years would I have expected this.'

'None of us did.' He grinned and possessed himself of her hands. 'Come, let me introduce you to my brother.'

Chapter Twenty-Two

When the introductions had been performed, Jamie took her hand and raised it to his lips.

'This is an honour I did not think to have,' he said.

Elena smiled. 'Nor I, my lord.'

'I had no idea that my brother's taste was so exquisite.'

'You have no idea how jealous a husband he is either,' said Harry, 'so you'd best have a care.'

Jamie grinned. 'How on earth did *you* find anything so beautiful? There's no justice.'

'I have no complaints to make about my lot.'

'I should say you haven't.' Jamie leaned confidentially towards Elena. 'I really must relate some of his boyhood adventures. You'll find them most entertaining.'

Her eyes sparkled. 'I should like to hear them, my lord.'

'Such formality is inappropriate between brother and sister. Won't you just call me Jamie?'

'If you wish it.'

'I do wish it. I hope we shall be good friends, you and I.'

Harry uttered a theatrical groan. 'I'm lost.'

'I rather think you are, brother.'

'If you plan to dredge up all the misdemeanours of my youth, I give you fair warning that I shall retaliate in kind.'

Jamie's expression was indicative of mock dismay. 'Hmm. Perhaps we might call a truce there.'

Elena eyed them both speculatively. 'You will do no such thing, for I am determined to hear all these stories, and once I have made up my mind I am not to be dissuaded.'

'Now you've done it,' said Harry.

'Can't you talk her out of it?'

'Not a hope.'

She laughed. 'How right you are.'

When they all met for dinner that evening Elena thought she had never seen Harry look so happy. It positively radiated off him. From time to time she would intercept a glance which only reinforced the impression. While it pleased her to see his joy it also saddened her to know that only others could call it forth. That, it seemed, was beyond her power.

With a determined effort she pushed these gloomy reflections aside, reminding herself that there was much to be thankful for. This outcome was beyond her wildest dreams. Now it had happened she settled down to observe. The longer she spent in their company the more apparent it was that these two men were brothers. They had the same quiet good breeding, the same polished manners, the same charm. They even shared some of the same mannerisms. Harry had once told her he'd looked up to his brother and it was true.

Yet there were differences too. Notwithstanding his obvious physical injuries, there was something about the older man that suggested private sadness, as though the experiences of the past two years had scarred him in other ways. Like Harry he was good at controlling his facial expression but his eyes were more eloquent. There were things that he had not said, events he had not yet recounted. However, they were none of her business. If he chose to tell Harry that was their affair.

It was late when the party broke up. Jamie eventually left them, promising to return on the morrow.

'You'd better keep your word,' said Harry, 'or there'll be the devil to pay.'

'Trust me.'

'I do.'

Jamie turned to Elena. 'I cannot recall the last time I spent so agreeable an evening. I hope to have the pleasure often repeated.'

'And I,' she replied.

'Until tomorrow, then.'

They went with him to the door of the inn and watched him mount his horse. Then with a final wave he left them.

'I like your brother very much,' said Elena as she and Harry strolled back to their room.

'He likes you, that's certain.'

'I'm glad.' She looked up at him. 'What an incredible day this has been. I shall never forget it if I live to be a hundred.'

'Nor I.'

'I did not believe in miracles, but I have been proved wrong.'

'I think we were both wrong about that,' he replied.

'We have been given more than I ever dreamed possible.'

'I know what you mean.'

'If anyone had told me three months ago that things would work out so well I should have called him a liar.'

He drew her closer. 'You helped to make it happen.'

'I'm glad of it,' she replied, 'and I'm happy for you, Harry.'

'There's only one fly in the ointment now, my sweet.'

'What fly?'

He summarised the relevant part of his conversation with Jamie. Elena was incredulous.

'You mean to say that Alicia is not his wife?'

'That's exactly what I mean to say.'

'Then the child is not…'

'The rightful heir? No, he is not.'

'The woman must be a most accomplished liar to have deceived everyone so well.'

'Indeed she is, though I suspect she was put up to it.'

'By whom?'

'That's what we need to find out,' he replied.

'What a shock this will be for your family.'

'It's better that they know the truth as soon as possible. That's why we shall have to leave for England immediately.'

'I can see that.'

'Shall you mind, Elena?'

'No, of course not.' She held his gaze. 'It is the start of a whole new adventure for us.'

'So it is,' he replied. 'The most exciting one yet.'

She knew that any adventure would be acceptable as long as she was with him. If she had only been able to win his heart life would have been perfect.

In spite of having retired late, Elena woke the next morning with the light. A sideways glance revealed that Harry was still asleep. She watched him for a little while and then, carefully, so as not to disturb him she rose and dressed. Wrapping her shawl about her shoulders she slipped from the room and closed the door quietly behind her.

After that she went to find Concha. As she had hoped the maid was already up and, just then, sitting in the public dining room engaged in quiet conversation with Jack. The room was empty but for the two of them, and, although they were sitting on opposite sides of a table, there was something about their expressions that rendered the little scene strangely intimate. For a moment she felt like an intruder. Then they became aware of her presence. Both reddened a little and rose hurriedly. Concha was first to recover her wits, regarding her mistress with concern.

'Doña Elena. Is something amiss?'

'Nothing at all,' she replied. 'However, there is something I need to do. Will you come with me?'

Concha nodded. 'Of course. I will fetch my shawl at once.'

As she hastened away Elena turned to Jack. 'If my husband asks for me tell him I am gone out but will be back soon.'

'I will, my lady.' Jack paused. 'Am I to tell him where you've gone?'

'No, I'll do that myself when I return.'

'Very good, my lady.'

A few moments later Concha reappeared and the two women departed, leaving Jack staring after them in silent bemusement.

Harry stirred and stretched lazily in a pleasant waking doze. As memory returned he smiled to himself, enveloped in a sense of well-being and contentment. After the uncertainty of recent weeks all was well with the world at last. He turned and reached for Elena, wanting to share the moment. His arm found empty space and a cooling sheet. He came to at once. Propping himself on one elbow he scanned the room swiftly and, finding no sign of her, frowned. A more detailed inspection revealed that her clothing was gone too. Feeling oddly bereft and vaguely disquieted now he rose and dressed in his turn. Then he summoned Jack. An enquiry elicited the message that Elena had left for him. Harry looked at the other man in astonishment.

'Gone out? At this hour?'

'Aye, my lord.'

'And she didn't say where?'

'No, my lord. She said she'd explain on her return.'

Harry couldn't imagine where she might have gone but, feeling reassured to learn that she was attended by Concha, he forbore to question Jack any further. No doubt the mystery would be cleared up in due course. He ran a hand over the bristles on his chin. In the meantime he needed to shave.

For a little while the two women walked in companionable silence until Elena noticed the covert glances directed her way.

'What is it, Concha? Is there something on your mind?'

'Jack has asked me to marry him.'

Elena stared at her. 'Good gracious! Has he?' Then, recollecting herself, she hurried on. 'Not that it's to be wondered at. He always did seem like a sensible man.'

Concha reddened a little. 'I think so too.'

'What did you tell him?'

'That I would consider his proposal.'

'I see.' Elena surveyed her steadily. 'You like him though.'

'Yes. I didn't at first…well, not much anyway, but he has grown on me since then.'

'I had a strong suspicion he liked you.'

'He says he loves me.'

The words caused a pang of something very like envy. Elena forced it down. 'Then if you both feel the same why should you hesitate?'

'I said that I could not think of marrying him until you are safely settled in your new home.'

'Concha, you have devoted years of your life to my welfare. It's time to think of your own happiness.'

'Jack says he doesn't mind waiting. Besides, I think it will be a wrench for him to leave His Lordship's service.'

'Is he planning to do so?'

'He means to set up in business.'

Elena's eyes widened. 'What manner of business?'

'A coaching inn, he says.'

'How exciting.'

'He has the means to do it. Apparently the war was not a total disaster, financially at least.'

'Shall you like living in a coaching inn?'

'The idea is not without appeal. I have the necessary domestic knowledge, and Jack is a good organiser. He was an army sergeant before so he'll be able to deal with staff, and he knows a lot about horses too.'

'You'll make a perfect team.'

Concha nodded. 'I think we might.'

'If it's what you want you have my blessing.'

'Thank you.'

'Has Jack spoken to His Lordship yet?'

'He will not, until he has my answer.'

'Then I will say nothing either. It will be our secret for now.'

They lapsed into silence again, each rapt in thought. The conversation had given Elena much food for thought. While she was pleased for Concha the emotion was also tinged with sadness because with her went the last connection to Spain. Concha had been like her right arm for so long that it was hard to imagine being without her. Adversity had drawn them close so that in many ways she had been more like a sister than a servant. Losing her would be hard indeed.

Elena pulled herself up sharply. If anyone deserved happiness it was Concha. Jack was a good man. He had proved his worth many times over and he would no doubt make a fine husband. She had won his heart besides. Elena was tempted to ask how it was done. If there was a secret she didn't have it. Harry might care for her, but it was Belén he loved.

These thoughts occupied her until she reached her destination and stopped outside an imposing building. Concha regarded the church with undisguised astonishment.

'Is this the place, Doña Elena?'

'Yes, this is the place.'

Now that she was here Elena felt unexpectedly nervous and she hesitated. Concha eyed her quizzically.

'Are you all right? You look a little pale.'

'It's just that, having turned my back on the Tenant for so long, it feels like a real cheek to turn up at His house out of the blue like this.'

'Well, I suppose you could have sent a note beforehand,' said Concha, 'but since the Tenant is reputed to be omniscient that would seem to be unnecessary.'

Elena smiled wryly. 'A fair point.'

'Besides, if we're not wanted here I expect He'll make His displeasure known.'

'Lightning bolts?'

'Possibly.'

'I think I'll risk it,' said Elena. 'Seriously though, if you'd prefer to wait here I'll understand. You don't have to come in.'

'Actually I think I do.'

'Right, then.' Elena took a deep breath. 'Ready?'

'Ready.'

Elena pushed open the door and together they went inside.

Harry was beginning to feel concerned. The two women had been gone over an hour and there was still no sign of them. He was about to send Jack out to look when Elena entered the private parlour. Relief replaced anxiety.

'I was starting to worry,' he said. 'Are you all right?'

'Of course. Did you not receive my message?'

'I did, but that was a while ago.'

'I didn't mean to cause you anxiety.'

He hesitated, wanting to ask her where she'd been but fearing to sound like a domineering husband. Elena took off her shawl and bestowed a kiss on his cheek. He slid an arm about her waist.

'I missed you.'

'I missed you too,' she replied, 'but I had to go out. It was important.'

'What was important, sweetheart?'

'I went to church.'

For a moment or two his expression registered blank astonishment. He'd thought of half a dozen possible explanations for her absence but none had even come close.

'Church?'

'It was time.'

He recovered his wits. 'If you felt it to be so, then it undoubtedly was.'

'I have been angry about the past for long enough, Harry. The events of recent weeks have made me see that clearly. I wanted to let go of it once and for all, but in order to do that I needed to make my peace with God.'

'You don't have to explain yourself to me, my sweet.'

'I know, but I want to all the same. Apart from Concha you are the only person who can truly understand.'

'An unorthodox trinity if ever there was one, but I'm proud to be part of it.'

'I want to make you proud.'

'You already do, in every way.'

'We have so much to be thankful for and so much to look forward to. There's no place for negative emotion.'

'You're right, there isn't.' He sighed. 'It's like a bad habit and just as hard to break.'

'But it can be broken—if we want it enough.'

'You never had anything to reproach yourself for.'

'Neither do you, Harry, and I think it's time you realised it.' Her gaze locked with his. 'What happened in Badajoz wasn't your fault. It was a chain of extraordinary circumstances that led to tragedy.'

'That's part of it.'

'That's all of it. You mustn't let it blight your life for evermore.'

His hold slackened. 'You speak as though I were somehow permitting it.'

It might have been wiser to let it pass, but she knew she wasn't going to. This had to be addressed. Too much depended on it.

'Aren't you?'

'Even you cannot understand…'

'Who should understand better than I? Or do you think that somehow you have a monopoly on shame and grief?'

'I have never claimed to do so.'

'Then stop wallowing in it.'

His gaze grew steely. 'Is that what you think?'

'It's exactly what I think,' she retorted. Then, as he opened his mouth to reply, 'How would I know? Because I did the same so I recognise all the symptoms. You bury the hurt and never talk about it with anyone, hoping it'll go away. But it never does. Instead it embeds itself more firmly and then festers like an infected wound.'

'It was my way of dealing with it.'

'Yet guilt consumes you still, even though it has no basis in anything but distorted imagination.'

His jaw tightened. 'Elena, leave this.'

'Pretend it isn't happening?' She shook her head. 'It's too late for that.'

'What do you want me to do?'

'I want you to forgive yourself and move on. You're throwing away the future because you won't let go of the past.'

'That isn't so. I want us to have a future.'

Elena's dark gaze burned into his. 'No, Harry, the woman you want is dead. She's the one you cling to, and she's the one who has your heart.'

'What?'

'You have made your feelings abundantly clear. I suppose I should just be grateful that you care anything for me at all.'

She turned on her heel and left him staring in thunderstruck silence at the open doorway. For a moment or two his mind was completely blank. Then the details of a former conversation returned with appalling clarity.

'Elena, wait!'

He strode after her and caught up as she reached their chamber. She tried to evade him but he bundled her unceremoniously inside and shut the door behind them. Elena glared at him.

'Leave me alone, Harry.'

'Not until we sort this out.'

'Can you pretend you don't love Belén?'

'When I spoke of those events I was describing my emotions then, not now.'

'Emotions you still felt a few days ago.'

'Not so,' he replied. 'I told you what my feelings were.'

'Ah, yes. You *care* for me. You *love* her.'

'If I had thought that you would so misconstrue the matter I'd have set the record straight.'

'You had the chance to set the record straight, but you didn't take it.'

'Because I'm a damned fool. You were right when you said that I hide my feelings. It has become a habit with me and perhaps a defence too.'

'A defence against what?'

'Against the knowledge of what you made me feel.'

Elena regarded him in surprise but checked the urge to interrupt.

'I tried to deny it at first,' he went on, 'but your honesty and your courage made me examine my own behaviour. It didn't make for comfortable viewing.' He paused. 'When you declared your feelings so openly... well, I wasn't expecting it even if they were the words I'd most wanted you to say.'

She swallowed hard. 'Do you mean that?'

'Yes, I do mean that. I love you, Elena.'

It was so welcome and so unexpected that it was hard to take in at first. 'Then you don't still...you're not...'

'No, I'm not. That chapter of my life is over. I want to move on—with you. You are my love now.'

'I want to be, Harry.'

His heart gave a painful lurch. 'I don't deserve that you should but I'm glad all the same.'

Elena regarded him in heart-thumping silence for

some seconds, then returned a quizzical look. 'How glad exactly?'

He took her in his arms and proceeded to show her with a lingering kiss that removed every last trace of doubt.

Later that morning Jamie arrived. They joined him in the private parlour. Elena thought his face had more colour now than it had erewhile, his eyes more sparkle. His whole manner seemed generally more animated. Perhaps the previous day's meeting had been good for him too. She hoped so. Her own happiness was such that she wanted everyone else to be happy.

'Would you like to talk alone?' she asked.

'No, please stay,' replied Jamie. 'Since what we must discuss now involves you as well.'

'As you wish.'

When Elena had sat down they followed suit.

'I'm glad you are come,' said Harry. 'Quite apart from the pleasure of seeing you, we need to discuss what happens next.'

Jamie smiled. 'Yes, we do.'

'Will you be returning to England with Elena and me?'

'I regret not, although I hope I shall not be far behind you.'

'The loose ends you mentioned yesterday?'

'Just so.'

'Very well.' Harry paused. 'I trust this won't involve you in further danger.'

'You need have no fears on that score.'

'That's a relief.'

'I plan to keep a whole skin, I promise you.' Jamie held his brother's gaze. 'The important thing now is to let the family know I'm alive and to expose the fraudulent claim to the title.'

'Trust me for that. We should be back within a month at the outside.'

'You should have no difficulty in getting a passage. Ships regularly ply their trade between here and England.'

'So I believe.'

'The sooner this scheming upstart is confronted the better. We need to know who masterminded the plan. He's the real villain of the piece.'

'We'll find out all right.'

'What will happen to the culprits?' asked Elena.

'They'll hang,' said Jamie.

She shivered inwardly. 'I wonder if this woman was aware of that when she agreed to the plan.'

'If not she's about to be made aware of it.' He eyed Harry. 'That may just be the leverage required to get the whole story.'

Harry nodded. 'Exactly what I was thinking.'

'I'll leave the matter in your capable hands for the time being.'

'Don't be too long.'

'I won't. In the meantime, we need to organise your passage home.'

Chapter Twenty-Three

A week later they left Cádiz on a merchantman bound for England. As the ship slid out of harbour Elena stood at the rail watching the coast recede. Now that they were under way she experienced a strange sensation in which anticipation was mingled with sadness. There was no way of knowing if she would ever see her homeland again. It seemed unlikely in the scheme of things.

'Are you all right, darling?'

Harry's voice broke the train of thought. She turned and smiled.

'Quite all right, I thank you.'

'Not too cold?'

She shook her head. 'To be on board a ship is a new experience.'

'I hope the experience will be a positive one.'

'Do you fear we shall be wrecked?'

'No, but we do have to negotiate the Bay of Biscay. It can be rough.'

'We have weathered worse, you and I,' she replied.

Harry eyed her keenly. 'With you beside me I believe I could weather anything that fate might throw.'

'So we'll take Biscay in our stride, then.'

He grinned. 'We may not even notice it.'

'It's exciting. Do sailors feel the same, I wonder, when they set forth on a new voyage?'

'I suppose they may. All the same, it's a hard life with lengthy periods away from home.'

'That must be the worst part of it.'

'Speaking of home,' he said, 'where do you wish ours to be?'

'Somewhere in the countryside. A farm, perhaps?'

'I think we can do better than that. I'm a reasonably wealthy man, after all.'

Elena threw him a mischievous look. 'Really? You didn't tell me this before.'

'I wanted to be married for myself, not for my money—hence our lengthy courtship.'

'I'm glad you took time to think carefully.'

'It was an important decision,' he replied. 'Besides, I hate to be rushed.'

'It may take a while to choose the house, now that we no longer have my uncle's guiding hand.'

Harry grinned. 'We'll just have to cope, won't we?'

'I'm confident that we shall.'

'So am I.'

She met his gaze and they both laughed. Then, out of the corner of her eye, she caught movement and glanced round. Then her smile widened further.

'Harry, look!'

He followed the line of her gaze. 'Dolphins! Well, I'm blessed!'

The graceful creatures were no more than twenty yards off, keeping pace with the ship, cleaving the water with effortless ease. Elena was enchanted.

'They're beautiful! I hoped we might see some but I wasn't sure we really would.'

He grinned. 'They must have come especially to greet us.'

'I think they have.'

'Sailors believe they bring good fortune.'

'Well, they should know.' She glanced up at him. 'We should take this as a good omen.'

Harry put his arm around her waist, drawing her closer. 'I do, my love. Very much so.'

As he watched the leaping dolphins Harry felt his heart lighten, as though the last remnants of a great shadow had dissolved. While he would never forget the events of the past he had come to terms with them at last, as he had come to terms with self-knowledge. All he had to do now was move on and embrace his future. Good omens told him so.

* * * * *

Read on to find out more about
Joanna Fulford
and the

series...

Joanna Fulford is a compulsive scribbler, with a passion for literature and history, both of which she has studied to postgraduate level. Other countries and cultures have always exerted a fascination and she has travelled widely, living and working abroad for many years. However, her roots are in England and are now firmly established in the Peak District, where she lives with her husband Brian. When not pressing a hot keyboard she likes to be out on the hills, either walking or on horseback. However, these days equestrian activity is confined to sedate hacking rather than riding at high speed towards solid obstacles. Visit Joanna's website at www.joannafulford.co.uk

Previous novels by the same author:

THE VIKING'S DEFIANT BRIDE
THE WAYWARD GOVERNESS
THE LAIRD'S CAPTIVE WIFE
THE COUNTERFEIT CONDESA

AUTHOR Q&A

What are you researching for your forthcoming novel?

My next project sees a return to the early medieval period—a sequel to *The Laird's Captive Wife*. This is an era I have become increasingly interested in and, along with the Regency, enjoy writing about. When I was writing the original book it occurred to me that Ashlynn's brother, Ban, might one day have a story of his own. Readers agreed and several people asked about a sequel. I'm pleased to tell them that this is now underway.

What is your hero's favourite childhood memory of Castonbury Park?

Harry has fond memories of the horse races he had with his brothers when they thought no one was watching. The pace was keen—a neck-or-nothing style that he and they found exhilarating. He enjoyed the competitive edge in those games and always hoped to beat Jamie, though he never did.

What would you most like to have been doing in Regency times?

I'd have liked to have been taught to drive a high-perch phaeton—preferably by one of the notable whips of the time. Those people made it look easy, though it was anything but. It would be wonderful to be able to 'drive to an inch', as they did, though I suspect I'd be lucky if I managed to drive to an ell.

Which stately home inspired Castonbury Park, and why?

Castonbury Park was inspired by Kedleston Hall. The latter is a magnificent property and is situated in Derbyshire—the setting for our series. The surrounding scenery is lovely too. This place ticked all the boxes with regard to the grandeur and the status required for the Montague family and it was easy to imagine our fictional family living there. Since the information and images are available online it was easy for all the authors to have a virtual tour of the place, even though they couldn't get there in person.

Where did you get the inspiration for Harry and Elena?

Harry came to mind first—a vivid and dramatic figure who wasn't anything like the man I'd originally envisaged as my hero, but who refused to go away. Moreover, he did not want to be at Castonbury—which could have been a problem given that the series is set there. However, I have learned to listen to my characters and eventually Harry came clean about his reasons for avoiding the place and for not wanting to go back to Spain. This was the basis for his emotional conflict. Elena arrived juxtaposed with the image of a convent. At first this seemed like a most unpromising scenario for the heroine of my story, but slowly the reasons began to emerge. As the layers began to peel away I became more intrigued about what she was telling me about herself. It became clear that she was the ideal woman for my hero. All this then had to be interwoven into the over-arching plot for the whole series. Amazingly, it was—and with fewer problems than anticipated.

AUTHOR NOTE

This series is set between the spring of 1816 and the late summer of 1817. Although the Napoleonic Wars have finished, the memory of Waterloo is still sharp. People are relieved that the lengthy conflict is over, but at the same time have to come to terms with the massive loss of life involved. There is scarcely a family that has not been affected in some way. The over-arching plot reflects this. Edward Montague dies in battle —a tragedy that has far-reaching consequences for his entire family.

Waterloo was the decisive blow for the coalition forces and the end of a campaign fought on many fronts. One of these was the Peninsular War in Spain, which had ended two years earlier. I was once fortunate enough to live in Madrid for some years and used it as a base to explore as much of Iberia as I could. The history of Spain also interests me very much, so this aspect of the Napoleonic Era is of especial interest. In the course of my reading on the subject I was riveted by accounts of events in the aftermath of the Siege of Badajoz in 1812, when British troops ran amok in a three-day orgy of pillage, rape and arson.

It was a shameful episode which, even at a distance of two hundred years, makes for very uncomfortable reading. Those accounts made me wonder what it must have been like for the individuals caught up in it—whether they were hapless officers trying to regain control of their men or innocent civilians who suffered the atrocities that occurred. How would an English soldier and a Spanish heroine come to terms with what had happened? How would they reconcile individual and cultural differences? This provided the basis for the deep emotional conflicts that my protagonists must resolve by the end of the story.

Don't miss the next instalment of Castonbury Park—
A STRANGER AT CASTONBURY
by Amanda McCabe

'It's hard to admit, but you're not the son I once knew…'

The obliterated battlefields of Spain are a world away from the privileged life of James Montague, Earl of Castonbury. Only nurse Catalina Moreno eases the deafening roar of mortar fire—and in a crumbling chapel by candlelight they make their vows. But before the sheets cool from their scorching wedding night Jamie leaves for a brutally dangerous mission…

Two years later, believing her husband dead, Catalina is shocked to see a man who looks and sounds like her Jamie at Castonbury—but where once there was warmth and charm now unflinching torment lies in the gaze of a man she barely recognises…

A STRANGER AT CASTONBURY

Amanda McCabe

It looked like the landscape of another world entirely—not a place where he had once lived and worked, fought and loved. It was a place he had never seen before except in nightmares.

Jamie felt strangely numb, remote from his surroundings, as he climbed stiffly down from his horse and studied the scorched patch of earth where the camp had once stood. The hot sun beat down from a clear, mercilessly blue sky onto the baked, cracked dust, but Jamie didn't even feel it. He was vaguely aware of Xavier Sanchez, sitting on his own horse several feet away and watching the scene warily, but Jamie felt as if he were the only living being left for miles around.

Maybe the only living being left on the planet.

There were no sounds—no birds singing or wind sweeping through the trees. Once this place had been filled with voices, laughter, the cries of the injured, the barked orders of a military operation. The ghosts of such sounds in his mind made the silence even heavier.

Jamie tilted back his head to stare up into the sky. He could smell the dusty scent of the air, the faint acrid remains of fire. The echoes of the violence that had happened here.

And Catalina had been caught in it.

His numbness was shattered by a spasm of pure, raw pain at the thought of what must have happened here. The fear and panic, the sense of being trapped amid fire and ruin with nowhere to run. No one to help her because he had gone.

'Catalina,' he whispered, his heart shattered at the thought of her being afraid.

Had she thought of him in that moment, just as he had pictured only her face when he'd been sure he was drowning? Had she called out his name?

Jamie walked slowly across the blasted, blackened patch of earth, not seeing it as it was now, abandoned and ruined, but as it had been that day he'd first seen Catalina. Her smile, her face like a beautiful, exotic flower, a haven of peace and loveliness in a mad world. She had given him something he had never known before—stillness, a place to belong. She had made him think of things he had never dared to before—like a future, a home. With her he had imagined even the grand halls of Castonbury could be that home, if she was there.

And then in only a moment that had all gone.

He remembered her hurt, pale face when she'd found out about the nature of his secret work. The doubts that had lingered in her eyes when they'd parted. He had foolishly imagined he would have time to make it all right later, to make everything up to her.

Jamie reached up and pressed his hand over the ring he wore on a chain around his neck under his shirt, against his heart. Cawley had said this ring—Catalina's ring—had been found here among the dead. Yet some stubborn hope clung to Jamie—what if she had somehow miraculously got away?

Castonbury Park

A brand new eight-book collection

A Regency Upstairs Downstairs

for fans of Regency, *Upstairs Downstairs* and *Downton Abbey*

On sale 3rd August

On sale 7th September

On sale 5th October

On sale 2nd November

On sale 7th December

On sale 4th January

On sale 1st February

On sale 1st March

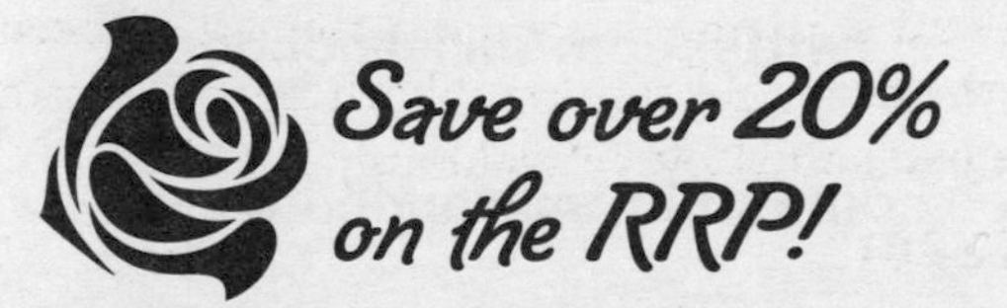

Find the collection at
www.millsandboon.co.uk/specialreleases

0912/MB385